CW00330464

Murder of an Amish Bridegroom

Also available by Patricia Johns

The Hope, Montana Series

Montana Mistletoe Baby
Her Cowboy Boss
The Triplets' Cowboy Daddy
The Cowboy's Valentine Bride
The Cowboy's Christmas Bride
Her Stubborn Cowboy
Safe in the Lawman's Arms

The Comfort Creek Lawmen Series

Her Secret Daughter
The Deputy's Unexpected Family
The Lawman's Runaway Bride
Deputy Daddy

The Home to Eagle's Rest Series

Her Triplets' Mistletoe Dad
The Lawman's Baby
Falling for the Cowboy Dad
Her Lawman Protector

The Montana Twins Series

A Rancher to Remember
Her Twins' Cowboy Dad
Her Cowboy's Twin Blessings

The Second Chance Club Series

Snowbound with Her Mountain Cowboy
Rocky Mountain Baby
Mountain Mistletoe Christmas
Their Mountain Reunion

The Redemption's Amish Legacies Series

The Amish Matchmaker's Choice
Blended Amish Blessings
Snowbound with the Amish Bachelor
Wife on His Doorstep
A Precious Christmas Gift
The Nanny's Amish Family

The Infamous Amish Series

Loving Lovina
The Preacher's Daughter
The Preacher's Son

The Amish Country Haven Series

A Cowboy in Amish Country
A Deputy in Amish Country

The Amish Country Matches Series

The Amish Marriage Arrangement
Their Amish Secret
The Amish Matchmaking Dilemma

The Butternut Amish B&B Series

A Boy's Amish Christmas
A Single Dad in Amish Country
Her Amish Country Valentine
His Unexpected Family
The Rancher's City Girl
A Firefighter's Promise
The Lawman's Surprise Family
A Baxter's Redemption
The Runaway Bride
A Boy's Christmas Wish
The Bishop's Daughter
Thursday's Bride
Jeb's Wife

Murder of an Amish Bridegroom

AN AMISH SEAMSTRESS MYSTERY

Patricia Johns

NEW YORK

This is a work of fiction. All of the names, characters, organizations, places, and events portrayed in this novel are either products of the author's imagination or are used fictitiously. Any resemblance to real or actual events, locales, or persons, living or dead, is entirely coincidental.

Published in the United States by Crooked Lane Books, an imprint of The Quick Brown Fox & Company LLC.

Crooked Lane Books and its logo are trademarks of The Quick Brown Fox & Company LLC.

Library of Congress Catalog-in-Publication data available upon request.

ISBN (hardcover): 978-1-63910-532-8
ISBN (ebook): 978-1-63910-533-5

Cover illustration by Ben Perini

Printed in the United States.

www.crookedlanebooks.com

Crooked Lane Books
34 West 27th St., 10th Floor
New York, NY 10001

First Edition: December 2023

10 9 8 7 6 5 4 3 2 1

To my husband and son, my biggest supporters. And to my parents, who tirelessly help me out in the background so that I can keep writing and the world keeps spinning. I love all of you! I couldn't follow my dreams without you.

Chapter One

Petunia Yoder's pies never turned out. Even in January, with crisp, cold, snowy days, her pies could not be counted on. That was one of many reasons she was teasingly referred to as the youngest old maid in all of Blueberry township. Petunia was absolutely unmarriageable in any reputable Amish community.

But her ice cream turned out most of the time, and when her father Elias—owner and proprietor of On the Yoder Side Amish Tours in town—took the wagonload of tourists on their trip around the Amish countryside, her job today was to stay home and have some fresh ice cream ready for them when they passed by on their way back to the tour office in Blueberry.

Well, that and she had a sewing job that she was working on too. Having given up on any Amish man wanting to take her as a wife, Petunia's main focus was on growing her seamstress business. She did most of her sewing at home, but her father had given her some space in the On the Yoder Side Tour office in town to sell ready-made Amish dresses, aprons, and *kapps* to the tourists passing through. A surprising number of tourists liked the idea of dressing like the Amish, it turned out. But if Petunia had to provide for herself eventually as a single woman—and she couldn't lean on her father forever—she needed to keep hustling.

Petunia opened the chest freezer—what the Amish referred to as the ice box, since the electrical cord had been removed, and it was filled with ice to keep cool food chilled—and while there were some melting ice blocks in the bottom, there was no fresh ice, and fresh ice was absolutely necessary in the ice cream churn.

"Oh, bother," she murmured. "So much for staying inside where it's warm."

Fresh ice was easy enough to come by once a week when Ike Smoker came through the community with his ice wagon and hauled several big blocks right to the door. And if they ever ran out between deliveries, they simply went down to the ice house and bought some. Ike even had some cloth bags of chipped ice so she wouldn't have to chip it herself.

Her sewing would have to wait.

So Petunia bundled up in a sweater, a winter coat, boots, gloves, a scarf, and her black woolen bonnet that she pulled over her white prayer *kapp*. Staying warm while wearing a dress in a Pennsylvania winter was all about the layers. She hitched up her little two-seater, uncovered buggy—typically called a courting buggy because it held two people in plain view for all to see—and flicked the reins. Her horse, Trudy, started forward, the wheels making perfect slices through the fresh snow, and she headed down the road and toward the ice house.

The ice house was located on the shore of Lapp Lake. Why it was called Lapp Lake, no one remembered. At some point someone named Lapp very likely owned that land. But the ice house was on the very edge of the lake, and in the winter, the ice man and whoever would come help him went out onto the frozen water and sawed blocks of ice and floated them to shore. The ice man and his assistant would pack up the blocks and take them to the insulated ice house. They did this a few times in the winter so that when the spring melt came, the ice house would be packed to the rafters with lake ice to get the whole community through the warmer months.

Petunia's father's wagon, pulled by the two quarter horses, was just approaching the ice house from the other direction. The wagon brushed past some overhanging evergreen boughs, and snow misted down onto the tourists. Petunia waved at Elias, and he waved back. Several Englishers leaned around him to look at her, and some cell phones popped out.

Petunia dropped her gaze. The Amish didn't like having photos and videos taken of them. Her father obviously said something, because the phones lowered.

She reined in and let Elias turn into the drive that led up to the ice house first, but all the tourists turned and stared at her as they passed, and a few smiled and waved. She waved back. They'd all see her soon enough back at the house. Then she flicked the reins and let her horse fall into pace behind the wagon.

There had been a fresh dusting of snow overnight, and a few different buggy tracks could be seen in the snow, along with hoofprints from horses. This was a distinctly Amish location. Englishers had no reason to come to an Amish ice house in winter, and it was the one place they could be guaranteed no car tracks would be seen, and as she scanned the tracks in the snow, her guess was right.

There were two buggies parked in front of the stable—one, an uncovered courting buggy with the horse still harnessed. The other buggy was Ike's, and his horse would be inside the stable. Was someone visiting Ike?

Her stomach sank when she pulled up next to the courting buggy. Of course. She'd know this buggy anywhere—especially with the scrape on one side that hadn't been painted over yet from when her good friend, Eden Beiler, had taken a corner too close around a building. Eden was having a not-so-secret romance with Ike Smoker.

They weren't about to interrupt something embarrassing, were they?

"What are you doing here, Petunia?" her father asked in Pennsylvania Dutch as he tied off his reins.

"We're out of ice for the ice cream," she said.

"Ah . . ." Elias nodded, then turned around to face his wagon load of tourists and switched to speaking English. "This is my daughter, Petunia. You can say hello to her."

There was a smattering of hellos, and Petunia smiled in return. The ice house was part of the regular tour—the list of things that amazed Englishers was rather long. Laundry washing, furniture making, sewing clothing, scrubbing floors, and even fetching ice. It left them in awe. Petunia tied off her reins too, and hopped down from her buggy.

"Is Eden here?" Elias asked, lowering his voice. His gaze flickered nervously toward the shut door. That was the delicate question, wasn't it? Had Eden come to see her boyfriend for a bit of privacy? And were they about to interrupt an inappropriate moment between a passionate couple with a wagonload of tourists to stare in on the scene? She could just imagine the online reviews that she checked weekly at the library…

"I think so," Petunia said. "That's her buggy, all right. Maybe I should go first, in case a *kapp* needs straightening, so to speak."

"Yah, for sure," her father agreed. "And make some noise . . ."

"What about that horse still hitched up?" someone asked from the back of her father's wagon. "How long will a horse be left outside like that?"

"Not long," she said. "Someone must be visiting. If we think it will be a quick visit, we leave our horses hitched up. But if we'll be a bit longer, we'll cover them with a blanket to keep them warm in weather like this. Or we'll put them in the stable if we'll be more than a few minutes."

Something Eden hadn't done, to her discredit, and if she was here for a romantic visit, then she should have thought of the horse.

"Are horses worth a lot?" a woman asked.

"Yah, they're our transportation, and our horsepower, so to speak . . ."

Petunia tuned out her father's explanation and adjusted her winter coat over her dress. An icy wind wound its way up her legs, and she determinedly ignored the cold. She eyed the ice house uneasily. Ike normally came outside and greeted the visitors. The Englishers loved this part.

"Hello?" she called, and she headed toward the door, her boots crunching over the snow. Just as she reached it, the door banged open and Petunia took a startled step back. It wasn't Ike in the doorway, but Eden, and her face was pasty white, her coat open at the front, and a strange crimson streak down the front of her purple dress. Her hands were trembling, and they had red on them, too . . . Blood? The details were only now starting to come together in Petunia's mind, and her heart hammered hard to catch up.

"Eden, are you hurt?" Petunia gasped.

"He's dead," Eden whispered hoarsely. "Petunia, he's dead!"

Petunia pushed past her friend into the ice house. A lantern sat on a shelf, illuminating the small room in a golden glow. Stacks of ice blocks loomed up in a wall—each layer of ice separated from the ice below by insulating wood shavings that also covered the floor. Lying on his back in a pool of crimson, his eyes wide open and an ice pick sticking out of his chest, was Ike Smoker.

"Ike?" Petunia said quietly, almost afraid that he'd answer. His eyes were glazed over, and a patch of blood seeped out of his woolen coat—hard to make out against the black wool, but it glistened oddly in the kerosene lamplight. She leaned over him, her heart thundering in her chest. There was no life left in him, but she leaned down to touch his neck all the same. He was as cold as the ice around him.

Petunia scanned the small room in the front of the long ice house. The front of the building was the only place where there was any space to move around, and the floor was covered in a layer of shaved wood that had been scuffed by boot marks. She noticed a small flask sitting open on a shelf. There were no glasses to show how many people had been consuming the contents, either . . . She recognized Eden's knitted scarf lying in the wood chips on the floor. There was no evidence of who had been in that room with him, besides Eden's scarf.

"Yah, he's dead," Petunia said, more to fill the silence than anything else, and when she looked up, she found her father first, and the tourists behind him, peering in the doorway with stricken looks on their faces. One man was on his cell phone, and he turned away, talking.

"Yes, a dead body. I'm pretty sure he's dead. We need emergency services here right away . . ."

Petunia let out a slow breath. Dead. He was definitely dead, and while she'd never liked Ike—he'd been a bad sort of man who was taking advantage of her friend—seeing him lifeless on the floor made her feel sick to her stomach.

She went out of the ice house, her head spinning.

The tourists were huddled in a group, the man with the cell phone seeming to rise up as the natural leader, and Elias went into the ice house next.

"The police are coming," the Englisher man was saying. "We shouldn't touch anything, so that they can properly investigate, and make sure that the young woman doesn't go anywhere—the one with the blood on her hands."

Eden stood a few paces away from the ice house trembling, and Petunia went over to her side and put an arm around her shoulders.

"What happened?" Petunia asked.

"He's dead! I'm sure of it . . ." Eden shuddered. "I came to see him, and—"

"You didn't . . ."

"Kill him?" Eden looked down at her hands and then tried to wipe them on her dress.

"Did he attack you, or . . ." Petunia began delicately. "Because if he attacked you, I'm sure the police will understand."

"Petunia, I came to talk to him! That's all. And I found him like this. I tried to wake him up. I thought he might still be alive, and I don't know what I was thinking because there was an ice pick—" Tears leaked past her wet lashes. "Who would have killed Ike? I know he was misunderstood, but no one hated him!"

Petunia's mind was moving past the shock now, and she looked at her friend in mild surprise. There were plenty of people who had reason to hate Ike—mostly Eden's own family. Ike had been acting far too familiar with Eden. He took her driving, kept her out late, and was seen with his hands wandering in full view of any curious gaze. It was damaging to Eden's reputation, especially since when asked about his intentions by Eden's father, Ike had gotten angry and said that he wasn't going to be pushed into marriage.

And Eden, blind lamb that she was, just adored him. She wouldn't listen to anyone who said anything against him. Petunia herself had tried and then given up.

"What did you come to talk to him about?" Petunia asked.

Eden looked ready to answer, then she shook her head. "It's private."

"He's dead!" Petunia replied. "There is no need to keep secrets now. And the police are on their way. They'll ask questions too. So practice on me. What were you coming to talk to him about?"

"About getting married." Tears welled in her eyes again. "I wanted to marry him, Petunia!"

But Ike had made it clear publicly that he didn't want to get married. He thought that just loving Eden was enough for now, and there was nothing less Amish than that. The Amish dated with intention, and simply loving a girl was in no way good enough. The goal was always marriage, and Eden had a reputation to worry about, even if Ike didn't seem to care much about his own. If Eden ever wanted a married life, which was at the heart of Amish living, then she should have been a lot more careful.

"Oh, Eden," Petunia sighed. "He was refusing to marry you, wasn't he?"

"It wasn't like that," Eden wept. "He loved me so much, but he knew everyone disliked him. He said he couldn't just marry me without my community's support. It wasn't his fault!"

A convenient excuse in Petunia's mind. Trample a girl's reputation, then when the community resents you for doing so, blame their displeasure for not making an honest woman of her. Ike was many things, but he was not stupid, and he'd set the situation up nicely for himself. It wasn't like people didn't try to warn Eden, either. *Everyone* had tried.

"But you wanted to change his mind?" Petunia asked.

"Of course I did! I had an idea. I wanted to get married outside the community," Eden said, lowering her voice. "I was willing to go to town and get married. They couldn't stop us then! Who cares if people didn't like it? It's my life! It was supposed to be our life together, Ike and me."

"But your family . . . ," Petunia said, shocked.

"I loved him!" Eden burst out.

"I'm so sorry," Petunia said. "I know. I know . . ."

Because whatever Ike's true character, which was clear enough to everyone else in the community, Eden had been utterly blind to it, and she loved him. Far off, Petunia could hear sirens on the way. The ice house was only a few miles from the town of Blueberry.

Petunia looked back toward the brown, wood-sided ice house where Ike's body lay, and she felt a guilty swell of relief. Ike Smoker had been a manipulative, bad man who'd taken advantage of an innocent young woman, but he wouldn't be doing it anymore. Whatever strings had held Eden under his sway, they were snapped.

Ike Smoker was dead, and Petunia couldn't help but feel glad of it. Now life could return to the way it was supposed to be around here . . . Mostly. The shocking reality remained—someone in this well-meaning Amish community had killed him. That fact wasn't just going to go away. And she knew that the killer was Amish because of the buggy tracks in the snow. There were no tire marks—she looked around once more just to make sure.

Elias came back out of the ice house, and he looked shaken—his face white. He met Petunia's gaze and grimaced. A police cruiser followed closely by an ambulance pulled into the drive, lights flashing, and Petunia gave her friend's shoulder a reassuring pat. Farther away, she could hear the wail of more approaching sirens.

"What do I do?" Eden asked, rubbing her hands down the front of her dress once more, but the blood had dried on her skin, sticking around her fingernails and in the lines of her hands.

"Tell the truth," Petunia said. "You didn't do it! They'll see the truth in that."

Wouldn't they?

* * *

The police took their time in going over the scene. They questioned Elias and the tourists, wrote down their statements, took their contact information, and then transported them back to town in police vehicles. The ice house was cordoned off with police tape, and black-booted police officers tramped in and out, until a stretcher with a body bag finally emerged from the ice house, carried between two somber police officers.

Petunia edged over to look inside the ice house again. There would obviously be fresh proof inside the building of who had actually killed Ike Smoker, and she felt an overwhelming desire to see it for herself.

"Miss," the uniformed officer said. "This is a crime scene."

"Yah, I know. I just wanted—" She stopped. There was no way to make her desire to see inside seem less macabre. So she stepped away and went back to stand with Eden.

A police detective wearing a gray suit brought woolen blankets over to where Petunia and Eden sat in the back of Petunia's wagon. He wasn't a tall man, but he was broad—almost a walking rectangle. Even his face was square. He wasn't particularly handsome, but his eyes held an intimidating intelligence. He strode over to where they stood and put his hands into his pockets.

"You're the one who found him, Miss . . ."

"Eden Beiler," she whispered.

"Eden Beiler." The officer's voice was gruff, but there was kindness under the gravel. "My name is Detective Asher Nate. I'm just going to ask you a few questions." He glanced over at Petunia. "And you are?"

"I'm Petunia Yoder—I was here to buy ice."

"Right." Detective Nate turned back to Eden. "Are you all right, Miss?"

"No," Eden said. "I just found Ike dead. I'm not all right."

"I have witnesses here who said they saw you come out of the ice house with blood on your hands." He looked down at her blood-streaked dress. "Can you explain that?"

"I came to talk to Ike," Eden said. "I went inside, and I saw him on the floor. I tried to wake him up—help him. I got blood on myself . . ."

"Hmm." He pulled out a cell phone and took a couple of pictures of her hands and dress. "And who was Ike Smoker to you?"

"He's my—" Eden stopped. "He *was* my boyfriend."

"Boyfriend?" He raised an eyebrow.

"We loved each other," Eden said. "Yes, he was my boyfriend."

Asher's gray-eyed gaze flicked over to Petunia for a moment, then back to Eden.

"This was his workplace, wasn't it?" he asked.

Eden nodded.

"So why did you come here today?" Asher asked. "A romantic rendezvous?"

"A what?" Eden squinted.

"A romantic meeting," Asher amended his phrasing.

"No, to talk to him."

"About what?" Asher chewed on his bottom lip, his gray gaze locked on Eden. Petunia felt like squirming for her. There were conclusions being drawn here, and she could feel it like a prickle against her skin.

"About . . . us. Our relationship," Eden said.

"How did that talk go?" he asked.

"It didn't happen! He was dead!"

"Hmm." He nodded. "Had you discussed your relationship before? At another time?"

"Yes, of course!" Eden looked over at Petunia helplessly, then back at the detective. "We were serious, but he didn't want to upset my family by marrying me."

"They don't like him?" Asher's eyebrows went up again.

"They—" Eden shook her head. "Petunia, you explain."

"No, I need you to explain. Petunia, if you could just walk over there for a couple of minutes, and then I'll come talk to you after I'm finished with Miss Beiler here."

Petunia looked at Eden. "Will you be okay?"

"I don't bite," Asher said curtly. "She'll be fine. Over there, please."

Petunia cast him an annoyed look. The ordering around wasn't necessary, and being sharp with Eden wasn't going to help matters.

She'd just found the man she loved dead on the floor of the ice house. She wasn't going to be in any shape to talk coherently, but what could Petunia do? The man was a police detective, just doing his job.

She walked a few paces off and scanned the area. The ambulance, lights off, pulled onto the road, taking the body with it. Officers were still circling the scene, putting down little plastic numbers next to clues in the snow that Petunia couldn't make out, and taking pictures. Her father stood off by himself, his arms crossed over his chest and a scowl on his face. She ambled over to where he stood and took her place next to him.

"Ike Smoker . . . ," her father said quietly.

"Yah."

There was really nothing else to say. Ike Smoker was not a good man, and the community would be better off without him. But murdered?

Across the parking area, Detective Nate stood with his legs akimbo, his steely gaze fixed on Eden's face. Petunia wished she could decipher what was being said, but she couldn't from where she stood. The icy winter wind swirled around her legs, and she pulled her coat closer. How long would it take for this detective to figure out that Eden was telling the truth and let them go home? Her gaze moved over toward Eden's horse, still hitched up to her buggy. Petunia would follow Eden home and make sure she got in okay before she headed back up to town again. Elias wouldn't argue about that, she was sure. Poor Eden . . .

From where Petunia stood, she still had a good view of Eden and the detective, and it took her a moment to even register what had happened when the detective pulled out a pair of handcuffs, and Petunia's breath caught in her throat. He said something to Eden, she turned, and he put the cuffs on her slender wrists. He put one big hand on Eden's arm and guided her toward a squad car.

"What's happening?" Petunia called, and she jogged back to her friend's side. She planted herself in front of Detective Nate and put her hands out to stop him. "What are you doing? Where is Eden going?"

"If you'll excuse me, please," the detective said. "I'll speak with you in a minute."

"No!" she shot back. "Where are you taking her? Eden is innocent! She found Ike's body—that's it!"

"Did you see her find the body?" he asked.

"No, but—"

"According to the other eight witnesses, this buggy was already on site when you arrived," the detective said. "Do you have anything to add to that?"

"Only the fact that I know Eden better than anyone, and there is no way she committed murder, let alone with an ice pick!"

"That will be taken into account," Asher Nate replied, and he beckoned to another officer. "But for now, Miss Beiler is going down to the station for further questioning."

Eden cast Petunia a hollow-eyed, helpless look as another officer snagged her by the arm and led her toward a police cruiser.

"Petunia!" her father called, and he strode over to her side.

She was doing it again—overstepping, being too much. She always was. Amish women did not argue with men. They didn't plant themselves in a man's path and demand he change his ways. It wasn't done!

"Detective Nate," Petunia said, her voice shaking as she struggled to sound more contrite. "She's been through enough. You have to let her go home."

"Miss Yoder," the detective replied quietly. "That is your name, right?"

"Yes. Petunia Yoder."

"I cannot tell you anything more, as this is a murder investigation." His voice was quiet, patient, unyielding, and Petunia had the urge to scream.

"Eden didn't do it!" What was wrong with this man that he couldn't spot an innocent woman when she was standing right in front of him?

"Petunia!" her father said, more firmly this time.

The detective glanced over at Elias. "It's okay, sir." Then he faced Petunia again. "Then who did?"

Petunia licked her lips, her mind flicking through the options. Who would hate Ike Smoker enough to plunge an ice pick into his chest? Would anyone in their little Amish community do such a terrible thing? Ike might not have been trusted or much liked, but no one would *kill* him, would they? And she couldn't very well give this man a list of members of their community who might have hated Ike enough to succumb to a crime of passion.

"I don't know," she admitted. "But it wasn't her."

"I have a woman with blood on both her hands and dress, who was seen with the body within the time frame of the death. He was killed very recently, Miss, and your friend came bursting out that door when you arrived. She was romantically involved with him, and you wouldn't believe how common it is for a romantic relationship to get out of hand—for an emotionally fueled argument to turn into a violent fight. If I simply let her go, I wouldn't be doing my job. She could easily disappear, and we'd have no way of finding her."

"She loved him," Petunia said. "Whether he deserved it or not, she did."

Detective Nate narrowed his eyes and crossed his arms over his chest. "Why wouldn't he deserve it?"

Petunia looked over at her father with his sensible beard and kind, brown eyes, and he just looked at her helplessly. They were knee deep in the problem now, and she wasn't going to be able to just back out.

"Look, I know for a fact *you* didn't do it," the detective said, softening his tone. "You arrived after the wagon of tourists, and this man was killed about an hour ago, give or take. Your demeanor isn't consistent with someone who is hiding anything at all."

"Thank you," she said. "I think."

"I have a very complicated case on my hands," he went on. "It always is out here in Amish Country."

"Why is it always complicated?" she asked. It sounded like an insult to her.

"Because the Amish culture keeps to itself," Detective Nate replied. "It solves its own problems and if someone were to want to disappear, they could easily do it. A young woman, for example, could nip off in the night in a buggy and go stay with friends in another community. There would be no paper trail, and she'd blend right in. Quite frankly, Miss Beiler could vanish this evening, and we'd never see her again."

"She's innocent. She has no reason to leave," Petunia insisted.

"But if she weren't innocent?" He spread his hands. "You have to look at it from my perspective, Miss Yoder."

"Just Petunia," she said.

"What?"

"We don't say Miss or Mrs. or Mister," Petunia said. "We call each other by our first names. Anything else is Fancy."

"Aha." He smiled then, and wagged a finger at her. "There are cultural nuances that we Englishers don't catch onto very quickly, and a murder investigation is all about the nuances."

"You know we call you Englishers, though," she said.

"I do know that much," he said, and he eyed her for a moment, chewing the inside of his cheek. "What I need is a sort of interpreter. Someone who will go with me, smooth the way for me. I tend to be a little intimidating, and I need someone with me to both offset that, and to fill me in on the cultural cues I'd otherwise miss."

"That would be helpful," she agreed, irritably. "Best of luck finding it."

No one in an Amish community would be willing to step in and do that kind of job—help him to incriminate one of their own. But what other way would there be to prove poor Eden innocent?

"I don't imagine you'd be interested?" Detective Nate asked. "You're someone I can be nearly positive didn't kill him, and you seem to be rather invested in finding out who did."

Petunia looked over at her father. Was this crazy? Maybe.

"What do you think, *Daet*?" she asked in Pennsylvania Dutch. "I know she didn't kill him, and I think you know it too, but if no one helps him navigate our community, they'll pin it on Eden, and she'll go to prison."

Her father chewed the side of his cheek. "This is the very thing that makes it so hard to find you a husband, Petunia."

"I know . . . but how can I think of finding a husband when Eden might end up in jail? I think it's the right thing to do."

Detective Nate was watching them in silence, and when Elias grudgingly nodded, Petunia turned back to the detective.

"I know for sure and certain it wasn't Eden Beiler," Petunia said. "And I would be more than happy to help you in your investigation if I could clear her name. I'm probably the only one really suited to helping you out, anyway."

"Why's that?" he asked.

"I'm the youngest old maid in all of Blueberry," she replied. "I'm mouthy, forward, ask too many questions, and am completely unmarriageable."

Her father grunted, and Petunia wasn't sure if it was agreement or annoyance.

The detective's eyebrows went up, and she saw a sudden twinkle in his eye. "The youngest old maid in all of Blueberry, are you?"

"It's a fact," she replied. "Ask anyone."

"Would they answer me?" he asked.

"Probably not," she conceded. "But if you want help finding out who killed Ike Smoker, I will be more than happy to provide it."

"And if we discover that your dear Eden Beiler is the killer?" he asked.

Petunia licked her lips and a shiver ran down her back. That was the problem, wasn't it? If all the proof pointed to Eden, would she accept that?

"No, I won't accept that she did it, but I won't stoop to lying or faking evidence to clear her, either," she replied. "I'm Amish. I tell the truth, even when it hurts me. I believe in personal integrity and doing the right thing—that anything less puts my very own soul at stake. The truth is the truth, Detective Nate. That's all I want."

"Okay . . ." The big man pressed his lips together thoughtfully. "Then I suppose you should start calling me Asher. And I will call you Petunia." He glanced over at Elias. "And you're okay with this, sir?"

"Yah, I'll agree to it . . . with reservations," Elias replied.

"Is it a deal, then?" Petunia asked. "Are we working on this together?"

"It's a deal." Detective Nate put out a meaty hand and shook hers in a surprisingly gentle grip. "Let's find our killer. And to start with, I'm going to need all the information you can give me about Ike Smoker."

Chapter Two

The police combed the area, from the ice house to the stable to the lakeshore. Passing buggies stopped to see what was happening, and within an hour, they'd returned with a couple of young men to bring Eden and Ike's horses back to the farms where they belonged.

Eden's buggy was returned to the Beiler farm, and Ike's horse was brought to the acreage where he was renting a room from an elderly couple.

"Why don't you give me a ride in your buggy over to that farm next door?" Asher said. "Then you can give me a ride back into town. What do you say?"

"Next door to question them?" Petunia asked. Was their arrangement starting so soon?

"Someone might have seen something," he replied. "It's worth checking. And better sooner than later before details are forgotten."

Petunia looked over at her father, but he was busy with the horses. She'd agreed to this, and she had her father's permission—sort of. At least he wasn't going to stop her.

"Okay," Petunia agreed. "I can do that."

Elias took his wagon back to the house, and she watched with a sinking feeling as he disappeared from sight. The last of the police cruisers pulled out, and Petunia sat on the buggy seat and watched as Asher locked the ice house door. It looked like he'd taken Ike's keys off the body because it was just the regular lock on the door knob. Then she got back up into her buggy, and Asher slid into the seat beside her. She flicked the reins and Trudy started forward.

Everything had changed in the span of a few hours—Ike Smoker was dead, Eden was being held in custody on suspicion of murder, and Petunia was riding over to the Hilty farm, neighbor to the ice house, with a police detective at her side. She shot him a wary look.

"So, tell me about you," Asher said as they rumbled over the snowy gravel.

"No," she said, shaking her head. "Tell me about you, instead."

That was unheard of in an Amish community—a woman questioning a man—but this man was as far from Amish as possible.

Asher shot her a wry smile. "All right. I'm a state police detective, and Blueberry County is my first assignment as a detective. I've been working out here for about six months."

"Ah." She eyed him. "Are you married?"

"Divorced."

"How old are you?" she asked.

"Twenty-seven."

"And divorced already?" She frowned. "What did you do?"

"Me?" He barked out a laugh. "You'd blame me?"

"Any marriage takes two, we say. You weren't completely innocent."

"It's a long and *personal* story." He shifted himself on the hard seat. "How about you? What do you do?"

"I'm a seamstress."

"I thought you'd say you help your father with the family business."

"I do, but the job that fills most of my time is being a seamstress."

"How long have you been doing that?"

"I started full time when I graduated grade eight when I was fourteen."

"No more schooling?" he asked.

"We don't go past grade eight," she replied.

"Right." He nodded. "And who do you sew for, specifically? I thought most Amish women do their own sewing."

"They do, but my father has given me a section of his tour office in town where I can sell some ready-made Amish dresses for tourists. Those sell quite well. And for our Amish community, when someone gets married, we need to sew matching *newehocker* outfits. The women wear the same color dress, and the men wear the same color shirt. It's a lot of work, and I do the sewing for some weddings around here. I also sew for some families that can afford to hire it out. But mostly it's weddings."

They came to the edge of the drive, and she guided the horse down the road away from town and toward the Hilty drive that led to their small farm. The watery afternoon sunlight gave no warmth, and she shivered.

"Weddings are a big deal," he said.

"Of course."

"Can you stay busy sewing for weddings?"

"Yah, I do. There's plenty of weddings. And like I said, sometimes a wealthier farmer's wife will hire me to sew children's clothing if she's too busy with other things. People pass word along that I do good work at a decent price. It keeps me booked up."

"And this Ike Smoker," Asher said. "Was he born here? Does he have family?"

"No, he moved here a couple of years ago from Ohio," she replied.

"You said he might not have deserved your friend's loyalty," he said.

"He didn't," Petunia replied. "She couldn't see it, though. With us Amish, we don't toy with dating and marriage. A couple will court in order to marry. That's it. But Ike wasn't interested in getting married. He wanted all the benefit without the commitment. Of course, he told Eden all sorts of different excuses as to why he didn't want to get married, but he was taking some very big liberties with her for someone he wasn't going to make his wife."

"Liberties?" Asher's voice was low. "As in . . ."

"As in kissing her in public, holding her close against him when people could see, monopolizing her time, demanding that she spend time with him instead of going to family events."

Petunia reined in the horse as they got to the Hiltys' drive. It was adorned by a simple green plastic mailbox that read HILTY in block letters written with white paint. The horse turned in, and a wheel thunked down into a pothole and back up again, jostling them so that both Petunia and Asher grabbed the seat to steady themselves.

"Sorry," Petunia murmured.

"Ike was controlling," Asher said, not distracted from his initial questioning.

"Incredibly. Eden didn't go to her cousin's birthday celebration because Ike was jealous that other Amish men were interested in her. That's what he said, at least."

"And he wouldn't just go to the party with her?" he asked.

"No, because he said her family hated him. And he wasn't wrong about that. But I can tell you, all the other Amish young men had seen the way she'd been carrying on with Ike, and couldn't very well take her home from singing, if you know what I mean."

"No, I don't," he replied. "Spell it out."

"Well, they couldn't respectably court her. Their families wouldn't approve."

She reined in the horse at the end of the drive. The farmhouse was set back a little farther, the stable being the closest building. A dog came running from around the house, barking.

"And what about these people?" he asked.

"Abram and Mary Hilty," she replied. "They farm."

"And?" he asked.

"That's it. They farm. What do you want to know?" she asked.

"Any relationship to Ike Smoker?"

"Besides living next to the ice house, not that I know of. You'd have to ask them."

The side door of the house opened, and a middle-aged Amish woman in an apron poked her head out. Her expression was stern, and even spotting Petunia didn't soften it at all.

"What's happening out there, Petunia?" she asked curtly in Pennsylvania Dutch.

"This is Mary Hilty. She wants to know what's going on." Petunia looked over at Asher, and he hopped down from the wagon.

"Hello, Mary," Petunia said. "I'd best let him explain."

"Oh?" Mary turned her iron look onto Asher.

"Good afternoon," he said with a cordial smile, unfazed. "My name is Asher Nate, and I'm a detective with the state police."

Mary moved back into the house by an inch or two, but it wasn't an inviting gesture. More like a retreat.

"Something very serious happened at the ice house," he went on. "Do you think we could come inside and talk a little bit? It's brisk out today. Pretty cold."

Asher rubbed his hands together in demonstration of just how cold it was.

"Yah, yah. I suppose," Mary replied reluctantly. "What happened, exactly?"

It was Mary's curiosity that would get them through the door, Petunia realized, and perhaps Asher was a little wilier than she'd given him credit for earlier. Mary stood back, and cast Petunia a questioning look as they came inside. They passed through the mudroom first, and Asher carefully wiped his shoes on the mat, then carried on into the kitchen.

"There was a murder," Petunia said, shutting the door behind her.

"A murder!" Mary stopped short. "What? Who?"

"Ike Smoker is dead," Petunia replied. "We found him this morning."

"Oh, that's terrible . . ." Mary grimaced. "How did he die?"

"Ice pick to the chest," Petunia replied.

Mary's eyes widened in what looked like genuine surprise to Petunia. "Well, now. Someone meant business."

"We wanted to ask if you saw anything," Asher said. He ambled across the kitchen—a more cluttered kitchen than was common for the Amish—and he stopped at the window and leaned over to look out. Then he went to the side window, on the other side of the dining room table that held an assortment of canning supplies. Asher's attention moved over the cans, lids, and various pincers of different sizes with which to grasp hot jars, and moved back to the window. "Yeah, yeah . . . I can see the ice house from here."

"There's not much to see," Mary replied.

"But you must have seen the police cars." Asher turned with a conciliatory smile. "Lights, sirens . . ."

"Of course, I saw that," Mary replied.

"Did you notice anything else, earlier today?" Asher asked. "Any visitors to the ice house, perhaps?"

"Well, Eden Beiler goes there often enough," Mary said. "I noticed her buggy there, yet again. No shame, that girl. She trails after that man like a puppy. I don't know why her family hasn't put a stop to it yet." She shot Petunia an apologetic look. "I'm sorry to say it so bluntly. I know you two are good friends."

"Have they tried to tell her?" Asher asked. "I'm not a father, myself, but I've got friends with daughters. It's not always so easy to tell a young woman that the man she's fallen for isn't worth her time."

"She's in her twenties now," Mary said. "So she can run her own life, I suppose, but my girls knew better by that age. Eden Beiler was known to be a good girl until she took up with that Ike Smoker. He was the problem."

"Did you see anything before Eden arrived?" Petunia asked hopefully.

"Not that I noticed today," Mary said slowly. "But yesterday there was a woman out there."

"Eden again?" Asher asked.

"No, a different woman," Mary said. "I only noticed because she was hollering at him and her voice carried. Couldn't make out words, but she sounded pretty furious. She came in a buggy and left in one."

"Someone from our community?" Petunia asked. "You'd recognize someone from here . . ."

"It wasn't anyone I knew," Mary said, shaking her head. "So I'd say not from Blueberry. But I've never seen a woman quite that furious before, either. She was yelling and shouting, and I saw her slap him across the face. Full force—" She mimed the slap, pulling her whole shoulder back and then coming around with an open palm. "He just took it, too. Didn't yell back at her or anything. Then she got into her buggy and drove off."

"Would you know her to see her again?" Asher asked, and he looked back out that window toward the ice house thoughtfully.

"I don't know . . . I couldn't really see too much of her face from here," Mary replied. "She was wearing a bonnet. I might recognize her again, and I might not."

Asher pulled out his cell phone and a stylus and wrote something down.

"Did she seem angry enough to come back and maybe . . ." Asher shrugged delicately.

". . . plunge an ice pick into his chest?" Petunia finished for him.

Asher cast her an annoyed look.

"Well, how angry does a woman have to be to do that?" Mary asked. "I'm not sure. That ice pick just feels like an overreaction in any situation. It's like old Barnie Stoltzfuz."

"Hmm . . ." Petunia nodded in agreement.

"What's this?" Asher asked.

"Barnie Stoltzfuz burned down his own barn in a rage when he and his brother were arguing about something," Petunia said. "An overreaction. That's the point."

"What were they arguing about?" Asher asked.

"A woman," Mary replied with a small smile. "What else would drive a man to burn down his own barn? They both were in love with the same widow."

Asher smiled faintly. "Indeed. Who ended up with the widow?"

"Neither of them," Mary replied. "She was rather put off by the burnt barn."

"Big red flag. Smart lady," he murmured.

"Smarter than Eden Beiler seemed to be," Mary said, shaking her head. "But if you'll excuse me, I do have laundry to get to today."

"Yah, of course," Petunia said. That was the polite way of ending a visit. Petunia led the way to the door, but Asher lingered behind her.

"Where is your husband?" Asher asked.

"He's out with the cows," Mary replied.

"Hm. Did he mention seeing anything by the ice house in the last day or so?" Asher asked.

"No," Mary replied. "Our herd grazes in the other direction. He wouldn't have seen anything."

"Well, thank you for your time," Asher said. "Much appreciated."

Petunia led the way back outside into the icy air and Asher stood in the snow, turning a slow circle.

"What are you looking for?" Petunia asked.

"What can be seen from here," he said, stopping at the spattering of bare trees that stood between this property and the lake beyond. "And on the other side of the lake is pasture that doesn't look like it's been used for cattle in some time. If anyone was going to see something, the Hiltys are our best hope." He looked back toward the house where Mary stood in the front window, watching them, her mouth pressed together into a thin, puckered line. He gave her a nod, and then strode toward the wagon. "Let's head back to town, then. I'm sure you're anxious to get home."

Petunia followed him and they both got into the wagon and resettled. She flicked the reins and the horse pulled them around in a circle and back to the road.

"She said she didn't know anything, and suddenly she remembers seeing a woman slapping Ike across the face," Asher said. "Interesting."

"Why?" she asked.

"She might be making it up," he said. "It could be a lie to put us off."

"I think it's true," Petunia replied. "Of course, she wouldn't tell you what she saw right away. You're an Englisher."

"Right."

"I'm sorry—I don't mean to offend, but she'd be inclined to talk it out with someone she trusted first."

"Fair enough," he replied.

"But I am rather surprised that there was a woman out there besides Eden," Petunia said thoughtfully.

"Why is that?" he asked.

"Ike Smoker was incredibly fixated on Eden. I didn't like him, but I also didn't think he was trifling with other women besides her. She was his sole victim."

"And your guess for this other woman is a romantic relationship?" he asked.

"For an Amish woman to slap a man across the face?" Petunia slowly shook her head. "We are not a violent people, Asher. We're calm, thoughtful, and we are quick to forgive. We also respect our menfolk. We don't make fun of them or insult them or belittle them like happens out there with other people. For an Amish woman to lift a hand in anger against a man—any man—would take . . . a lot."

"Agreed," he said. "It would take a lot to get anyone to stab someone in the chest with an ice pick, too."

"That's a good point," Petunia said, tipping her head to the side while she considered that. "Maybe it was the slapping Amish woman who did it. She obviously had some strong feelings and an inclination toward violence."

"It might not have been an Amish person," Asher said.

But then an image suddenly flashed into Petunia's mind of the snowy parking area for the ice house.

"I looked at the drive when we came in," Petunia said. "There were only buggy tracks. No tire tracks."

"You noticed that?" Asher asked.

"It's the sort of detail my father's tourists tend to enjoy," Petunia said. "They like being in a strictly Amish area. It feels special to them. I just . . . noticed."

Asher shot her a small smile. "Would you swear to what you saw? Any bit of doubt in your mind?"

"No doubt. I know what I saw."

"You're very observant."

Petunia looked over at him, silent. This wasn't good. If there were no tire tracks, and only an Amish presence, that meant an Amish murderer.

"That's a compliment," Asher added, facing forward again. "It's very helpful having you around. I appreciate your help."

She might be helping her own community straight to perdition. Trudy plodded on, the weak winter sunlight splashing over the road ahead of them as they made their way back to the town of Blueberry.

No, an Englisher murderer wasn't going to get them off the hook with this one, and that distinct possibility was gnawing at Petunia's mind. Someone had killed Ike Smoker, and the killer had arrived and left in an Amish buggy. Chances were someone in their very own faith community had killed the man.

* * *

Early that evening, Petunia sat in the kitchen of the little farmhouse on the outskirts of Blueberry. The farms that close to town had been chopped up into small acreages decades ago, and they were just big enough for an Amish family to maintain their traditional way with a stable, a small pasture, a decent garden, and enough space to feel like they had elbow room to live. But the Yoders relied upon Englisher curiosity and tourism to make their living. Most businesses in town were the same.

The kitchen was clean—counter scrubbed, with a plate of Danishes waiting for them to finish their dinner. These were store-bought. Petunia couldn't make a decent Danish to save her life.

"I know I agreed to this, but I don't like it," Elias said, getting up with his emptied plate and heading toward the compost bin. "Getting caught up in a murder investigation like that—it's not the sort of thing a nice young woman does. How are we supposed to find you a husband if you keep running off after murderers?"

"I don't run after murderers as a habit," Petunia said. "This is my first time for this particular thing."

"But knowing you, you'll like it," he muttered.

"*Daet*, they have Eden in custody. They think she did it! If we don't find out who killed him, she'll be the one to pay."

Her father scraped his plate, then turned back. "I don't like that, either. Poor Eden. She's not been wise in her choice of boyfriend, but I don't believe she killed him. Not Eden."

"Who might have?" Petunia asked. "It does seem like it was someone Amish . . . But who? Her brother? Her father? They were upset that Ike was taking advantage of her. I know that. But I find both of those hard to believe too. Anyone here in Blueberry—why would they kill a man? Especially like that?"

"An ice pick to the chest . . . that's a lot of hatred in one blow," her father agreed. "That is a heart not right with Gott. But Ike Smoker inspired a lot of hard feelings wherever he went—even in the best of Christians. He gambled, he flirted with women, he owed money to several people that I know of firsthand, and he generally caused trouble. I mean, was it enough trouble to kill the man in a fit of anger? I don't know. But someone was good and mad to the point of abandoning his own soul to get revenge."

"Who did he owe money to?" Petunia asked.

"Obie Schlabach, for one," Elias replied.

Obie . . . his name could still make her heart squeeze with some nostalgia. Back in her teenage years, she'd been in love with Obie from afar. For being so opinionated and vocal, she'd never breathed a word about her feelings for him. But they'd been teenagers then, and Obadiah had his sights set on Eden Beiler. A great deal had changed over the years.

"How do you know Ike owed Obie?" she asked.

"I heard him complaining that he needed the money back. He wanted to start thinking of marriage, and he couldn't do that without a little bit set aside. And then there was Jacob Weir. He said he was trying to do the Christianly thing and help to get Ike out of debt. He gave him the money, and they agreed that he'd pay him and make monthly installments. But Ike never paid one installment. Not even one!"

"Jacob . . . he lost his carpentry business," she said.

"Yah, and while that business was struggling before Jacob helped Ike, that money going out the door and never coming back surely didn't help."

Jacob Weir had shut his doors in the spring, and Petunia's heart gave a squeeze of sympathy even now, remembering how despondent he'd been. Jacob's wife had had to start working as a house cleaner then. There was no way to avoid it.

"I know for a fact that Eden didn't kill him, *Daet*. There are others who might have had reason enough to hate him—Jacob being one of them. I saw Eden when she came out of that ice house, and she was shaking. She was heartbroken, shocked . . ."

"And yet he wouldn't marry her." Her father fixed her with a pointed look. "Jacob lost that money and his business months ago. This wasn't new. But Eden's relationship with him was very much in the present."

"She loved him!"

"And he was stringing her along. We all could see it. What if she figured it out? What if he said it in so many words? What if he told her that he'd never marry her? Would she be upset enough to . . . lash out?"

"She couldn't have hidden it from me if she had," Petunia replied. "But I can understand why they suspect her. We found her on the scene. She had blood on her hands. She was his girlfriend, and he was taking her for granted and ruining her reputation. I can see exactly why they think Eden killed him. But she didn't, and that's why I have to help Asher Nate find out who did."

"And if you find out that Eden did kill him?" her father asked. "Will you be able to face her parents on a service Sunday if you helped to gather the evidence against their daughter to lock her away for the rest of her life?"

Petunia's heart knocked to a stop. Could she do it—face her friends and family knowing that she'd helped to put her very best friend into prison?

"*Daet*, I'm positive she didn't do it. But if I leave the investigating to an Englisher cop, he'll come to his own conclusions—very Englisher conclusions. I can help show him what our culture is like and explain a few things that might otherwise mislead him. It's Eden's best chance."

Elias was silent for a moment, then he sucked in a slow breath.

"I have to grudgingly agree," her father said at last. "But it doesn't matter who did it—if they're a part of our community, it's going to be a blow when you discover them."

"Less of a blow than my best friend, *Daet*."

"Please be careful, Petunia." Her father cast her a pleading look. "You know how you can get . . ."

And she did know—but Petunia's quick temper and daring nature might actually help Eden at this critical time. *For such a time as this*, if she wanted to quote the Good Book.

That evening, Petunia's father left for a meeting of the town council. They were attempting to put more buggy parking into some downtown Blueberry parking lots, and Petunia was on her own for the evening. Her father wouldn't get back until quite late. She had a sewing order to complete, but it was harder to do in the kerosene light than in proper daylight. She'd get more done by getting up with the sun.

So Petunia puttered around the house, cleaning up the kitchen, and then she headed up the creaking staircase to the second floor where her workroom was located in the extra bedroom. She looked over the cape dress that she had set up on her dress form in the softly hissing light of the kerosene lamp. But her mind kept going back to her friend who was sitting in a jail cell right now, her heart broken at the loss of her boyfriend. Poor Eden—that was what everyone said. Poor Eden. But what were they doing to help her? Because even Petunia's own father could make a convincing case against her.

Petunia's mind kept going back to the ice house that the stern officer had turned her away from. If there was evidence that proved Eden innocent, that was where it would be. It was a place to start, at the very least. Ike was already dead, and whoever killed him would be lying low if they were smart. The door to the ice house was locked, but it was possible she might be able to look inside the one narrow window and get a glimpse of whatever it was that was so off limits.

Petunia slipped outside into the early evening darkness. A half moon hung low in the sky, and the snow glowed in the dim light that it cast. Petunia didn't take the time to think any further about her plans. She took a lantern, a flashlight, and some extra batteries along with her. She bundled up with her winter coat and an extra scarf since the night would be considerably chillier than the daytime. Then she hitched up Trudy again, flicked on the battery-operated headlights that stuck out on either side of her buggy, and headed out into the dark winter evening.

The roads were deserted at that time of night, except for a few cars. She didn't like coming out in a buggy late at night because her vehicle was far less visible than automobiles. She had two headlamps and a reflective triangle on the back of the buggy—that was all the bishop and elders allowed. But by the time she got out to the road that led to the ice house, all Englisher traffic had melted away, and it was just her and the looming, leafless trees on either side of the road. Even Trudy pranced uneasily as they turned into the drive toward the ice house.

The snow was sliced through with buggy wheel marks, and then flattened by the tire treads from police vehicles. Yellow police tape fluttered from around the ice house doorway, flapping free in the frigid wind. Another buggy—a black, covered buggy—sat a few yards off, and a large quarter horse stamped uneasily. She flicked off the headlights and reined in Trudy, her heart stuck in her throat. The door was ajar, a slim line of lamplight shining out into the night.

That door had been locked when they left. Asher had the key . . .

Who was here? Dare she look?

Petunia tied off her reins and dropped as quietly as she could to the snowy ground. Then she crept toward the ice house door. A faint light came from inside, glowing eerily in the darkness, and it occurred to her just then that she hadn't left a note to say where she'd gone.

Had the killer come back to the scene of the crime? A little voice in the back of her head whispered that she should be careful not to find herself on the business end of another ice pick.

Who'd come to the scene of the murder?

Petunia crept closer to the door, and she could just make out a slice of the inside of the ice house. She could see the tall form of a man standing there—his black felt hat pulled down over cold reddened ears. He wore work gloves on his hands, and his married man's beard was sparse and curly. She knew him immediately, and pushed the door open all the way.

"Jonathan Beiler," she said, and the man whirled around, his face ashen. "What in the world are you doing here?"

Chapter Three

Jonathan stared at her, his mouth half open, and then he exhaled a shaky breath that hung frozen in the air between them. He looked quickly down at his palm, closed his gloved hand over something, and pushed it into his coat pocket.

"I could ask you the same, Petunia," he said, shaking his head. "We had the police at my *daet*'s farm today, and you know why, I think. They said your *daet*'s tourists were the ones who'd found my sister with . . . with . . ." He swallowed.

"With the body," she finished for him.

"Yah, the body." He looked relieved to have a way to say it.

"And it wasn't the tourists only. I was there too. I'd come out to buy some ice."

Jonathan shot her a sympathetic look. "So you saw . . . the scene."

"Yah," Petunia said. "I'm not sure many will miss Ike Smoker except your sister, but it's still strange to think of him being gone."

Jonathan's gaze darkened. "He was horrible. Did you know that Eden had a farmer asking about her from another community? A well-off farmer who was recently widowed. He would have given her a good life, and *kinner* of her own. He had three little ones. And then he heard the stories about her and Ike, and he was no longer interested."

"She was in love with another man," Petunia said softly. A sweet widower, no matter how kind he might be, wouldn't tempt her in the least.

"She was in love with a man who would never marry her. Don't tell me you think Ike was going to step up, marry her, and support a family. That's tough to do on a gambling income."

"I know, I know . . ." Petunia sighed. "I didn't like how he treated her, either. But that is why the police think she did it—because he was ruining her life."

"She was blind to that," Jonathan said with a sigh. "Completely blind to it. The rest of us could see it clear as day, but she thought we were unfair to him and should be more charitable. She didn't do it, Petunia. I know that!"

Jonathan Beiler was very certain his sister was innocent—because he knew his sister's nature, or because he knew who'd really killed the man?

"I think she's innocent too," Petunia replied. "So what are you doing here?"

"Looking for clues as to who did it," Jonathan said.

"The police did that," she said.

"They might have missed something." He met her gaze, mildly challenging.

"Did you find anything?" she asked. She'd seen something in his hand—something small that she hadn't been able to get a good look at.

He paused just a fraction of beat. "No."

"Are you sure?" She leaned against the doorframe, and he shot her an annoyed look.

"Are you accusing me of something, Petunia Yoder?" he asked, his voice low.

"No!" She forced a laugh. "I just thought . . . it doesn't matter."

He'd lied to her, and she couldn't very well call him out in it, could she? Not alone in the dark.

"What did the police find?" he asked. "You were here, after all."

"They didn't show me," she replied. If he wasn't going to show what he'd found, she wasn't revealing information, either. "They know I didn't do it, though, because everyone saw me arrive just behind my *daet*'s wagon. And Ike had been killed quite recently. Plus, apparently, I don't hide things very well, and the detective could tell that about me."

"A good alibi."

Yah, Asher seemed to think so too. But what about Jonathan? Where was he yesterday? Did he have an equally strong alibi?

"Can I look inside?" she asked, nodding toward the ice house.

"Yah, yah, of course." He stood back and as Petunia walked inside, she felt a chill run up her spine. She'd just turned her back on a man who'd lied to her.

"How did you get in here?" Petunia asked, scanning the small room. There wasn't much to see—a patch of blood on the sawdust-covered floor, an unlit lantern on a shelf, some prepackaged food next to the lantern, and the long-handled saws and chisels for harvesting ice hanging on the wall.

"My sister had a key hidden in her bedroom. I knew about it," he replied.

"What? I didn't know that," Petunia said, feeling a little betrayed at her lower level of knowledge when it came to her best friend's romance. "How did you know?"

"My mother knew," Jonathan said. "As mothers do. She told me about it a long time ago. She was worried about Eden's reputation, like we all were. So when she found out that Eden had a key for the ice house, she was worried about . . . well, about what liberties Ike was taking with her, to start with, and how it would look."

"Yah . . ." Petunia nodded. She didn't have her own mother anymore, but she understood a mother's ability to understand her children's lives, just by cooking for them and cleaning up after them.

She wasn't sure what she was looking for in that room, but when she turned again, she found Jonathan's gaze locked on her with a guarded expression on his face.

"He's dead now," Petunia said. "Are you relieved?"

"My sister is arrested," he snapped back. "No, I'm not!"

"I am . . . a little bit," she admitted. "At least he can't continue stringing her along. She was so determined to believe him."

"Well . . ." Jonathan shrugged. "I am relieved that much is over. But I'll feel better still when she is back at home where she belongs."

"Me too," Petunia agreed. There was nothing else to see in the ice house, and she moved toward the door. "I'd best get home. It's late."

"Yah, me too," Jonathan said. He paused. "Perhaps it's better we don't tell anyone we were here. It's just you and me. No one else knows . . . do they?"

His words hung in the air with his frozen breath. No one else did know they were here in the dark, miles from town. If someone found another body—hers—lying out here in the ice house, there'd be no explanation about what happened . . .

"Uh, my father does, actually," she lied brightly. "You know how protective he is. He won't let me out of the house without knowing exactly where I'm going and when I'll be back."

It had come out of her mouth so smoothly that she felt a pang of guilt. It shouldn't be that easy to tell an untruth, even to protect herself.

"That's wise of you, Petunia," Jonathan said with a nod. "I'm glad you keep your head on straight. And I know you were trying to help my sister to see what kind of man Ike really was, too. So thank you for that."

Petunia let out a slow breath. "Yah, I did try."

Was she being ridiculous, worried that Jonathan would hurt her? All the same, she felt a little better as she got back into her buggy and turned on the electric headlights.

"Goodbye!" Petunia called, flicking the reins, and Trudy trotted eagerly forward, seeming as anxious as she was to get back onto the road. She looked over her shoulder.

Jonathan Beiler stood there in the soft light of his kerosene lamp, watching her go, and she shivered. Jonathan was her best friend's older brother—someone she'd known all her life. But someone had killed Ike . . . and Jonathan had just as much reason as anyone to do the deed.

Petunia urged Trudy faster, but she hardly needed the encouragement as her hooves rang against the pavement. An engine rumbled behind her and bright headlights suddenly blazed all around her. She attempted to look over her shoulder, but all she could make out was the blast of headlights. Her heart hammered against her ribcage, and she flicked the reins, urging Trudy faster still. The lights made the barren trees look like whitewashed fingers, stretching upward, and their shadows shot out long and thin. Who was following her?

Then there was a whoop, and the addition of some red and blue to the blaze of lights, and she reined in the horse. The police . . . She was actually relieved. The last thing she wanted was to come across some local yahoo in a pickup truck looking to spook horses for drunken fun.

A police marked SUV pulled up next to her as Trudy came to a stop, her eyes rolling in fear, and the passenger side window lowered.

"Petunia?" Asher's voice came from inside the SUV, and he put on an interior light so she could see his face. "What are you doing out here?"

"Asher!" She heaved a sigh of relief. There was something so reassuring about that square jaw and his direct, gray stare, and the relief was making way for the anger behind it. "You scared my horse!"

"Sorry about that." He didn't sound terribly concerned.

"That's very dangerous, you know. She could just as easily have taken off and I'd be in a runaway buggy. Don't do that to a buggy—people die that way!"

Her anger was rising now, replacing her earlier fear, and Asher stared at her, his eyes wide.

"I'm sorry. I'll be more careful next time, but you were coming away from the scene of the crime at"—he looked at his watch—"half past nine at night."

"That late?" Her heart thudded to a stop. Her father would be home by now, and he'd be worried sick. She'd be the one enduring a lecture tonight.

"What are you doing out here?" Asher asked, frowning.

"I'm . . ." And then she realized she *had* to explain herself. "I came out to take a look at things on my own, and I didn't think it through all the way, apparently."

Like what she'd do if she stumbled across someone else back at the scene of the crime.

"Hold on. I'm going to park. I'll be back in a minute . . ." Asher drove his vehicle ahead, pulled over to the side of the road, and then came out of his vehicle and back to where she sat in her buggy. He crossed his arms over his broad chest. "All right, I'm glad it's you. I was just patrolling the area, and I saw two buggies come out from the ice house drive. I have to admit, I was wondering who might want to visit the place at this time of night. I picked one to follow. Who was in the other buggy?"

"Jonathan Beiler," she replied.

"What?" His gaze swung behind her, down the road. "That's . . . Eden Beiler's brother, am I right?"

"Yah. He was doing the same thing I was—worried about his sister and wanted to prove her innocent." She really had no proof that he'd found something there, and she wasn't sure that cuffing Jonathan and bringing him into the station was going to improve matters.

"He might have some good reason to kill the man—since Ike had been tarnishing his sister's reputation . . ." Asher fixed her with a thoughtful look. "A guilty conscience, returning to the scene of the crime? Maybe worried we'd find some evidence it was him?"

She wanted to say no, that Jonathan couldn't possibly, but there had been something about him out there in the darkness—something cold and distanced.

"He hated Ike," Petunia admitted. "He didn't like the way Ike was treating his sister. But he didn't hate him any more than any other member of his family did." And then, with Asher's reassuring presence, and her heartbeat returning to a normal rhythm, she started to feel silly for her earlier panic. "Besides, Jonathan has a wife of his own now. She's pregnant with their first child. He has his own life to focus on, no matter what he feels about his sister's choices. He might have hated Ike, but I don't think he'd sacrifice his own family and future to avenge his sister's bad choices. That doesn't make sense."

"Crimes of passion aren't logical," Asher said.

"I don't know what to say to that," she replied, and she hunched her shoulders up against the cold.

"Do you always drive around at this time of night on your own?"

"Not usually," she admitted with a rueful smile. "But I couldn't get my mind off the ice house, and I decided to go check it out instead of losing sleep over it."

"Will you sleep better now?" Asher asked, a smile turning up one side of his lips.

"Not really." She shook her head. "It was worth a try."

"Go on home," Asher said. "I'll follow at a distance to make sure you get back safely. I'll come by your place tomorrow morning and we can sort out a plan."

"I'll see you then." Petunia picked up the reins. She'd feel a whole lot braver in the light of day . . . and old friends like Jonathan Beiler would feel less menacing then too, she was sure. "Good night, Asher."

She flicked the reins and Trudy started forward again. The night did feel less frightening with Asher out in the darkness with her. And now all she wanted was to settle in next to the wood stove at home and warm back up behind a nice, solid, locked door. More sleuthing could wait for the light of day.

* * *

Petunia was right that her father would be both home and worried enough to be absolutely furious by the time she came back. Elias stomped outside, helped her unhitch, got the horse settled with some fresh hay, and then stomped back inside, his spine rigid with fury.

Elias's lectures weren't like ordinary Amish fathers'. His lectures tended to meander all over the place, touching on "truly stupid things" she'd done over the last decade, at least, that had worried him sick. Tonight's lecture ended with, "Someone was murdered, Petunia. Murdered! And you're trotting out in the middle of the night, trying to catch a killer! This is precisely why you aren't married!"

"What?" Petunia attempted to control her tone, but she had little success. "I'm not married because I can't keep my mouth shut and I don't bat my lashes and tell a man he's so superior to me. That's why I'm chronically single! Me trotting about after dark looking for a murderer is entirely beside the point!"

But in the end, she did apologize, tell her father how very sorry she was for worrying him, confess that she knew she should have at the very least left a note, and finally retired to bed at half past eleven with her mind filled with suspicions of her neighbors.

The next morning, Petunia awoke to an even colder day, with ice on the inside of the windows. Elias decided that they wouldn't do the regular tour, specifically because there were several Englishers asking to be taken past the ice house after the murder hit the news.

"It isn't right to use a person's death as an idle curiosity," Elias said. "And out of respect for the dead man, I think we should shutter the tour business for a day. Ike Smoker might not have been a popular man, but he was one of us."

"Yah, *Daet*, that does seem appropriate," she agreed. "I do need to get some more groceries into the house, too. I'll bake for us this afternoon, but I'm low in everything."

"You're baking, are you?" he asked warily.

"We have to eat, *Daet*!"

"Yah, but your last pie . . ."

Petunia was not great in the kitchen, but she did try. Some of her pies turned out. Some ended up just about inedible.

"I will be very careful this time. And I'm not making pie. I'm baking bread. I won't leave the kitchen for a second until it is safely cooling on the cupboard."

And what choice did her father have? She was the woman, which made her the cook of the home. That was how an Amish family worked, even if it wasn't always the most logical setup. He'd just have to let her get on with it. Baking flour, white sugar, yeast, lard. They were all on her shopping list.

"Just . . . be careful, Petunia," her father said, and Petunia wasn't sure if he meant in the kitchen, or in town.

So Petunia took the big, black buggy into town. The town of Blueberry was a perfect hybrid of Amish and English conveniences. There was buggy parking with hitching rails in the biggest parking lots from the Walmart to the grocery store. Several downtown streets had Amish shops—no electricity, except what was required for food preservation and safety codes. There was a dry goods store that Petunia preferred to the regular grocery store. She got less attention there, and more Amish people shopped in the Amish stores, making her presence less likely to attract pictures and videos. The Englishers thought they were very discrete. They were not.

She parked her buggy in the back parking lot that was mostly filled with Amish vehicles. A few cars were parked at the far end of the lot, and one Englisher couple who got out of a pickup truck didn't even give her a second look, which meant they were local and Amish people weren't a curiosity for them.

Inside the dry goods shop, Petunia pushed a cart through the aisles. The store was very plain on the inside—just shelves loaded down with bags and cartons. Plentiful windows allowed in a good amount of natural light. There were hooks hanging down from chains attached to the ceiling. They would support hanging kerosene or battery-operated lanterns when the day got darker before closing time. The signs at the top of each aisle were handwritten in English: Flour, Dry Cereals, Baking Goods, Canning Supplies . . .

She picked up a large bag of flour and a second bag nearly as big of granulated sugar. There was a sale on brown sugar, and large containers of cinnamon and nutmeg, and as Petunia headed in that direction, her cart nearly collided with another, and she looked up to see Lovina Schlabach.

Lovina was a middle-aged woman with wire-framed glasses and iron gray hair pulled back under her black *kapp*. She was a single woman still—one of the more established "unmarriageables," and Petunia had always liked her. She was the bishop's maiden sister, and she lived with Bishop Felty Schlabach and his family. It gave her a strange position in the community—one of respect, but also a woman with perspective. She saw more than most people had the chance to see, just because she lived with such an influential man.

"Oh!" Lovina pulled up short before the carts collided, and a distracted smile came to her face. "Petunia, how are you?"

"I've been better," Petunia said. "I'm sure you've heard about the ice house."

Her smile faded. "Yah, I did."

"It was awful, Lovina, I don't mind saying. I don't know how you felt about Ike, but he's now facing Gott."

"I didn't feel anything about him," Lovina said.

"Nothing?" Petunia asked. "I know he owed your nephew Obie a good deal of money, and he needed it back."

"Yah, Obadiah was kinder than he should have been with Ike Smoker, I'll give you that. But it's business between men," Lovina said, and her words were pointed. A remonstrance, or was Lovina trying to avoid that line of conversation for a reason?

"How did you hear about the murder?" Petunia asked.

Lovina moved her cart closer to keep their words private, and they settled next to a shelf holding large containers of pickling salt.

"Menno Lapp came by with the news, and he'd heard it from someone else. And when my brother Felty heard, he stopped right then and there, fell to his knees, and prayed. It was a beautiful prayer, too."

"Just . . . dropped and prayed?" Petunia asked. It was a strange image. The bishop was normally very dignified.

"Yah. Well . . . he cares about this community. Really cares."

"He's a good bishop," Petunia said, trying to smooth over her earlier criticism. "What did he say in his prayer?"

"He begged Gott's forgiveness for the murderer," Lovina replied, pushing her glasses up her nose. "He said that whoever did this wicked thing knew not what he'd done. And Felty shed a tear right there on his knees. We all got a little misty listening to him."

It was an incredibly emotional response to the death of a ne'er-do-well. Petunia paused, trying to imagine the bishop weeping on the floor, praying on his knees in front of Menno Lapp with his awkward overbite and too narrow shoulders . . .

"How did the bishop know that the murderer didn't know what he'd been doing?" Petunia asked. "A good many people had reason to dislike Ike. It stands to reason that someone might have killed him knowing exactly what they were doing."

"Well . . ." Lovina shook her head. "No one here would do something like that with premeditation, I'm sure."

"Does the bishop have any suspicion of who might have done it?" Petunia asked.

"None."

"With a reaction like that, it sounds like he might," Petunia pressed.

"My brother is very sensitive to spiritual things," Lovina replied, giving Petunia's hand a gentle tap. "He feels things deeply, including the sins of others."

"Ah." Petunia wasn't sure how to answer that.

"And what about Eden?" Lovina whispered. "I heard they took her away. I'm worried about her, the poor girl."

"She's heartbroken," Petunia whispered back. "She loved Ike—whether he was worthy of it or not. But the police are keeping her because she was the one who was with poor Ike closest to his death, and they seem to blame the romantic partner first."

"Eden wouldn't kill him," Lovina said with a sigh. "I don't think she's strong enough."

"Emotionally?" Petunia asked. Because Petunia had to agree. It would take a stronger nerve than Eden's to kill a man where he stood.

"Physically," Lovina replied. "She's just a slim little thing, and I heard that . . . it was . . ."

"An ice pick. Right in the chest," Petunia said, and her mind went back to that gruesome scene. "You're right, Lovina. It was very far into his chest, too. I'd say it was about four or five inches deep. That would have taken strength."

"Someone should mention that to the police," Lovina said, her voice low. "Because anyone can see that Eden is innocent. I can't believe they're keeping her like this. She should be at home with her family, recovering from the shock."

Petunia couldn't disagree.

"Who do *you* think did it?" Petunia asked softly.

"An Englisher." She sounded so certain, so logical. She almost found herself nodding in agreement based on Lovina's tone alone.

"Wait . . . why?" Petunia asked.

"Well, who else? Not one of us. I'm sure it was an Englisher who snuck up on him. Someone he upset. Ike wasn't a good Amish man, if you know what I mean."

"I do know," Petunia agreed. "But I was there that morning, Lovina. It had snowed the night before, and the only tracks in the parking area were from buggies. I looked at it especially. There were no car tracks."

Lovina's face paled.

"So it wasn't an Englisher," Petunia went on. "It would be so much easier on all of us if it were. But it was someone Amish—someone who hated him, obviously."

"Are you sure?"

"Yah."

"Maybe you didn't notice some tire tracks?"

"I'm very, very sure."

"One of us," Lovina said weakly.

"Yah."

The older woman licked her lips and swallowed hard. "I don't like the sound of that one bit."

"Me neither," Petunia replied. "But we'd best face it, because I won't let Eden stay locked up for something she's innocent of committing. Whoever did this is better off admitting their own guilt and facing Gott. And quite frankly, Lovina, I want to know who did this awful thing. And *why*."

"Who do you think did it?"

"Who do I think?" Petunia sucked in a deep breath. "My first thought was maybe someone protecting Eden's reputation. Maybe someone who was furious about how he was treating her."

"Maybe . . ." Lovina's eyes lit up. "That's true. Maybe it was."

"But when you put a name to that—Eden's own brother or father—it's harder to believe, isn't it?" Petunia said. "But someone did it."

"A crime of passion, perhaps," Lovina said. "Someone who would never do such a thing if they weren't so worked up. Like my brother the bishop said."

"I think that stands to reason," Petunia agreed. "But all the same, their conscience must be pricking them by now. You can't stab someone in the chest, no matter how worked up you are, and feel nothing."

"I don't think I want to know who killed him," Lovina said weakly. "I'd rather . . . let it go. Bury Ike, bring Eden home, and forget about the whole nasty business."

"Eden doesn't come home unless we can find out who did it," Petunia replied. "That's the catch. Someone has to pay for the crime, and I'd much rather it be the person who did it than my innocent friend."

"I know," Lovina murmured, and her worried gaze moved toward Petunia's cart. "Are you baking today? Even with . . . everything that's happened?"

"Yah," Petunia said. "Food still needs cooking. Bellies still need filling. Life still keeps marching on."

"True." Lovina smiled sadly. "I was feeling guilty for coming out for groceries at a time like this, with my brother deep in prayer and my sister-in-law locked away in her room with her Bible. But you're right. Families still need feeding, and someone needs to keep things rolling." She reached past Petunia and picked up a box of pickling salt. "I think we're low on this, too . . ."

It seemed that the bishop was taking this murder very seriously, on a spiritual level at the very least. But a spiritual response to the murder wasn't going to do Eden a bit of good. She needed evidence that proved her innocence. So while the bishop prayed, Petunia had other plans.

Someone in Blueberry had killed Ike Smoker, and she was going to find out who.

Chapter Four

When Petunia got back from the store, she peeled off her winter coat and headed into the kitchen to start some baking. She was worried that her bread would flop, considering her mind was elsewhere. Petunia's success with a decent loaf of bread seemed to be anchored in her mood, more than the actual mixing and kneading. And her mood today was irritable.

This was part of her problem. It wasn't that she didn't try to be a good cook, but her mind wandered off a lot—frankly, there were more interesting things to think about than her baking. And right now, her mind was moving through the members of her community, sifting them for who might have had reason to kill Ike Smoker. When Petunia put the rounded loaves into the oven, she did so with a prayer that Gott would bless them into some decent shape, for her poor father's sake, if nothing else.

An hour later, Petunia was standing with her arms crossed, frowning at the big, black wood-burning stove when someone knocked at the front door. Anyone who knew them personally would come around the side. She headed through the sitting room, and when she pulled open the door, she was met with a blast of cold air and the serious face of Detective Asher Nate.

"Come in," she said, "and hurry. It's cold out there."

Asher stepped inside and slammed the door shut behind him. He stamped his boots off on the mat.

"Are you free to go visit a suspect?" he asked.

"I've got bread in the oven," she replied.

"Oh." He nodded. "Uh . . . how long until it's done?"

"I'm about to check it now," she said. "Come on through. Hopefully it's done."

She led the way into the kitchen. She opened the oven door and put on some oven mitts. Two of the loaves were nicely domed and browned, but the third had collapsed. She pulled them out one at a time and put them on top of the stove.

"This one flopped," she said, pulling out the last loaf. "But two out of three isn't bad for me!"

Asher chuckled. "It smells great."

"They've got to cool, but I can leave the house now," she said. "*Daet* is at the tour office in town catching up on some paperwork, so he won't miss me. Who are we going to visit?"

"You mentioned that Ike owed money to two men in the community," Asher said.

"Two, *at least*."

"Well, two *for sure*," he said. "I can only work with facts, not hunches."

"That's too bad," she replied. "A gut feeling can take you a long way."

"Judges tend to disagree with that." He shot her a rueful smile, but then he sobered. "They also don't like a flight risk . . ."

"What do you mean?" This felt important, but she didn't see how.

"I mean . . . my boss has decided to press formal charges against Eden Beiler for the murder of Ike Smoker."

"Press charges!" Petunia said. "But we haven't done the investigation!"

"It's possible to drop the charges, but we can only hold her for so long, and that's what I meant about a flight risk," he replied. "If we let Eden go, chances are she'll disappear somewhere, and if we come back to press charges again, we won't find her."

It was true. Her parents would immediately ship her off to some family member, and the community would remain silent about it. He wasn't wrong . . .

"So what do we do?" Petunia asked.

"We keep investigating. The problem is, Eden was found with blood on her hands standing over the body. That's pretty damning evidence. But my boss agreed to slow things down on our end so that we can keep Eden in custody here in Blueberry. We have a few days yet to figure out who else had reason to want Ike dead."

"Oh . . ." Petunia's heartbeat was still slowing down. "Okay, so . . . what do we do now?"

"I want to start with Obadiah Schlabach. Is there anything you can tell me about him?"

"He's the bishop's son," Petunia said. "He's very well respected in these parts. His whole family is."

"Where would he have gotten the money he lent to Ike?" Asher asked.

Petunia shrugged. "I don't know. He probably saved it up."

"What does he do for a living?" Asher asked. "The bishop owns a farm, doesn't he? So there'd be a family business there?"

"Bishop Felty does own a big farm, but Obie and his father have a tense relationship," Petunia replied. "They have very different personalities, you see. Bishop Felty is very strong and opinionated. Obie is gentler, and he goes along with his *daet*'s ideas because it's easier, I think. So Obie helps his *daet* at the farm, but he also works at the farmers market, selling their goods there. It gives them all some space from each other."

"Ah. So we're more likely to find him at the farmers market this time of day?" Asher asked.

"I'd say so."

"Good. I'd rather speak with him away from the rest of his family, anyway." He looked down at his cell phone. "Can we go?"

"Yah, I suppose we can," she replied, scanning the kitchen one last time. Petunia closed the damper to the stove to limit the air getting to the fire, and then fetched her thick, woolen winter coat and her outdoor bonnet. A tickle of worry worked its way up her spine.

Obie Schlabach was a nice man, but he was also the bishop's son . . . she just hoped that Asher stepped lightly, because if he didn't, Petunia dearly hoped not to have offended the whole Schlabach family by the end of this. That family was influential and connected. She had a life to live in this community, too.

The drive to the farmers market was blissfully warm despite the blowing cold outside. Heat pumped against her legs from the inside of Asher's police cruiser, and it felt almost wickedly cozy. And Englisher men were different from the Amish. You could smell the reassuring scent of a man's job on him when he was Amish, or the soap he'd scrubbed with. But Asher smelled of a faint musk she couldn't place. It was warm, a little spicy, and it made her insides melt. She did her best to ignore that—it shouldn't matter. It *didn't* matter. The Englisher world was a strange and confusing one, and she much preferred her Amish life where things made sense, and everyone had their place.

Almost everyone. Petunia was proving to be difficult to file away, it seemed. But she was working on that. There had to be a way to settle in.

The Blueberry Farmers Market was located on the far side of town on the fairgrounds. In the summer this area was much busier, but during the winter months, the indoor farmers market gave the locals somewhere to browse local crafts and farm fresh goods. About half of the booths were Amish, and the Schlabach Amish Family Farm booth was located in a far corner.

Where the bishop was tall, strong, and powerful in both personality and physique, his son Obadiah Schlabach was a "middling" man. Of middling height, middling weight, middling looks, and he could blend quite easily into a barn door. His hair was a mouse brown, and he was clean-shaven, as all unmarried men were, but he wore his black felt hat at a jaunty little angle that defied the mediocre rest of him.

"Hello, Petunia," Obie said as they walked up. His gaze flickered back toward Asher. "Just a moment, sir." Then he switched to Pennsylvania Dutch. "How is Eden doing?"

"She's been charged with murder," Petunia replied in English for Asher's benefit.

A look of annoyance flickered across Obie's face, and he continued in Pennsylvania Dutch. "Murder? That's ridiculous. She didn't do it."

"I agree," she said. "But until we find out who did kill Ike, she's the one who will take the blame. This is very serious."

"Yah . . ." Obie breathed. "It wasn't her. I know her. She's not capable of something like that."

"I agree," Petunia said earnestly. "But that's why we're here. This is Detective Asher Nate."

"Oh." Obie turned his attention to Asher for the first time. "She didn't do it, Detective. Eden isn't capable of something like that."

Asher's expression didn't change even a little. "I was told that Ike Smoker owed you money."

Obie froze for a moment. "A little."

"How much?"

"Four thousand dollars."

"Four thousand dollars?" Petunia burst out. "That's a lot of money, Obie!"

"I know." Obadiah cast her an irritated look.

"Why would you give Ike that kind of money?" she pressed. "Did you really think he'd pay you back?"

"Yah, I thought he would." Obie's tone was terse. She was overstepping in a major way, but so much money felt wrong—very wrong.

"Were you friendly with him?" Asher asked.

"No."

"Four thousand dollars is pretty friendly," Asher countered.

Obadiah sighed and looked down at the ground.

"I mean, we all knew what kind of man Ike was," Petunia said. "Well, everyone but Eden, it seems. I don't understand why you'd give him that money, unless you didn't need it back again. But I don't see how. That's a lot of money. You could buy a quality used buggy for that."

And hadn't her father said Obie was thinking of marriage? Years ago, Obie had set his sights on Eden Beiler, but she hadn't been interested in return. And none of them were teens any longer.

"I'm a man who made a choice!" Obie retorted, giving Petunia a no-nonsense look.

"And I'm a man with a badge asking why," Asher said quietly.

Obie's attention snapped back to Asher, and he deflated a little. "Ike said he'd leave town if his debts were cleared, and four grand should take care of it."

Well, that was more believable, but not completely. He wouldn't have given that kind of money to get Ike away from Eden, would he?

"You were willing to part with that kind of money just to see the back of Ike?" she asked cautiously. Did he still hold some feelings for Eden?

"I—" Obie grimaced. "Ike Smoker was a bad man. He claimed the Amish faith and lived like he was heathen. He—"

An Amish girl came up behind them, murmured an "excuse me," and passed behind the counter. It was Hadassah Schlabach, Obie's teenage sister. She looked over at Petunia questioningly.

"Haddie, go get some lunch," Obie said.

"I just came back from lunch," she replied.

"Then . . . go find someone to talk to."

"Why?" she asked.

No one seemed to be taking Obadiah's authority terribly seriously, and his face turned red.

"We're asking some questions about Ike's death," Petunia supplied.

"Oh! Ike . . . ," Hadassah said. "He was always nice to me."

"Of course he was nice," Obie snapped. "He was nice to every girl!"

"He wasn't flirting," Hadassah said seriously, turning to Petunia. "He was kind. He saw something in me no one else did."

That was worrisome . . . Petunia stepped closer to the girl.

"What did he say to you?"

Hadassah took a step back. "Nothing. Nothing really."

Petunia looked over her shoulder and saw Asher staring at her with blazing eyes. Yah. Unhelpful. But it was possible that Obie was wanting Ike to go away for reasons other than his feelings for Eden.

"Come here, Haddie," Petunia said. "And Asher—" She shot him an annoyed look. If he wanted her help, he'd have to trust her to have a conversation without him over her shoulder. She led the girl a little way off.

"There," Petunia said. "Men don't understand this stuff anyway."

"But Ike seemed to," Hadassah said, tears welling in her eyes. "He was so kind."

"What did he say?" Petunia asked.

"Oh, he just said I was very smart. He said he wished he had been as good in school as I was. And he said"—Hadassah blushed—"he said my blueberry muffins were the best in the county. He said he wouldn't tell anyone else that, because they'd get jealous, but he said any man who married me would be lucky."

Smooth words for a man who was sullying Eden's reputation at the same time.

"But he was courting Eden," Petunia reminded her.

"Oh, he didn't mean it that way," Hadassah said quickly, shaking her head. "He was—" She stopped short. "He was like a big brother. He told me I should find a nice man and marry him when I was old enough. He said he wasn't going to get married, though."

For a grown man to be giving a teenage girl that kind of attention wasn't appropriate. Or to be talking to her about his personal life. Had anyone besides Obie noticed Ike's "kindness" to a teenage girl?

"He told you he wasn't going to get married?" Petunia asked.

"Yah . . ." Hadassah looked like she might have said too much.

"Did you worry about Eden?" Petunia asked. Where were Hadassah's loyalties here? "If he didn't want to get married . . ."

"Then she shouldn't have been carrying on with him," Hadassah replied. "I don't know why she did."

"Because he wasn't telling her that," Petunia replied. "He was telling her that he wanted to marry her."

Hadassah's brow furrowed. "He . . . lied to me?"

"No, sweetie," Petunia murmured. "He told you the truth. He lied to her. There is a certain kind of man who lies and lies. And they can be very smooth about it. They're very charming, but liars all the same."

Hadassah's lips flattened and she seemed to be considering this new possibility. While the life lesson was an important one, that wasn't why Petunia was here.

"What did your *daet* think of Ike hanging around you?" Petunia asked, tugging the girl's attention back.

"He didn't know," Hadassah replied. "Ike didn't come to our house. I only ever saw him here at the market."

"And Obie? What did he think of it?"

"You know Obie," Hadassah said. "He can be so proper all the time that he forgets how to be friendly. I know people didn't like Ike, but I did. I don't think even Eden really understood him. He was very kind to me, and I'll miss him." Hadassah wiped a tear off her cheek. "I can't believe anyone here would do that to him."

So Ike had a different version of himself that he shared with young, vulnerable women. That was interesting to know. And Petunia didn't think that was the kind of secret Obadiah would keep from his father. So maybe that was why Obie was willing to part with four thousand dollars—to get Ike away from his little sister!

But would Obadiah go further to keep his sister safe? Would he confront Ike and in a rage, strike out?

Petunia looked up and found Asher's dark gaze pinned to her.

"Are you helping to find who killed him?" Hadassah asked.

"I'm trying," Petunia replied.

"Good," Hadassah said. "Because whoever did that to poor Ike deserves to be punished for what he did. Ike was kind."

Ike was many things, but his interest in Haddie was far from "kind," Petunia was sure. Regardless, they were now a step ahead in this investigation.

* * *

Back in the cruiser again, Petunia looked over at Asher. His expression was like a stone. He started the car and the warm air immediately began to blow against her legs again. Such luxury . . . such comfort. She'd have to be careful not to get too used to this. The Plain life wasn't always the most comfortable, especially in winter, but it did come with a deep and undisturbed sleep at night. Or it used to.

"Well?" Asher asked, turning toward her. "What did Obadiah's sister have to say? It looked like a pretty intense conversation from where I was standing."

"It seems Ike was sweet-talking her too," Petunia said with a wince. "And it sounded . . . inappropriate in a way I can't exactly prove, but . . ."

"What did she say, exactly?" Asher asked.

Petunia repeated everything she remembered.

"Yup." Asher put the car into gear and pulled out of the parking space. "It is inappropriate for a grown man to be forging a friendship with a teenage girl. I don't care where you're from, that's not normal behavior. So it seems Ike Smoker had eyes for women other than Eden."

"I didn't think he did," Petunia admitted.

"I know. Because you were seeing it through Eden's eyes. But guys like that are the same everywhere. It sounds like things might have been getting a bit too high pressure with your friend. There were expectations that he'd marry her, and people were leaning on him to commit to her—to man up. When that starts happening, the guy tends to start looking for something new and fresh. That's what they enjoy—the chase."

"So you aren't surprised," she said.

"Not at all. We'll probably turn up a few more women he was sweet-talking, too."

"Maybe I shouldn't be shocked, either," Petunia admitted. "I suppose I just wanted him to be faithful to her, at the very least. But I knew he was a bad man."

"Go with your gut on that stuff," Asher said. "Bad men behave badly."

And Eden had been devoted to Ike, sacrificing her own reputation and her relationships with her family and community for that man. Ike might not have deserved to be killed the way he was, but he'd definitely deserved more community consequences than he'd faced!

"Does the fact that Ike was looking around make Eden look more guilty?" Petunia asked. "Will you be thinking she might have gotten jealous or something?"

"It did occur to me."

"That's what I was afraid of," Petunia said. "But we can't forget Obie, either. He had some good reason to give Ike that money. But it looks like after he handed the cash over, Ike didn't follow through on his promise to leave the community."

"And that would make any man angry," Asher agreed. "If he thought that Ike was turning his attention away from Eden and toward his younger sister, it might make him angry enough to lash out."

Petunia tried to imagine Obadiah coming at Ike with an ice pick, and it was hard to do. Obie was gentle, a little full of his own position, yet not the violent type. But he was very protective of his younger sister . . .

"Do you think we'll catch the killer?" she asked.

"Of course."

At least Asher was optimistic. But then, he'd never seen how tightly an Amish community could close up when they felt like Englishers were needling into their business a little too much.

"Are you hungry?" Asher asked.

"A little," she said.

Asher signaled a turn and headed in the direction of a burger joint. He took them through the drive-through behind an Amish buggy. They were probably young people in there, because most times Amish families liked to go inside and sit down and eat together, not try to balance a drink and burger in a buggy seat.

When it was their turn, Asher ordered two bacon double cheeseburgers and fries, and a few minutes later, they were at the far end of the parking lot next to where two harnessed buggies stood—one of which was the buggy that had gone through the drive-through ahead of them. Petunia leaned forward to see who it was—she recognized a young married couple, and she smiled to herself. Good for them.

Asher handed her food over, and for a couple of minutes, they put their attention into eating. Petunia's gaze moved to the horses as her mind clicked through the facts they had so far. The horses stamped in the cold, and their breath hung in clouds in front of them. The buggy without anyone inside had blankets flung over the horse's back to keep him warm while he waited on his owners.

How was Eden doing right now? She'd be fed and warm, but probably incredibly confused and heartbroken . . .

"Tell me something," Asher said, swallowing a bite, and then taking a sip of his fountain soda. "What was with Obadiah's attitude he was giving you?"

Petunia pulled her attention back. "It's Amish roles for men and women."

"And?" he prodded.

Oh. He didn't fully understand that.

"You see, with us Amish, we take our roles very seriously. Men protect and provide. They work hard, and they shoulder the worries. We women take care of the home. We cook, clean, sew, and take care of the men's needs. We're very serious about what's a woman's business and what's a man's business. I'm a woman. My place is not to question a man and ask for details about his financial situation, no matter how odd it might seem."

"And what seems odd about Obadiah's financial situation to you?" he asked.

"I'm supposed to keep my nose out of it," she said, shooting him a joking smile.

"Yeah, yeah, but I'm not Amish, am I?" He met her smile.

"Fine . . . four thousand dollars is a lot of money," she said. "Especially to give it to someone who obviously would never repay it . . . that's not smart. Besides, Obadiah is of an age where he'll be wanting to get married. My *daet* mentioned he was thinking of marriage, and that was why he needed Ike to pay him back. He'll need some financial security of his own to start up a home. He'll need money in the bank, frankly."

"Is there someone he's dating?" Asher asked.

Petunia shook her head. "Not that I know of, but that doesn't mean anything. A matchmaker could find him a quality girl from another community, and a marriage could be arranged without any of us being the wiser before the banns are read in Sunday Service."

Easy-peasy for a man. Less easy for a woman like Petunia.

"Okay."

"So that didn't make sense, him wasting money that way. Besides, he might inherit his *daet*'s land, but his *daet* is far from retirement. If Obie wants a life of his own, he'll have to prove he's financially secure enough in his own right to provide for a wife and children. And that isn't based on his father's farm. That's based on his own personal financial situation."

"But with his sister in the mix?" Asher prompted.

"I suppose that makes him parting with the money make more sense," she replied. "But there is still something that doesn't sit right with me. We all knew about how Jacob Weir lost his carpentry business, and even when Jacob pleaded with Ike to repay him, Ike couldn't do it. So Ike was completely broke, and not likely to repay. There was an easier solution for Obie. Why not just have his father, the bishop, and the community elders step in? If Ike was angling for Bishop Felty's own daughter, don't you think the bishop would do something about it?"

"You'd think," Asher agreed.

"So why give Ike the money?" Petunia rolled it over in her mind, and it still seemed . . . off. "You see? It doesn't make sense . . ." She took the last bite of her burger, then licked off her fingertips.

"I see your point," he said. "It doesn't. There were easier ways to deal with that."

Petunia nodded. "And that right there is what makes me unmarriageable. A nice, sweet girl would let a man take care of his business and she wouldn't question him again."

"And what will you do?" Asher asked with a short laugh.

"I'm probably going to keep bringing it up with him until it does makes sense," she replied. "I'm a real pain in the neck."

"I like it," Asher said with a chuckle. "I'm the same way."

Petunia popped a fry into her mouth. "My father has been begging me for the better part of a year to mend my ways, but I've got a brain of my own, and there are times a man is downright wrong. However, if I want an Amish man to marry me, I can't say that. I have to pretend that he's right, even if he isn't. The only place where I can call the shots is my own kitchen—and I'm not much of a cook. The truth of the matter is, I don't behave in a demure and submissive way, and there are enough women who do that I won't have any men asking me home from singing."

"Hm." Asher nodded. "Just getting married doesn't seem worth smothering your personality for anyway."

"I couldn't do it if I tried," she replied. "Which leaves me single, and I've made my peace with it."

"Really?" He arched an eyebrow. "You have no hopes for romance?"

"None." She slurped the last of her orange soda and jiggled the ice cubes in the cup.

"Because in our Englisher society, you wouldn't be discounted from love and marriage just because you're smart and have opinions," he said. "In fact, we figure that if a man is intimidated by a woman, that's his problem, not hers."

"That's very nice for all of you," Petunia said. "But I'm Amish."

"You don't have to stay Amish," he countered.

"It's who I am, Asher," she said. "It's not a choice."

The big man nodded slowly. "Understood. Forget I said anything."

"Besides," Petunia said. "I have more to offer than just my hand in marriage. Blueberry needs a few free-spirited old maids to keep things running. I might not make a very good Amish wife, but I make a very good Amish *woman*. That's one thing I learned from Lovina Schlabach. She's the bishop's sister, and she never did get married, but she's a well-loved member of our community. She's strong, opinionated, and often right, even when men don't want her to be. When someone needs help in the kitchen, or advice about gardening . . . or even just a shoulder to lean on, Lovina is there. She's shown me that being an old maid isn't a terrible fate. My community needs me. Even now, I'm the only one who can really show you what our culture is like, aren't I? Every community needs a few people who rattle around loose."

"Well, I for one am glad to have your help," Asher said. "Truly."

Petunia popped her last fry into her mouth and wondered just how much of this detective's trust she'd earned today. "Asher, can I see Eden?"

Asher looked over at her thoughtfully.

"She's alone right now," Petunia pressed. "She's accused of a murder she didn't commit, and she's lost the man she loved. Let me see her, at least. You can be there supervising, if you want to, but I know it will make her feel better knowing that I'm looking for the truth. Please?"

"It's not a good idea," he said.

"You think Eden killed Ike because she was the closest one to him?" Petunia said. "But she also knew him better than any other person in this community. She might know something that she doesn't even realize she knows! And if you question her, you'll never get to it. I might."

"That's a good point," he admitted, and he pressed his lips together, then sighed. "Okay. A brief visit. But it'll be supervised."

"I have nothing to hide!" Petunia said, shooting him a grateful smile. "Thank you, Asher."

And Petunia was almost certain that Eden didn't have anything to hide, either. At least she hoped so . . . because Eden couldn't afford to have more dredged up against her right now.

Chapter Five

The Borough of Blueberry Police Department was situated at the corner of Main Street and Gvild Road, on the end of Main, far from the clustered Amish shops that drew in the tourists. It was a single-story brick building with crisp, white trim. There were two planters flanking the doors with small evergreen trees growing in each one, and the light from inside shone cheerily through a paned window. The whole building looked far more welcoming than Petunia thought it should for the job that it did.

Asher opened the door for her and Petunia walked in first, Asher close behind. A uniformed officer sat at the front desk. She had short-cropped hair and a Bic pen tucked behind one ear, and was writing something down with another pen in her hand. She shot them a distracted smile as they came inside.

"Hello there," she said to Asher.

"Hi, Dot," Asher said. "Busy day so far?"

"Surprisingly!" she replied. "Must be a full moon or something. There have been three stolen bicycles in the space of one morning."

Outside, Petunia heard a raucous voice talking loudly in a mixture of English and Pennsylvania Dutch, and the front door behind them opened again for an officer to lead a hatless, red-faced Amish man into the station. Petunia knew him immediately. He was Jacob

Weir, a middle-aged man with a graying beard and a bald spot now fully on display without his hat.

"I didn't do anything," he was slurring. "Not a thing. I was sitting there and having a drink like anyone can do, and then you came in!"

"This way, sir," the officer said, sounding tired.

"It's perfectly awful to drink!" Jacob went on loudly.

Everyone stopped and looked at the drunk man in mild confusion then, because it was clear Jacob had been doing little else since early that morning by the state of him. Petunia could only wonder what his poor wife, Bonita, would do about that money poured down his throat in the bar.

"It's perfectly . . . per . . . perfer. . . ." He was slurring more now, and he pursed his lips for a moment, then said even louder, "Perfectly *lawful* to drink."

Then he nodded so exuberantly at having gotten the words out that he nearly tipped over.

"Maybe so, but it is *not* perfectly lawful to urinate in the corner," the officer replied.

"I don't think I did that—" Jacob sounded genuinely shocked.

"Sir, you absolutely did," the officer replied. "I watched you do it."

"I don't think so . . ." Jacob swayed on his feet and blinked a few times while he attempted to focus his alcohol-fogged gaze on Petunia. "Petunia Yoder? What are you doing here, Petunia? Are you in some kind of trouble, Petunia?"

"Don't be worrying about her," the officer said. "Come along now. You're going to lie down and sleep it off."

"Somebody needs to worry about Petunia," Jacob whispered loudly. "If you knew how Ike Smoker talked about her, you'd be worried, too!"

"Would I now . . . ?" The officer wasn't listening, but Petunia froze, and so did Asher.

"What did Ike say now?" Asher asked.

"That she puts her nose where it doesn't belong." Jacob reached out a finger toward Petunia's nose, and then seemed to change his mind, darted forward, and planted a wet, foul-smelling kiss on Petunia's forehead.

"Jacob!" Petunia snapped, wriggling free. Bonita would certainly have an opinion about *that*!

"You be careful, Petunia Yoder!" Jacob said earnestly. "Ike hates you."

"Let's go," the officer said.

"Ike is dead, Jacob!" she called after him.

"Oh, that's right . . . ," Jacob said, his gate wobbly as he allowed himself to be guided by the officer. "It's okay then! Never mind!"

Petunia stood there, her breath shaky. She mutely accepted a wet wipe from Officer Dot at the desk and used it to wipe off her forehead.

"Did you know Ike felt that way about you?" Asher asked quietly.

"No . . . ," she breathed. "I don't think I've ever been hated before."

It wasn't a nice feeling, either. Like having a rug pulled out from under her. She'd always been liked—even if no one would want to marry her. Being likable had been enough. But maybe she should get used to this feeling, because she was going to help Asher prove that someone else had killed Ike Smoker, and that would affect more than just the killer. Even murderers had families.

"Who is that man?" Asher asked, keeping his voice low.

"That's Jacob Weir," she said weakly.

"Jacob Weir . . . ," Asher repeated. "He's one of our people of interest. Ike owed him a good deal of money, didn't he?"

"He did."

"And Ike seemed to be quite open with Jacob, if he was telling him he hated you so much," Asher said. "Were they friends?"

"They used to drink together," Petunia said. "And that was shameful—I'll tell you what. But after Jacob lost his business, all that friendliness stopped. If Ike had paid him back, he might not have gone under."

"Indeed," Asher said thoughtfully, then he shot her a sympathetic look. "Are you all right? I'm sorry I didn't get between you sooner, and I can only imagine how scary that was. I'm sorry . . . I get used to erratic behavior. But I'm a cop, and you aren't."

"It's okay . . ." Petunia's heartbeat was returning to normal, and she scrubbed at her forehead with the scrunched-up wet wipe.

"Let me . . ." Asher took another wet wipe from the counter and took Petunia's chin in his strong fingers, keeping her immobile, then gently wiped her forehead. His touch was strong, but gentle, and she felt her heart skip a beat as he eyed her from one side, then the other, and released her. "You're good."

"*Danke*," she said breathlessly, forgetting herself for a moment. Then she added in English, "Thank you."

Dot shot Petunia a little smile. Yah, a woman would understand how that would feel, and her cheeks grew warm.

"I'm going to interview him once he sobers up," Asher said, seemingly oblivious to the effect of his tender gesture. "But I have a feeling after today, it will be better if I talk to him man to man."

Asher led the way into the bullpen. It was a cozy area with desks separated by chest-high walls, making little cubicles. But most of those cubicles had something more personal in them—a potted plant, a World's Best Dad mug, a glass container of jelly beans. There were two police officers at their desks, heads down and typing. One looked up and gave her a nod in greeting.

"Any idea why Ike would have hated you so much?" Asher asked, looking back at her.

All business again.

"Besides the fact that I saw through his act with my best friend?" Petunia asked. "None. I was civil and polite. And so was he."

"Hm." Asher nodded. "But you were a threat to his plans."

"I wish I had been," Petunia replied soberly. "Because then Eden would have seen the man he really was. But she only saw who she wanted him to be. He might have hated me, but I didn't have any effect on her feelings for him at all."

"But it does show that Ike was insecure," Asher said. "It goes to show the victim's state of mind."

"What does that tell us?"

"I'm not sure," he replied. "It'll all come together, eventually. Speaking of Eden, shall we?"

"Yes, please."

Asher led the way past an office with Detective Nate written on the door, and to an unmarked door that had a thick square of glass about eye height. She looked over her shoulder at the closed office door. What personal items would Asher have in his office, she wondered? There might be all sorts of clues that would tell her more about this man. He punched a number into a panel, then pulled the door open. Inside was a linoleum-floored room with two barred cells inside. All was cool and bland here—no softening touches. The cells were separated by a cinder block wall so that the inhabitants of each cell would not see each other. That was a blessing—a little bit of privacy for Eden, at least. Eden sat in the far cell, but she had a few comforts—a quilt on the narrow bed, a pillow from her home, and a few books piled on the floor, the top of which was a Bible.

"Petunia!" Eden said, springing to her feet.

Petunia pushed past Asher and clasped Eden's hand through the bars of the cell. Eden looked relieved to see her, and Petunia was equally relieved to see that Eden seemed to be well cared for.

"Did you know they're charging me with murder?" Eden asked, her voice shaking.

"I know," Petunia replied. "But they are moving very slowly on it, and we're still looking for who killed Ike. So we have a bit of time. I won't rest until we find out who really did it, Eden. I promise you that!"

Eden deflated. "That's the plan?"

"I'm afraid so . . ."

"Do you have any ideas yet?"

"A few," Petunia replied. "He owed some people money."

It didn't seem wise to tell Eden that members of her own family might have killed Ike. She'd never cooperate with putting her brother or father in jail in her place.

"Who did he owe?" Eden asked breathlessly.

Asher cleared his throat, and when Petunia looked over her shoulder, he shook his head slightly. That wasn't information he wanted shared.

"It doesn't matter, really," Petunia said. "The point is, we are leaving no rock unturned. Ike wasn't well liked around here—" Eden's expression turned sad. "And you know that, Eden. That is no surprise. Especially since someone killed him! So we need to find out who hated him enough to do that."

"Like who?" she asked dismally.

"That's what we're looking into," Petunia said. "We'll find out more. I know it. But you might know more than you think."

"About what?"

"About Ike's past, and his enemies," she replied.

"He came from Shipshewana. If he had any enemies, they'd be there, not here," Eden said.

"But he was killed here," Petunia pressed. "Did he ever mention anyone who made him feel uneasy?"

"Besides my family?" She shook her head, then froze, and her gaze flicked over to Asher. "I didn't mean it that way! My family would never hurt Ike. Ever!"

"It's okay . . . ," Petunia said. "Did he mention anyone he spent time with when he wasn't with you?"

"He worked," Eden said. "That was all. I was his whole life."

But she wasn't quite his whole life, though, was she? He'd been making friends with Hadassah Schlabach, and borrowing money from men in the community . . . there had been more to Ike Smoker's life than he'd shared with Eden.

"Did you ever get a feeling that Ike might have . . . I don't know, been interested in another girl?" Petunia asked.

"What?" Tears rose in Eden's eyes. "Not once! He loved me, Petunia. I know you didn't like him, but he loved me!"

"Okay, okay," Petunia said. "I'm sorry. I know you loved him too. I don't mean to tarnish his memory, but we need to find out who did this to him."

Eden nodded and let out a slow, shaky breath. "How are my parents doing?"

"I haven't gone to see them yet," Petunia admitted.

"You haven't?"

"I'm sorry . . . I . . ." Petunia winced. "I was more worried about you than them, but I will go see them. I'll tell them I visited you. I can pass along a message, if you like."

"Okay," Eden said. "Thank you. My *daet* brought me my quilt and pillow, but they wouldn't let him stay long, and the look on his face, Petunia . . . and I haven't seen my *mamm* at all."

"Is there anything you want me to tell her?" Petunia asked. Maybe she could offer some comfort by bringing her mother a message.

Behind them, the door to the holding area opened and a police officer with Jacob Weir came through. Jacob stumbled and looked around blearily.

"Here we are, Jacob," the officer said. "Now you can sleep it off."

"I'm just fine," Jacob slurred. "You can drop me off at home . . . my wife is going to worry."

"Your friend went by your place to tell her already," the officer replied.

"Oh dear . . ." Jacob staggered toward the cell. "Then lock me up, I'm safer inside. She'll be furious."

The officer got Jacob settled inside his cell, and by the time the officer was locking it back up again, Petunia could hear Jacob softly singing an old Amish hymn. His wife, Bonita, wouldn't be shocked, but Petunia's heart did go out to her. She'd endured a lot over the years, and a choice in husband could ruin a woman's life.

That was a warning that Eden hadn't taken to heart.

"We should get going," Asher said.

"Wait!" Eden said, gripping the bars with both hands. "Petunia, you said you'd give a message to my mother."

"Of course," Petunia said.

"When you see her, tell her that I'm so sorry!"

"This isn't your fault!" Petunia said earnestly. "You have nothing to be sorry for!"

"Yes, I do," Eden said, her eyes brimming with tears. "She'll understand. Tell her I'm sorry."

But for what? Petunia looked over at Asher and he angled his head toward the door. It was time to go, and if Petunia didn't cooperate now, he'd never bring her back here. She couldn't linger.

"Okay," she said to Eden. "I'll tell her. And try not to worry too much."

Eden nodded, and Petunia headed back past Jacob's cell to the door. Jacob's eyes were shut, and he lay on the narrow bed singing quietly to himself.

It was then something occurred to Petunia. Bonita Weir's life had altered, too, when her husband lost his business. She'd been forced to start cleaning houses . . . That money that Ike owed her husband would have gone a long way to making their current hardship a little easier.

And Bonita had spent a good many years storing up anger . . .

It wasn't only a man who might feel some rage over all the Weirs had lost. Could Bonita Weir have been angry enough to kill?

* * *

Back in the cruiser again, Petunia watched as Asher put the key in the ignition. She had a fresh wet wipe in one hand, and she absently scrubbed at her forehead once more. Asher pulled a hand through his hair, then looked over at her.

"What do you make of Jacob Weir?"

"Drunk as a skunk," she replied, wadding up the wet wipe in her hand.

"A man that drunk would be spilling over with emotion if he'd killed a man," Asher said. "He'd be confessing, or dropping hints, or something."

"He did say that Ike hated me," she said.

"He did let that much slip . . ." Asher put the car into gear and started to back out. "I'm going to talk to him when he's sober. But I'm not thinking he's a real suspect."

Asher signaled and turned out onto the street. "You promised Eden you'd go visit her parents. I don't mean to push myself into something personal for you, but if we could go together for that little visit, it would be helpful for me. I went to see them before, and it was like talking to a bunch of tree stumps. They just stared at me and gave me one word answers."

Yah, that sounded about right. They wouldn't open up to a police detective who'd just arrested their daughter. They'd be relying on prayer right now, and divine intervention to rescue her, and that didn't include opening up to outside scrutiny.

"You don't think Eden's family did it, do you?" Petunia asked.

"I have no idea," Asher replied. "But the more complete my understanding of the situation, the better chance of us finding the real killer."

The real killer. That was a reassuring turn of phrase. It meant that Asher didn't think that Eden did it!

"Let's go see them now, then," Petunia said. "You can come with me."

"Thank you." He shot her a smile. "I appreciate it."

Asher knew the way to the Beiler farm, and Petunia watched the town disappear outside her window, and the rolling Pennsylvania snow-covered farmland took its place. Cattle stood out in the fields, and red barns stood like cheerful sentinels in the snow. In the front yard of a school house, she saw some Amish children building snowmen, topping their snowball heads with old summer straw hats. It must be recess time. The teacher stood on the steps of the school, a bulky shawl wrapped around her shoulders. She raised the bell in her hand. And then they whisked past, the faint, retreating sound of the bell disappearing behind them.

The Beiler farm was a couple of miles past the school, and when they turned into the drive, Petunia saw Eden's father, Amos Beiler, just disappearing into the house with his familiar limp. Another buggy was parked by the house, unhitched. That meant visitors who were staying for a while. People would be coming by with food and compassion during a time like this, and Petunia felt a stab of guilt that she'd stayed away so long.

Asher parked the car behind the buggy and turned off the engine. He got out of the car and waited for Petunia. He was about to head for the front door, and Petunia tapped his arm and pointed toward the side door.

"That way," she said.

"Ah. Thank you."

The front door was for visitors who didn't have any real business being there. The side door was for people they knew.

Petunia knocked on the door, and it opened almost immediately. Amos and Jonathan were washing up at the sink. Snowy boots sat on a rubber mat by the door.

"Hello, Petunia," Amos said. "How are you?"

Amos's gaze slid past her toward Asher, and his lips tightened into a disapproving expression.

"I'm as good as can be expected, considering everything," Petunia said. "This is Detective Asher Nate. He's letting me help him investigate the murder. We're going to prove Eden innocent."

Amos eyed Asher uncomfortably. Maybe he didn't believe that.

"You charged her with murder."

"But I'm not stopping there, either," Asher said. "I know you don't have much reason to trust me right now, but I do want to find who killed Ike. If that isn't your daughter—and Petunia here is convinced she didn't do it—then I want to find who did."

"I just came from seeing Eden," Petunia added. "She misses you all a lot."

Susanna Beiler, a middle-aged woman with a thick waist and a sad smile, poked her head into the mudroom.

"Well, you might as well come into the kitchen," Susanna said. "You're here to prove my daughter innocent, right?"

"I'm here to find out the truth," Asher said.

It wasn't quite a confirmation, but it was close enough. They took off their boots and everyone moved together into the fragrant warmth of the kitchen. A roast was cooking in the oven—Petunia could smell it. Susanna's roasts were better than anyone else's in Blueberry.

A young woman stood at the counter. She was very obviously pregnant, and she was peeling potatoes into an ice cream bucket. She cast Petunia a tired smile. This was Beth Beiler, Jonathan's wife. She had been a couple of years ahead of Petunia in school.

"How are you doing, Beth?" Petunia asked.

"Okay," Beth said.

"We're hoping to get some information about Ike—anything you might know that we don't," Petunia said. "Eden thinks he was a wonderful, trustworthy man. But we all know better than that, don't we?"

"Ike was a fool," Beth said, her lips turning down in disgust. "He was using her."

Amos cleared his throat and Beth's gaze flickered in her father-in-law's direction and she stopped talking.

"Look, we know that," Petunia said. "Asher knows all of that. So don't worry that you're making things look worse than they are for Eden. Right, Asher?"

Asher was using the tip of his pen to flip through a pile of mail on the table. He looked up.

"Yes, we are quite clear about the victim's character," Asher said. "He was using your daughter for his own pleasure, and had no intention of marrying her from what we can tell. He borrowed money and didn't repay it, even when the ones who lent it were in a tough position. He was rude, arrogant, and didn't care if he ruined the rest of your daughter's life. Does that cover it?"

The room fell silent.

"Yah," Jonathan said at last. "That covers it. My sister couldn't see that he was using her, but everyone in the community could see it clearly."

"I need to ask where each of you were on the night of the murder," Asher said straightening.

"Didn't we do this before?" Amos asked.

"Let's do it again," Asher said. "The time of death was somewhere between six and seven in the morning. Starting with you . . . Amos, right?"

"I was in the barn, probably, mucking out stalls," Amos said tiredly. "I farm. That's the job that time of day."

"And you?" Asher turned to Susanna.

"I was with my husband. The work goes faster if we do it together, and his leg has been bothering him this winter," she said.

"I don't like to tell people that," Amos added. "I'd rather let my wife stick to the housework, but it couldn't be helped."

"What is wrong with your leg?" Asher asked.

"An old farming injury. I broke it as a young man and it never healed properly."

"You?" Asher turned to Jonathan abruptly.

Jonathan and Beth exchanged a stunned look. Beth shrugged slightly and Jonathan heaved a sigh.

"I was in the stable. My wife was in bed asleep."

"Why were you in the stable?" Asher asked.

"Because I was cleaning it," he replied tersely.

"And why was your wife still in bed?" Asher's eyebrows went up again. So he did notice a few subtleties. Beth should have been up making breakfast already.

"My wife and I had been arguing." Jonathan's face reddened. "And I was cooling off outside. She was . . . upset with me and stayed in bed."

That was an embarrassing admission. Petunia never thought about tiffs between married people, normally.

"What were you arguing about?" Asher asked, turning his attention to Beth now.

She opened her mouth, then shut it.

"You can say," Jonathan said softly.

"About Jonathan spending so much time over here with his parents," Beth said, casting an apologetic look at her in-laws. "My family is from another community, and I get lonely. He kept coming here to help his *daet*, and they were always worrying over Eden. There is always such upset and focus on Eden's poor choices, and . . . I feel bad about it now, but I needed more of my husband's attention."

Susanna's mouth opened in a small, silent "oh." Everyone was silent then, and Beth was nearly writhing with embarrassment.

"You weren't worried about Eden too?" Petunia asked.

"Other girls have fallen for bad men," Beth said. "Of course I cared, but she was an adult who made a choice. Enough was enough. At least, that's what I thought . . ."

She dropped her gaze, the earlier fire in her answer drifting away.

"That means that both you and you"—Asher pointed with the tip of his pen at Jonathan and Beth—"can't account for your whereabouts at the time of the murder. All we have is your word."

"I'm pregnant!" Beth said, shaking her head. "And it is very cold out there!"

She had defended herself, not her husband, Petunia noticed.

"True," Asher said. "But your husband could have been anywhere. How long was Jonathan angrily cleaning the stable?"

"I fell asleep. I don't know," Beth whispered.

At seven in the morning . . . she fell back asleep? That was either a lie or a shocking admission of laziness.

"I was only gone for about an hour," Jonathan said quickly. "I was out in the stable, praying."

"Not, say, driving out to the ice house?" Asher asked.

"Why would I?" Jonathan demanded. "No one was supposed to be there that time of morning. Ike rented a room at a nearby farm, and my sister was at home."

"How do you know?" Asher pressed. "As Beth stated, your sister was a grown woman."

"I assumed!" Jonathan snapped. "Where else would she be? And why would I go driving out in the cold to an empty ice house? I was cooling off in the stable after an argument. I had some time to think. I realized I was being too hard on my wife, and I went back inside to apologize. She was asleep when I got back in, so I stoked up the fire in the kitchen myself and I started breakfast."

Asher pulled out a piece of paper and jotted something down. "And what about Eden?"

Everyone looked around at each other.

"She *was* home," Amos said at last.

"Doing what?" Asher asked.

"She was upstairs in her room doing some mending," Susanna said.

"For how long?"

"For a couple of hours."

"Mending what?" he pressed.

"I don't know!" Susanna replied. "Just mending!"

"Did anyone check on her?" Asher asked.

"She's twenty-two!" Susanna said. "We no longer check on her like that. She's grown."

Asher wrote something down.

"I thought you believed she was innocent!" Susanna burst out.

"Madam, I have to prove it," Asher said dryly. "That's the difficulty. Can I ask something?"

"Yah . . . ," Amos said uncertainly.

"Did you go to the bishop about this difficulty with Ike and Eden?" Asher asked.

"Of course we went to the bishop!" Amos said. "He sat down with Eden and said that Ike was a bad sort, that she should break off the relationship with him immediately."

"And?" Asher prompted.

Susanna just shook her head.

"She wouldn't do it?" Asher asked.

"She loved him," Petunia supplied. "She thought he was misunderstood."

"Could you force her?" Asher asked.

"That is not our way," Amos said. "We do not force anyone. Even our children."

"Could the bishop expel Ike from the community? Send him on his way?" Asher asked.

Susanna's gaze snapped fire for a moment, and then she managed to cover by turning toward the kitchen again.

"He could have," Petunia answered for her. "But he didn't do that."

"Why not?" Asher looked around innocently enough.

"It might be that he thought Eden would just follow him anyway," Jonathan said. "My sister could be very stubborn. And she truly thought Ike loved her."

"I still don't understand why Bishop Felty didn't do more," Beth said softly. "What use is there having a bishop and elders if a man can walk into our community and behave that way without any consequences?"

"There *were* consequences," Jonathan countered. "He was lectured and told to improve his ways . . . but no one wanted to force him to marry Eden, either. We wanted him to move on, to go away."

"And for Eden to stay," Petunia supplied.

"He could have been shunned, right?" Asher asked.

"He wasn't baptized yet," Susanna said. "He told us that plainly. We did ask about it. If he'd been baptized, we could have done more. But he hadn't made his ultimate choice for the church yet. So he couldn't be shunned."

"And he couldn't get married, either, not being baptized yet," Amos added.

"Ah. Thank you for explaining."

Asher turned back to flipping through the envelopes. Amos walked over and snatched up the pile of mail, casting Asher a baleful look. Why on earth was Asher acting this way? Was he trying to annoy the Beilers on purpose?

"I heard you say that you saw Eden?" Susanna said hopefully.

"Yah, I was just at the police station. She's keeping okay, but she's obviously very upset," Petunia replied.

Asher walked slowly around the kitchen, looking out the window, then moved a curtain to look behind it. He moseyed around looking generally nosy. What was he doing?

Susanna watched Asher with a frown on her face. He wasn't being polite.

"Susanna," Petunia said. "Eden asked me to tell you something."

Susanna moved quickly over to where Petunia stood.

"Yah?" She lowered her voice and switched to Pennsylvania Dutch. "Say it in our language."

"She said she's terribly sorry," Petunia said quietly, complying and speaking in her mother tongue.

"Oh . . ." Tears rose in Susanna's eyes. "She said that?"

"Yah, she did."

"Anything else?"

"Just that. She wanted me to tell you she was sorry, specifically. But don't worry, I told her that none of this was her fault, and that she had nothing to be sorry for," Petunia went on. "Because I didn't want her to sit in that cell blaming herself. She's innocent, and someone else has caused all this grief, not her."

Susanna nodded mutely. Surely that would be a relief to Susanna, to know that Petunia had already assured her that she'd done no wrong.

"She's very upset," Petunia went on. "I don't think she's thinking straight."

"If you see her before I do," Susanna said, her voice low and urgent. "Tell her I forgive her with all my heart. Tell her that."

"But she didn't kill him," Petunia whispered. "I know it for a fact, Susanna. There is no way she killed Ike!"

Unless she was apologizing for something else . . . but for what? Eden *hadn't* killed Ike. Or did her family believe she had? That was a sobering thought.

But before she could ask anything further, Asher held up a small bottle he'd picked up from the counter.

"Whose are these?" he asked.

Petunia squinted to get a better look. They were prenatal vitamins. She was about to point out to him that Beth was pregnant—although why she'd leave her vitamins at her in-laws' place, she had no idea—when Susanna spoke up.

"They're mine!" Susanna said, her voice just a little too loud.

Asher looked more closely at the bottle. "This is a new bottle. They don't expire for another two years."

"Yah, well . . . they're still mine," Susanna said firmly.

"Are you expecting?" Asher asked pointedly. He raised one eyebrow.

"I'd have to be, wouldn't I?" Susanna said.

Petunia looked over at Susanna in surprise. She was in her early fifties, and she had a grandbaby on the way, but that wasn't all . . .

"Congratulations," Asher said. "I mean that sincerely. What a wonderful surprise for you and your husband."

Amos didn't say anything, and when Petunia looked over at him, the Amish man forced a smile.

"*Danke*," Amos said.

It meant thank you, and Petunia's heart hammered to a stop.

The Beilers had just lied. It had obviously taken some effort for them to do so, but it was a lie all the same. Susanna wasn't any more pregnant than Petunia was. Susanna had had a hysterectomy two years earlier. The easier explanation would have been to say the vitamins belonged to Beth, but they hadn't said so. It hadn't occurred to them fast enough because they weren't Beth's, either . . .

Petunia swallowed hard.

Eden was terribly sorry about something, and her mother had given her forgiveness. There were prenatal vitamins in the Beiler kitchen for someone who was expecting a baby.

"Oh my . . . ," Petunia breathed.

Susanna shot her a warning look, and Petunia pressed her lips together. Watching people she respected and cared for telling blatant lies felt uncomfortable and shameful. The truth mattered in the Amish world. Lies could sink a soul. But this time, she understood why.

"Well, thank you for your time," Asher said. "We'd best get going."

The Beliers all stared at Petunia mutely, and she felt heat in her face. If Asher wanted to go with her on these visits, then why was he behaving so rudely? These were people she'd need to get along with again when this was all over!

"I'm sorry about all this," Petunia said in Pennsylvania Dutch. "I really am doing my best to find out who killed Ike and get Eden home. I promise."

When they were finally driving away from the Beiler farm, Asher drummed his hands cheerfully on the top of the steering wheel.

"That was very productive!" Asher said.

"For you?" Petunia cast him an annoyed look. "You were incredibly rude, Asher!"

"And they opened up, didn't they?" Asher kept his eyes on the road. "Annoy people enough, and they'll finally snap and say something true. Jonathan and Beth hadn't said anything about their fight. And Susanna told us that Eden was upstairs sewing, not down where everyone could see her."

"It only looks worse for Eden," Petunia said.

"It's something the prosecution would dig up eventually. It's better to be ahead of things," he replied.

Petunia looked out the window irritably. The Beilers had told some truths . . . and some lies. She'd never heard the Beilers lie before, and it left her feeling a little shaken. They were good people.

"I'm sorry if I embarrassed you," Asher said, softening his tone. "They were a tough family to interview. They really pulled together last time, and you helped a lot."

"Why did you behave that way?" she asked. "Is that how Englishers are when they visit people they don't know?"

"What?" Asher shot her a surprised look. "No! I was putting them off balance. I annoyed them on purpose. You kept asking questions, and I kept annoying them. It's a great way to shake loose some new information."

"Oh . . ." So he'd done it on purpose. She wasn't sure if she should be relieved or irritated. "That makes things very difficult for me."

"I assume you were apologizing before we left," he said.

"Of course."

"They'll forgive you. Me—they can hold it against me all they like. See? You'll be fine. I'm a lout of an Englisher, after all." He sounded downright cheerful about it.

But there was more information there that Petunia had sussed out, and it wasn't the kind of secret that would keep. If Asher thought it was better to be ahead when it came to things that might incriminate Eden, there was one more . . .

"Eden needs her prenatal vitamins," Petunia said with a sigh. "Susanna isn't pregnant."

"I gathered as much," Asher replied.

"You figured that out?" Petunia asked in surprise.

"Susanna and her husband were obviously lying," Asher replied. "People who aren't used to lying have it all over their faces. They had all the signs."

"Oh . . ."

"Petunia, I'll make sure she gets some prenatal vitamins this evening. And I'll make sure she sees a doctor and that she gets everything she needs to be comfortable."

"Will you let her go home?" Petunia asked sadly. "She's pregnant. I didn't know that before, but it makes her very vulnerable, Asher."

She looked over at Asher hopefully. Did he have any compassion at all for Eden's situation?

"I know, but she's been charged with murder," he replied. "I can't do that. The best thing we can do for her now is to find who really killed her boyfriend."

And now knowing about Eden's pregnancy, they'd better move quickly.

Chapter Six

The next morning, Petunia woke early as she always did, and for the first few minutes she lay in her warm, quilt-laden bed, her mind flipping through the events of the last day.

Everyone had something to hide, it seemed. Little things, big things, embarrassments, or simply things that were too personal to share. Like a marital argument, or a daughter's unexpected pregnancy . . . Where was the line between private information and hiding something?

For Petunia, she tended to say too much. Everyone warned her about it. She needed to keep some things—many things!—to herself. The Amish lived in a tightly knit community where everyone needed each other and depended on each other . . . but that was balanced with an equally tight code of conduct. Some things were acceptable, and some things were not. People kept their personal business private—it was the only way to keep things balanced when you lived so closely with one another.

And now, Petunia was privy to details she shouldn't be . . . and it felt both uncomfortably intimate and thrilling at the same time. She was used to noticing details and wondering what was behind the odd behavior, or even discussing with her father what she thought might be behind it. She certainly wasn't used to finding out for true and certain what was going on!

She got up then, pulled on her cape dress and tights, and combed her thick, honey brown hair into a bun at the back of her head. She pulled a fresh *kapp* out of her top drawer and secured it over her bun with two bobby pins. She regarded herself in the mirror and deemed her appearance acceptable for the day.

Petunia had a young engaged woman named Priscilla Kempf coming for a fitting. The wedding banns hadn't been announced at church yet, which meant that most people didn't know about the wedding officially, but many were probably expecting it. Most weddings happened in the fall after harvest when things settled down a bit, but a few weddings were interspersed throughout the rest of the calendar year, especially for people whose work didn't revolve around a farming schedule.

Petunia made breakfast for herself and her father—oatmeal, buttered toast, some scrambled eggs, and two hot mugs of coffee. Her cooking turned out that morning, which put Elias in a good mood, and Petunia was rather pleased with herself.

Priscilla Kempf arrived at nine sharp. She drove up in a covered buggy, and Elias went out to help her unhitch and put the horses into the stable where it was warm. Priscilla would be staying too long to leave them outside.

When Priscilla came in, she unwrapped a shawl from around her shoulders and stepped out of her boots, then headed toward the stove to warm up quickly. She passed an envelope to Petunia on her way past.

"I found that on the step," she said.

"*Danke*." Petunia looked down at it. Was it a bill for her father? A note from a neighbor? There was nothing written on the front of the envelope.

"I'm so glad you're able to do the sewing for me," Priscilla said. "My *mamm* took that extra job at the hotel in town cleaning rooms, and she and my aunts are working on my wedding quilt, but I had to choose which I wanted them to finish for me—the dresses, or the quilt."

"It's going to be a beautiful quilt," Petunia said, tucking the envelope into her apron pocket. "It's more important that your relatives make the quilt, I think. That was the right choice. It'll be on your bed for decades."

"Yah . . . I can't wait until this wedding has been announced. Right now, I feel like it isn't really official, you know?"

"I can understand that," Petunia said. "But I've been to a lot of weddings, and every bride felt that way until the banns were read, and they all ended up married."

"True." Priscilla cast her a grateful smile.

"Should we go upstairs and try on your dress?" Petunia asked.

"Yah." Priscilla blushed. "It's all really happening, isn't it?"

Petunia led the way upstairs into her sewing room. She had bolts of cloth, baskets of thread, and the blue cape dress that would be for Priscilla's wedding day was on a dress form in one corner. Petunia had ironed it, and all that was left was to find the right length for the hem.

First Petunia showed her the *newehocker* dresses for the girls who'd stand with her at her wedding. They were sunflower yellow, and would be just beautiful for an early summer wedding. Then Petunia let the young woman get into the blue wedding dress behind a screen, and when she came out, Petunia positioned her in front of a full-length mirror.

"This is it . . ." Priscilla gazed at her own reflection in awe. She turned to one side, then the other, her cheeks pinking with happiness.

Petunia let the young woman glow in the emotions of her upcoming wedding, but Petunia's eye was on the fit of the dress. The waist was perfect, and she squatted down next to Priscilla to fold under the unhemmed edge of the dress and looked into the mirror to judge the length.

"About there?" Petunia asked.

"Yah, I think so."

Petunia added some pins to hold up the hemline in a few strategic places, then stood up.

"You know more about Ike Smoker's death than most," Priscilla said as Petunia undid the clasp at the back of her neck so that she could get out of the dress again.

"Well, the detective needed my help to understand our culture," Petunia explained. "We need to find out who killed him. It wasn't Eden—I know that for sure and certain."

"I don't think she did, either," Priscilla replied. "But Ike wasn't a nice man."

"No, he wasn't," Petunia agreed.

"Did you find out anything about why he left Shipshewana?" Priscilla asked.

Petunia shook her head. "No, not yet. All I heard was that the people there didn't like him and he felt unwelcome." That had been what Eden told her, at least. But he'd felt equally unwelcome here in Blueberry, and for good reason . . .

"It was more than that," Priscilla said. "I heard from Edith Smucker that he got a girl pregnant in Shipshewana. And then left her."

"What?" Petunia asked, and stabbed her thumb with a pin. She winced and popped her thumb into her mouth, then looked down at the puncture wound. "Really?"

"Yah. That's why he left, and why he can't go back there." She lowered her voice. "I'm not saying it's a good thing that he's dead—that would be wicked—but Eden will do much better without him. Can you imagine discovering you had stepchildren after the wedding?"

"Yah . . . ," Petunia breathed.

"My Benji says that Ike was the kind of man who took advantage and didn't see why he should get married at all," Priscilla said. "He says that Ike lied as smoothly as cutting butter."

"Did Benji know him very well?" Petunia asked.

"Not really." Priscilla went back behind the screen to change again, and her voice was a little muffled. "But he heard the way Ike talked when he was around the men, and he said he had no intention of making an honest wife out of Eden. I'm so glad that Benji wants a proper wife and *kinner.* He wants all the comforts of a proper home. He's a good man. He always said that our community should set Ike straight. I don't know why they didn't."

The envelope fluttered out of Petunia's apron and fell to the floor. Petunia picked it up. The blue dress flopped up over the top of the screen. She looked down at the envelope and tore it open.

"I'm not sure, either," Petunia said, her gaze falling to the single page that she pulled from the envelope. "Why didn't the elders take him aside and make it clear that . . ." The note was handwritten, and her breath caught in her throat.

"Clear that what?" Priscilla came out from behind the screen dressed in her old dress again.

But Petunia's attention was on the note in her hand:

> There are many ways to stop a heart. Ike had it coming. Leave it alone, and I'll leave you alone. Stop bringing Englishers into our community problems. This is why you can't get married. You never mind your own business!

"Well, that was just plain rude," Petunia said.

"What?" Priscilla asked.

"The letter," Petunia said weakly. "Where did you find it?"

"On the step," Priscilla said. "Why? What is it?"

"It's a threat," she said, almost in disbelief. "A rather insulting threat. They could have stopped at threatening to hurt me. There was no need to bring up my single status."

That last barb had really hurt. Hate her for getting too close to the truth, but no need for snide comments.

"A threat?!" Priscilla's face paled, and she snatched the page out of Petunia's hand and scanned the page. "Is this referring to you helping the detective?"

"It must be," Petunia said.

"I think that's the part you should be focused on!" Priscilla said. "Who cares about the rest?"

"I do. I might be more inclined to back off without the insult," Petunia said. "Now I'm just angry. Do you know what this means?"

"It means you're in danger!" Priscilla said.

"No! Well . . . maybe. But more importantly, it means that Ike's killer is getting nervous. There is no way Eden could have sent this."

"Or . . ." Priscilla handed the page back. "Or it was someone who was glad he was killed and resents Englisher involvement in our community."

Petunia looked at the note again:

> There are many ways to stop a heart. Ike had it coming. Leave it alone, and I'll leave you alone. Stop bringing Englishers into our community problems. This is why you can't get married. You never mind your own business!

"Yah, you're right," Petunia agreed. "There is no confession of guilt here, is there? But I know that Eden is innocent, and from the sniffing about that we've done already, we've made someone very nervous. This is good news, Priscilla."

An idea suddenly occurred to Petunia, and she dashed to the window. A skiff of snow had fallen last night, and the only tracks in the snow were from horses and buggy wheels.

"That confirms it," Petunia murmured.

"Confirms what?" Priscilla asked, her voice sounding strangled.

"The only tracks are Amish vehicles," Petunia replied. "And the letter writer is upset that I'm bringing an Englisher into our midst. Our killer is undoubtedly Amish."

Priscilla pressed a hand against her stomach. "Oh dear . . ."

"I knew it before, of course," Petunia said. "But this does confirm it for me. It's nice to know I was right."

And here Petunia was upsetting poor Priscilla. She needed to focus on her wedding, not worry about a killer lurking about.

"There's a killer out there . . . ," Priscilla breathed. "There really is. And it isn't an Englisher who hated Ike? I'd just assumed . . ."

"I think a good many Amish people hated Ike," Petunia replied distractedly.

Priscilla's eyes widened. "An Amish murderer? It's impossible."

The girl still seemed to be struggling with that part of it, but then Petunia had had more time to adjust to the idea.

"If we had an Amish philanderer, I see no reason why we can't have an Amish murderer, too . . ." Petunia was going over the facts in her mind. Was there a woman with a baby in Shipshewana who had reason to hate Ike too? Perhaps she had some family who'd wanted to get their hands on Ike . . .

When she looked over at the slim woman, there were tears standing in her eyes, and her hand was on her throat. Petunia felt a wave of regret.

"Oh, Priscilla, don't you worry a bit," Petunia said. "No one is after you. You're just going about your business. Ike was targeted for a *reason*. You know what a bad man he was. And if they come after anyone, it will be *me*."

"And they're already threatening you!" Priscilla's voice was rising.

"I know!" Petunia flashed her a brilliant smile. "I love being right."

"Do you like being targeted by a killer?" Priscilla demanded.

"Not so much," Petunia acknowledged.

"Petunia," Priscilla said seriously. "Leave it alone. Just stop digging into it. This is the job for police, not for you. Besides . . . maybe the writer has a point about us Amish taking care of our own business . . ."

"They've arrested my best friend," Petunia said. "The Englishers are already involved, and I'm not leaving Eden to rot for a murder she didn't commit. Period."

Priscilla nodded. "You're right about that. I understand."

But did she? And why was Priscilla suddenly arguing on behalf of the letter writer? Had she found it on the step, or had she simply delivered it by hand? Petunia regarded Priscilla thoughtfully for a moment, then looked back down at the letter. She'd show this to Asher the next time she saw him. It might not be solid proof that Eden wasn't the killer, but it was pretty compelling evidence.

"Don't worry," Petunia said. "I'll be careful. And I'll have your dresses done next week."

But Petunia didn't like the way that Priscilla scurried away as soon as she could, dashing out the door before she'd even wrapped her shawl around herself properly.

Being the target of a murderer was going to hurt business. The sooner this was sorted out, the better.

* * *

"Hurting business? That's your biggest worry?" Elias scrubbed his hands through his hair. "I withdraw my permission for this!"

It was after dinner, the tours were done for the day, and the meal had been cleared from the table. Elias sat at the head, where he always sat, with a mug of tea in front of him.

"Withdrawing your permission now will only let a murderer go free!" Petunia argued. "A rude murderer, at that!" She nodded to her father's cloth napkin. "Pass me that, please."

"Do you listen to yourself?" her father asked, passing her the wadded napkin.

"I know I'm making light of something serious," Petunia said. "I know the rudeness isn't the worst thing. I'm not a complete fool. But look at it rationally. There is a murderer among us. And that fact will not change. Someone was willing to plunge an ice pick into a man's chest, and is threatening me harm too. This is not a safe person, and we need to know who it is. Ignoring it will not make us safer, *Daet*."

She took the napkins and the day's kitchen towels over to the laundry basket in the other room, then returned to a knock on the side door.

"I'll get it," Petunia said.

"You will do no such thing!" her father retorted, and he rose to his feet, casting her an irritated look. "You get threatened and then start answering the door after dark?"

Petunia sighed and stood back while her father stomped to the door and pulled it open. Petunia could see Asher on the step over her father's shoulder.

"Good evening, sir," Asher said. "It's nice to see you again. I was hoping to have a word with your daughter."

"Come in," Elias said, stepping back. He looked out the door after Asher, then closed it and flicked the lock. "My daughter has something to show you too."

"Oh?" Asher fixed Petunia with a curious look.

Petunia pulled out the envelope from her apron and handed it over to Asher. "I was threatened today."

Asher opened the envelope and expression turned stony as he read. "This is an official threat."

"Which means I've ruffled the murderer," she said.

"I agree," Asher replied.

"This also suggests that the murderer is loose—wouldn't you say? It isn't absolute proof. Priscilla pointed out that all it really says is that the writer doesn't like me bringing you onto the scene . . ."

"Technically, this could be a threat more about you and less about Ike. It might not stand up in court," Asher said. "But I take this as some substantial evidence that we're on the right path."

"Well, you two are just two peas in a pod, aren't you?" Elias said, shaking his head. "Asher, my daughter has been threatened by a killer! I want her protected!"

"Of course, sir," Asher said. "From now on, I'll make sure there's a police presence in front of your home. We won't play with this. But this does show us that we're shaking loose the actual murderer."

"And that Eden is innocent, *Daet*!" Petunia added.

Elias shook his head. "And if my daughter just stopped helping you right now?"

"Would the murderer believe that?" Asher raised his shoulders. "Hard to tell. There's no safety in simply complying with a threat. Someone is rattled enough to leave a letter—" He turned to Petunia. "Where did you find it?"

"One of my clients found it on the step," Petunia said.

"How many people have handled it?"

"Me, Priscilla, my father . . ." She winced. "Fingerprints. That's what you're considering, isn't it?"

"Yep. I'll send it off for prints, but I have a feeling we won't get too much." Asher pulled a plastic bag from his coat pocket and slid the letter inside.

Elias looked between them, shaking his head. "Both of you think this is something to celebrate."

"Well, I wouldn't celebrate it," Asher said. "But it's a good sign."

Elias sighed. "Can I count on you to keep my daughter safe, Asher Nate?"

"Yes, sir, you absolutely can," Asher replied. "Your daughter's safety is my top priority, and I appreciate her help."

Petunia smiled. "See, *Daet*? I'll be fine."

"What brought you by?" Elias asked irritably.

"Right," Asher said. "I actually wanted to run something by the two of you. I want your input, too, sir, if you don't mind."

Petunia worried for a moment that Elias would throw Asher out, but he didn't. He slowly shook his head, then nodded toward the kitchen table with a jerk of his chin.

"All right," Elias sighed. "Sit down."

Asher took a seat at the kitchen table, and when Petunia slid a mug of tea in front of him, he gave her a murmur of thanks.

"Petunia may have mentioned that she saw Jacob Weir sleeping off a morning of hard drinking in the drunk tank yesterday," Asher said. "I went by his house last night—he was home again—and I had a word with him and his wife."

"He's a suspect," Petunia supplied for her father. "Since Ike owed him a good deal of money, refused to pay, and as a result he lost his business."

"Well, I wouldn't say it was a result of only the money he gave to Ike," Elias said.

"No?" Asher looked over expectantly.

"Jacob has always been rather susceptible to flattery," Elias replied. "He's been lending money to his brothers for years, and they seldom repay. Since he inherited the family carpentry business, his younger brothers thought he owed them. And I think he felt like he did, too. The problem was, Jacob is terrible with money."

"He's been doing this for a while?" Petunia asked.

"Oh, yah," her father replied. "All his brothers needed to tell him was that he was the successful one, and he'd hand over the money."

"That explains Bonita, then," Petunia murmured.

"What about her?" Asher asked.

"A couple of years ago at a quilting bee, Bonita and I were working on the same corner of a big quilt, and we got to talking," Petunia replied. "She was giving me some advice about marriage and choosing a husband, and she told me to make sure I married a man who knew his way around a checkbook, because otherwise, he could impoverish the family, and there would be nothing at all a woman could do about it."

"Nothing?" Asher asked with a frown.

"In our culture, the men handle the money," Elias said. "And Jacob is very traditional that way. He's started drinking lately, mostly because of the financial pressure. At least that's my guess. His financial plan consists mostly of caving in to the flattery of people wanting to borrow from him, and then praying for a miracle."

"Has no one tried to set him straight?" Asher asked.

"His wife certainly does try, and I did try once," Elias replied. "I sat him down and showed him how to keep track of his finances in a ledger. He thanked me kindly, and I doubt he opened the book again."

"He's embarrassing when he's drunk," Petunia added. "But he's very kind and patient when he's sober."

"And Bonita?" Asher asked. "What's she like?"

"She's the smart one," Petunia said. "But it doesn't do her any good because he won't listen to her."

"Would you call her frustrated?" Asher asked.

"Yah, incredibly," Elias said. "She's done her best to hold things together, but when Jacob finally declared bankruptcy on the carpentry business, she had to go to work."

"Which is a bit of a mixed blessing," Petunia added. "She's working now, and being paid into her own bank account. He can't touch that."

"How do you know that?" Elias asked.

"Gossip and rumor," Petunia replied. "But Bonita is finally able to control some of the finances, just by refusing to take more money out of her account than she chooses. And the bishop and elders won't say a word to her, because they know she's right."

Asher nodded soberly.

"Do you really think Jacob Weir could have killed Ike?" Elias asked.

"His personality doesn't seem compatible with that kind of violent crime," Asher said thoughtfully. "But then again, many a gentle man has been pushed past his limit until he finally snapped and lashed out."

"Or perhaps Bonita had enough, went to see Ike about the money, and snapped," Petunia suggested. "That's a lot of anger stewing inside one woman for many years . . ."

Asher pointed at Petunia and nodded. "A good point."

"These are our friends!" Elias said.

"And one of our friends is a killer," Petunia replied quietly.

"One of your friends is threatening your daughter, too," Asher added. "I know this is difficult, Elias. I can appreciate how uncomfortable this is, but I've learned that even the gentlest seeming people have a limit. Even our neighbors are capable of lashing out in a moment of anger. And once a person kills, there is a powerful drive to cover it up, to hide it, to make it go away. They have a hard time believing they did it, too."

Elias sighed. "Then I suppose I should tell you that Jacob Weir did have a stronger side to him that he didn't show too often."

"How so?" Asher asked.

"But he didn't hate Ike," Elias qualified. "I think he idolized him. Ike was strong, irreverent, and did whatever he wanted. He was Jacob's opposite. Jacob had started drinking, and he'd often sit and drink with Ike. That's how Ike convinced him to lend him the money. It was based upon a friendship."

"And the stronger side to him?" Asher prompted.

"I was coming through town, and I saw Ike and Jacob come out of the bar together," Elias said. "I noticed because I didn't approve.

They were talking loudly, laughing, and slapping each other on the back. I didn't even recognize him like that. But with Ike, Jacob acted more belligerent, louder and more swaggering. Very unlike himself, and not a good Amish example, to be sure."

Yah, she'd seen Jacob's drunken side when he kissed her forehead in the police station. It was not an attractive side to the man.

"Maybe he didn't like who he became around Ike," Petunia suggested. "Maybe he was embarrassed by his behavior when he sobered up again."

"Maybe he realized that he was ruining his own life by giving away so much money," Elias suggested. "Maybe he used some of that newfound gumption to demand to be paid back."

"If Ike said just the right thing, Jacob could have been set off," Asher agreed. He pulled out the note and laid it down on the table in front of the three of them.

Petunia reread the now familiar words:

> There are many ways to stop a heart. Ike had it coming. Leave it alone, and I'll leave you alone. Stop bringing Englishers into our community problems. This is why you can't get married. You never mind your own business!

Had Jacob written those words?

"It was spiteful," Petunia said softly. "Adding in that I can't get married . . ."

They were all quiet then for another few beats.

"I don't see Jacob being quite that cruel to me," Petunia said at last. "Jacob is many things, but why would he feel acidic about my ability to find a husband? It doesn't make sense."

Asher nodded slowly. "That's a good instinct."

"Is it?" Elias asked.

"She's got a good sense of these things," Asher confirmed. "I know it's countercultural for you, but she's good at this."

Petunia felt a wash of warmth at the words. It wasn't empty flattery. Asher meant it—she could tell by the way he said it. She was good at this. And it took away the sting of the insult in the letter.

"Consider the source of criticism, Pet," Elias said quietly. "Don't ever take criticism from someone whose life you wouldn't want to live. And this is a letter from a murderer. I don't think you can take that to heart."

"I agree with your father," Asher said.

"*Danke*," Petunia said.

It did make her feel better.

Chapter Seven

That evening, Elias stood silently in the kitchen as Asher took his leave. Her *daet* was sticking close, and he wouldn't be leaving her alone with Asher here in his own home. Asher shrugged back into his winter coat and pulled on his gloves. He gave Elias a smile and a nod, but Petunia doubted that would do much to win him over.

"Did you mean it?" Petunia asked quietly, keeping her voice low.

"Mean what?" Asher asked. He met her gaze—a frank, open look that made her stomach take a tumble. He wasn't a traditionally good-looking man, but when he focused all of his attention on her like that, it was hard not to notice that he was indeed a man, and she wasn't used to being looked at quite that way. Petunia was forced to avert her eyes.

"That I'm good at this," she said.

"I meant it," Asher said. "I don't waste my breath. You'll learn that about me. I work with fellow cops and detectives all the time. Some people have an instinct for sniffing out the truth, but not every cop has it. You do."

"Huh." Was that what made her different? Was it some instinct toward following clues and solving puzzles? She'd always suspected she was put together differently—and Heaven knew the whole community of Blueberry seemed to sense she wasn't like the other women. Even the murderer.

"Well . . . ," Asher said.

"Good night," she said, forcing a smile.

"Good night, Pet." He'd picked up her father's diminutive of her name, and he shot her a half smile, then marched out into the cold, and Petunia was forced to shut the door after him.

The night was dark and moonless, clouds scudding across the sky, a patch of stars here and there managing to poke through, but never for long. The wind moaned over the countryside, and Petunia crawled into bed with her three quilts on top of her to keep warm. In her father's bedroom she heard the comforting sound of creaking floorboards as he walked around, getting ready for bed too.

But as she fell asleep, her mind kept going back to Asher's observation. Maybe she wasn't so much unmarriageable as she was a natural sleuth. If few people had that talent, and she was one of them, it would stand to reason that she was different. Perhaps she could add to the title of youngest old maid in all of Blueberry, and be the youngest old maid *sleuth* in all of Blueberry. She liked that one better. At least it gave a good reason for why she was different.

She drifted off to sleep that night feeling like she'd grown in some small but important way, and she dreamed of a summer ice cream gathering with the entire Amish district, all together. There was a warm summer wind that smelled of strawberries and gardens, and grass that tickled her bare feet. In her dream, everyone was happy and getting along. Some of the youth were singing songs, and Eden slipped her arm through Petunia's and said, "What a beautiful day! Isn't it beautiful, Petunia?"

Petunia had looked at her best friend and struggled to remember why it wasn't simply a beautiful day. All the worries and stress of reality had simply slipped away to a mild, nagging discomfort in the back of her head that she couldn't explain.

When Petunia awoke the next morning, she wondered if their community would ever get back to an easy, happy balance again. Or had this murder changed them for good?

* * *

That day Elias had a tour group, and Petunia stayed home to sew those dresses. The work did improve her state of mind. There was something about cutting cloth and stitching seams on her pedal-powered sewing machine by the window that made the world feel like it made sense again, or like it *would* make sense again. And she would be part of setting it all right.

They were getting close to finding the killer—she could feel it!

Petunia made her father a thick ham sandwich to take with him for lunch, and then started a nice large pot of chili for dinner. And this time it turned out rather well, which improved her mood even more. It bubbled slowly on the big wood-burning stove, and the smell wound its way around the house.

Petunia went next door to her neighbor to borrow ice. She'd considered going and fetching some ice for herself at the ice house, but after her last encounter with Jonathan at the ice house, she was less inclined to go out there by herself. Her neighbor, elderly Hester, understood.

Ice cream might be a cold treat, but it was something that always turned out. Her mother had an ice cream recipe from years and years ago that Petunia followed, and for some reason, an ice cream churn could not be thwarted, even by the likes of Petunia. That recipe included egg yolks, canned milk, cocoa powder, and just a touch of cold coffee. And "sugar to taste." As she turned the crank on the old machine, she churned up some nice fresh coffee-chocolate-flavored ice cream for the tour group when they passed by on their way back to the tour office in town. It was a little on the sweet side, since Petunia could never remember how much sugar was the perfect amount, but all in all, that was forgivable.

The tour group loved the ice cream. They always did. A few commented on the cold treat for a cold day, and Petunia ignored them. Better good ice cream on a cold day than burned pie, but she wasn't about to explain herself to strangers.

When the tour guests left, Petunia stood at the sink washing dishes. The warm, sudsy water felt good on her hands after the cold work of churning.

"You know, *Daet*, I was thinking," Petunia said.

Elias looked up from the *Budget* newspaper he was reading at the kitchen table. "Oh?"

"Yesterday, Priscilla told me a rumor she heard about Ike," Petunia said. "I probably should have told Asher, but I was caught up with the letter."

"What rumor?" Elias asked.

"Apparently, Ike left Shipshewana to come here because he got a girl pregnant."

Petunia looked over at her father, waiting to see his response. Elias looked thoughtful for a moment, then nodded. "I could see that happening."

"You aren't shocked?" she asked.

"Is it disgusting behavior?" Elias asked. "Yes. It's appalling. First of all, getting a woman pregnant before he's married her, but more than that—running away from it. If he cared enough about her to get her in the motherly way, then he should care enough to marry her and take care of his new family. But it's not surprising where Ike was concerned."

"I don't have proof," she said. "It's just a rumor, but rumors can be true. And I was thinking that it's possible we have a whole other town of suspects to consider. Maybe there's an angry young woman who wanted more from Ike. Or maybe an angry family member who wanted him to come back and make an honest wife of her."

"That complicates things," her father agreed. "But it's heartening to think the murderer might be from another community than ours."

"Wouldn't it be nice?" Petunia cast her father a rueful smile and turned back to the dishes. "And come to think of it, Mary Hilty did tell us that she saw a woman she didn't recognize out by the ice house the day before the murder. She was angry and shouting."

"Shouting?" Elias sounded surprised. "She wasn't Amish, I take it."

"That's the thing. She was Amish. She arrived and left in a buggy, and"—Petunia paused for effect—"she slapped Ike across the face."

"Slapped him?!"

"I know. For an Amish woman to go to those lengths, it would take a great deal. A great deal."

Elias sucked in a slow breath.

"Maybe she was the woman he got pregnant," Petunia suggested.

"Mary would have mentioned if she were obviously pregnant," Elias said. "And while I don't have a lot of experience with pregnant women besides your dear departed mother, I do know that they don't tend to pick physical altercations with men."

"Then maybe it wasn't her," Petunia said with a sigh. "Or maybe the rumor was just that, and there was no truth in it. Maybe some other strange woman had reason to hate him enough to slap him."

"Hmm." Her father frowned. "I wish you would just leave this to the bishop, Pet."

But Petunia wasn't convinced that the bishop would do anything about it. He was more concerned about the state of their souls than the meting out of justice.

"Bishop Felty has a different job to do, *Daet*," Petunia said. "Besides, if he wanted to find the killer, he'd be the one in search of clues. But he isn't."

"True," her father replied.

"All the same, if anyone would know about an unfamiliar Amish woman spending time in our area—or maybe visiting one of our families—it would be the bishop, don't you think?"

"Probably," her father agreed.

"And a visit to the bishop is safe enough," she said. "No one can fault me for stopping by the bishop's farm to talk to him about something. I don't think that would draw any undue attention."

She looked over at her father, and Elias nodded. "I will agree there. You should go talk to him. Maybe he'll even take the case over for you. I'll feel better if the bishop is taking this in hand."

Petunia certainly hoped Bishop Felty didn't try to take it over, but she was glad to have her father's support all the same.

"Then I'll go see him," she said.

"But Petunia," Elias said, warning in his tone. "Perhaps don't bring your detective with you this time. You don't have to take him everywhere you go, and he seems to be upsetting people."

"He is, but it's part of his plan," Petunia said.

"I don't like my daughter being used in anyone's plans. You should be making your own," he countered.

"That is sound advice," she agreed. "But you don't trust Asher?"

"He doesn't know our ways," Elias said pointedly. "And he doesn't understand the mess he'll leave behind when he's finished with his investigation."

"I was worried about that too," she agreed.

"And I feel it is my duty as your *daet* to point out that you are an attractive young woman," Elias said. "I don't say it to puff up your head or make you vain, but I wouldn't want him to get any Englisher ideas about you."

"Me?" Petunia laughed. "I'm just an Amish woman willing to help. That's all. You're safe there."

"All the same." Elias didn't sound convinced.

And maybe Petunia liked the idea of Asher developing a small crush. Not that she thought he had. Asher was from a different world than she was.

"But please, Petunia, be safer. Don't go out at night, and when visiting anyone else besides our bishop, you should probably take your police friend, even if it is attracting attention. I don't want you taking risks. You young people think you're invincible, but you aren't."

"I'll go by the bishop's farm in the morning," Petunia said. "In the light of day."

"Much better," Elias replied.

And Petunia had to admit that after that threatening letter, she wasn't keen on creeping around in the dark either. They'd gotten *someone's* attention!

* * *

The next morning was bright and cheerful. Her father took the first group of tourists on the road past their house, lap blankets over their legs and thermoses in their hands. The bells on the horses' harnesses jingled cheerfully in the winter air. Those bells were rather close to being considered Fancy, but since they helped others to hear the buggy coming and were therefore considered a safety precaution, the bishop had allowed them.

Petunia let her father's wagon go by first, and then she flicked Trudy's reins on her little two-seater, topless buggy, and headed out into the glittering, cold morning. She spotted a police car driving slowly down their road, and she waved at the officer, who gave her a smile and a nod in return. Asher was keeping his promise, it seemed, and she felt better for it.

The bishop lived on a large farm a twenty-minute buggy ride away, and Petunia enjoyed the brisk wind and the way Trudy's breath billowed out in front of her. Out in the sunshine, it was possible to let the weight of her worries go as Trudy trotted along at a brisk pace. She waved to a young family who were outside shoveling their drive together, everyone with a shovel. The girls' dresses were bright pink against the brilliant snow, and the boys' dark clothes brought out the sparkle in their eyes and the red in their cheeks. The parents looked a little more sober—word had passed around the community about the murder—but the children were still living up the winter morning to the fullest. She loved her life in Blueberry. It was a friendly, happy community, and she'd feel better once they'd sorted out this ugly business of murder.

Another buggy came down the road toward her, and she recognized the Hiltys sitting side by side.

"Good morning, Petunia," Mary Hilty said as they drew close enough to hear each other. Her husband had the reins, and he looked over at Petunia with a solemn expression.

"Good morning!" Petunia called back.

Abram Hilty didn't so much as give her a nod, and Petunia wondered at that. She wasn't exactly friends with the Hiltys, being so much younger than they were, but people around here normally were friendly with each other, at least.

The Hiltys carried on past, and Petunia's mind went back to that visit. Mary had been certain that Abram wouldn't have been able to see anything at the time of the murder. But had he seen something earlier? Could *he* identify the woman who'd shouted and slapped Ike?

It was something to mention to Asher. Wives liked to think that they knew everything their husbands knew, but they didn't always.

The Schlabach dairy farm was large by Amish standards, but could still be run by a single family. The farm itself was far back from the road, and a long winding drive led the way to a large, three-story house, nestled next to two large greenhouses, and a freshly painted red barn farther back on the snow covered slopes.

Petunia parked her buggy next to the buggy shed. There were three unhitched buggies all lined up; which belonged to the Schlabachs and which might belong to a visitor, she didn't know. But the Schlabachs often had someone over, Felty Schlabach being the bishop and all. Petunia threw a blanket over Trudy's back to keep her warm while she waited.

The stable door opened, and Benji Stutzman came out, leading a horse. One of the buggies must be his.

"Benji!" Petunia said with a smile. "I just saw Priscilla yesterday."

He'd know why, and she left the rest hanging. Benji smiled shakily. "Oh . . . Right . . . Yah."

That wasn't the reply of an engaged young man looking forward to his banns being read.

"Are you all right, Benji?" she asked.

"Yah. Yah . . ." He didn't sound convinced of that, and she knew for sure now that something was wrong. She gave him a sympathetic look and waited.

"Well, things might be changing here . . . ," Benji said.

"Changing?" Petunia's heart skipped a beat.

Benji looked around, then led his horse closer to Petunia. "I'll pay you back for your work, Petunia, but I don't know if the wedding can go forward."

"Why not?" Petunia whispered.

"My uncle told me for years that I'd be inheriting his hardware shop," Benji said. "And that's changed."

"Why?" Petunia asked.

"Because he doesn't approve of me marrying Priscilla. He says that her family are good for nothing, and he won't have them sucking the money out of his business after he's gone." Benji shrugged weakly. "And Priscilla's family were counting on me inheriting for their daughter's comfort. I didn't know that those old grudges would matter so much to me and Priscilla. Her family won't support the wedding if I'm just the third son of a chicken farmer. I don't think it'll happen."

"Have you talked to her?" Petunia asked. "Because I know she loves you."

"I just talked to the bishop, and I'm going to talk to her now," Benji said dismally.

Had Petunia just done all that sewing for no wedding? Or had she perhaps done a lot of sewing for an Amish wedding that wouldn't happen, and perhaps the couple would go off to town and get married civilly? It did happen . . . but it made things awfully complicated in the Amish community. That was why they had a bishop and elders. They often rolled up their sleeves and waded into all sorts of family dramas in order to sort out problems.

Benji led his horse over to the first buggy and began to hitch up.

"Benji, if you call this off, you'll break her heart completely!" Petunia said. "She's head over heels for you!"

"Can I ask her to marry a poor man?" Benji asked. "She'd agreed to marry a man who was getting a healthy inheritance."

"Just tell her what's happening," Petunia pleaded. "There are *ways* . . ."

Benji met her gaze, then shook his head. "I'm not marrying her without her family's blessing. That's asking for a lifetime of misery. Families don't just go away, Petunia."

And Benji was right about that. Petunia felt some heat come to her cheeks at the reminder from someone younger than she was. But who knew? Maybe the bishop could sort this one out yet . . . Maybe Benji's uncle could be made to see that if he didn't forgive the Kempfs, then he'd be risking his own immortal salvation.

Fingers crossed.

"Where is the bishop now?" Petunia asked. "Is he home?"

"Yah. Inside," Benji replied. "But milking starts soon, so I have to hurry."

Petunia wondered if there was anything else she could say, but Benji didn't seem open to talking anymore. He turned his back and continued hitching up his horse. As much as Petunia wanted to help, it could often accidentally become meddling.

She sighed and headed toward the side door of the house. She knocked, and there was no answer. The wind picked up, and Petunia shivered as the cold wound its way around her legs. Behind her, Benji's buggy started moving and the clop of his horse's hooves melted into the sound of the wind.

Petunia turned and watched the buggy disappear down the drive, and then she moved off the step and looked up at the big farmhouse. The Schlabachs hadn't heard her, obviously . . . They wouldn't be avoiding her, would they? Unless word had already spread that she was working with the detective. And if the bishop himself ignored you, that was flirting dangerously close to some community discipline.

Had she gone too far? Her heart fluttered at the thought.

Inside the house, she heard a shout, then a scream. The thunder of running on hardwood floors could be heard all the way outside, and then the front door flung open and a soapy, wet dog came streaking out into the snow.

Bishop Felty came running after him first, no hat on his head. His teenage daughter Hadassah came out behind him, his wife Rosie right behind the girl, her sleeves rolled up and a big, gray work apron wrapped around her. The bishop's sister, Lovina, was at her heels, and the four of them spread out, trying to fence the dog in. The animal, covered in suds, seemed to have no desire to be caught, and seemed to prefer the cold to the bath.

"Hello!" Petunia shouted. "Can I help?"

"Just wait inside, please!" Bishop Felty shouted back, then, "Rosie, go left!"

The dog swerved between the Felty and Rosie, and all four of them were after him again, shouting after the dog to get himself back there and behave.

Petunia paused for a moment, wondering if she should join in the chase, but decided against it since some dogs would only get more excited with extra people in the mix, and she did as she was asked. She went in the front door, because it was the one hanging open, wiped her feet on the mat, stepped out of her boots, and stood in the silent sitting room.

There was a muddy, sudsy trail that led through the room and out again. Petunia followed it in her stocking feet, careful not to step in the mess. It went through the kitchen, and up the stairs. She found herself at the bottom of the staircase, and to her left she saw the bishop's study. The door was ajar.

Petunia could hear the shouting from outside still, and she stood motionless for a moment, wondering how terribly wrong it would be to peek inside.

She tiptoed over to the room and poked her head inside. It was a cozy room, heated from the vents that were fed from the stove in the kitchen, and since it was right next door to the kitchen, the room was warm. There was a desk, a bookshelf with a few books on it, and a large, heavy German Bible sitting on a little table all its own. There were a few Bible verses in Pennsylvania Dutch cross-stitched and framed, hanging on the walls. Likely those were Rosie's handiwork. A calendar hung on one wall, and she could see neat little notes written on several days over the month.

And lying across the desktop, scattered among bills, Petunia saw a tattered card with a photograph sticking out of it. Her breath caught in her chest. Photographs were forbidden. What was the bishop doing with one? He'd recently preached about putting all temptations behind them . . .

She crept closer to get a better look, and the photo looked a little ragged, like it had been around for a while. There was a coffee ring on one side of the card, and when she slipped the photo free of the card, she noticed that it looked a little bent. It was of an Amish man, smiling into the camera. She knew that smile, and the breath rushed out of her lungs.

It was Ike. He was sitting on a step in the middle of a hot summer day. His sleeves were rolled up, and he was leaning forward, resting his elbows on his knees. He was looking directly into the camera, an easy smile on his face. He was breathtakingly handsome!

On the back of the photo, she read the words written:

This is Ike. He'll be coming your way. You owe me.

What did that mean? Who did Bishop Felty owe? And was this a threat? Why had Ike come out to Blueberry, of all places? And why had the bishop known he was on his way?

She stood there, her breath stuck in her throat.

Who was Ike Smoker to Bishop Felty? And who had given the good bishop a warning that he was on his way? When had this warning come?

Overhead, a floorboard squeaked, and she froze. The house wasn't empty . . . But then she heard the front door open, footsteps, and voices. Petunia's heart galloped in her chest, and she pushed the photograph into her coat pocket.

Stupid! She shouldn't have done that, but it was too late now, because the door opened and she turned to see the bishop looking at her in surprise.

"There you are, Petunia," he said, wiping his hands on a towel. "I'm sorry about that. That dog is a rascal, and he got himself dirty in some cow patties, and when my wife gave him a bath, he made a run for it."

Rosie's voice echoed from the kitchen and moved up the stairs. "Naughty dog! Now you are getting that bath, and that's that! Haddie, don't let him past you . . ."

Petunia smiled weakly. "Sometimes they get something into their heads . . ."

"Yah, yah," the bishop agreed. "Now since you've come to my office, I imagine what you came for is of a personal nature?"

So he wasn't assuming she was snooping! That was a point in her favor, even if undeserved.

"Well, it's delicate," Petunia agreed. "May I sit?"

"Of course, and take off your coat," the bishop said kindly.

Petunia slipped out of her coat, sat in the chair in front of the bishop's desk and laid it over her lap. "Thank you."

"How can I help?" he asked gently.

"As you know, I'm helping the Englisher detective in his investigation of Ike Smoker's death," Petunia said.

"Yah, I'm aware," the bishop said. "Are you here to ask permission after the fact?"

"Do I need to?" she asked, a new worry suddenly joining her current ones.

"You should have," Bishop Felty said with a nod.

"Oh . . . Well . . . The reason why I agreed was that I'm doing my best to show him our way of life so that he isn't falsely accusing anyone from a misunderstanding. And I know Eden didn't kill Ike! I know it. But they're ready to send her off to a trial! They don't understand us, and that's incredibly dangerous. I'm just trying to protect one of our own."

Bishop Felty nodded slowly.

"Do I have your permission?" she asked breathlessly.

"Yah, you do," he said. "I agree with you—we need the police to understand us, and I don't believe for a minute that our Eden Beiler is a killer. We need to get her home. But I want you to be careful."

"I will," she said earnestly. "But that wasn't the reason I came . . ."

"No? What's the issue, then?"

"In the course of the investigation, it's come to light that there is an Amish woman here in Blueberry who must be visiting from somewhere else. She knew Ike—" Petunia paused, wondering how much to say, but having the bishop's kind face in front of her, the rest just spilled out. "She visited him. Someone saw her. And she was angry enough that she was shouting and she . . . she slapped him."

"Hm."

"As a woman, Bishop, it takes a lot to get to that point. Especially for an Amish woman. We don't do that . . . you know? And Ike was killed, so someone who felt strongly enough to go to his workplace, shout at him, and hit him, that's someone we need to talk to."

"Things are not always as they seem," Bishop Felty said, steepling his fingers.

"I agree. Things can be all muddled up—as they are right now. Nothing makes sense. But this woman might know more about Ike's history, and that could help us discover who killed him," Petunia said. "For all we know, she's the one who did it! The murderer might not be from Blueberry, Bishop. Wouldn't that be a relief to discover? Anyway, I don't even know where to start in finding her. I thought that if anyone might know about who she is, it might be you."

Bishop Felty cocked his head to one side. "Why me?"

"Because you're the bishop. You . . . you know people," she said feebly. "And my father said I should come to you, because you'd be the one who might be able to set all of this to rest. We have a murderer in our midst, Bishop! A murderer!"

"Where is your detective?" he asked.

"I didn't tell him I was coming," she replied. "This is between an Amish woman and her bishop. I wanted to come alone."

"I appreciate that," Bishop Felty said. "I've been in prayer over this, and perhaps you arriving here is the answer I've been looking for."

"Answer to what?" Petunia asked.

The door behind her squeaked softly, and Petunia turned to see a woman standing in the doorway. She was short, plump, and had a pleasant face. Her dress was clean, albeit a little wrinkled from sitting, and she had a handkerchief knotted in her fingers in front of her.

"Come in," the bishop said with a kindly smile. "This is Petunia Yoder."

"Hello," the woman said quietly.

"Petunia," Bishop Felty said. "I would like you to meet Verna Smoker. She arrived from Shipshewana a few days ago."

"Smoker . . . ," Petunia murmured. Would this be a sister? A cousin? Likely one of Ike's relatives, and she felt a rush of compassion. Whoever she was, she'd be grieving Ike's death in a different way from the rest of Blueberry. Blueberry hadn't liked him.

"I'm sorry for your loss," Petunia said.

"Thank you."

"Are you a relative?" Petunia asked.

"You could say that," Verna said. "I'm Ike's wife."

And Petunia's heart hammered to a stop.

Chapter Eight

"You're—" Petunia licked her lips, struggling for the words. "You can't be!"

"No?" The woman eyed her warily.

"I mean—" Petunia felt the heat hit her face. "What I mean is, none of us knew he was married."

"Yah, I was told that he'd not mentioned my existence. That tends to hurt a woman's feelings, as you can well imagine."

How much did Verna know about her husband's activities here in Blueberry? Ike and Eden had been talking about ways to get married . . . Unless that cad had been simply lying to her, giving her false hope, and stringing her along worse than any of them feared. Anger slowly began to replace the shock.

"It was more than not mentioning you," Petunia said. "Ike is—or he *was* involved with my best friend, Eden. They were quite serious."

"He did that sort of thing," Verna said, then pressed her lips tightly together. "He told a girl anything she wanted to hear."

"But . . . ," Petunia sighed. "I'm sorry. This is all just very surprising."

"I understand," Verna said.

"I am sorry for your loss," Petunia said, at last, not sure what else to say.

"I'm not." Verna's chin trembled. "I know this is terrible of me to say, but I'm glad he's gone. He was a terrible husband."

Petunia searched inside of herself for some sort of judgment against Verna's words, but she found none. Verna had married a bad man who left her, and that meant that she couldn't marry again. Not in his lifetime. So with Ike gone, her problems were solved. Petunia would have something new to say if Verna killed him, but if she just wasn't sorry to see him go, she couldn't blame her.

"Was that you who went to visit him at the ice house?" Petunia asked.

"Yah, that was me. He didn't know I was in Blueberry or that I'd tracked him down. Your bishop was kind enough to help me with that. And when I confronted Ike, he laughed at me."

"And you . . . killed him?" Petunia whispered.

"No, I didn't kill him!" Verna said. "I slapped him! He's the father of our two children, and he walked out on me, pretending he was single and free. Well, he wasn't either of those things. He had me and the *kinner* at home in Shipshewana, and as you know, marriage is for life. There is no getting out of that. I told him I was going to tell all of Blueberry about me and the *kinner* at home, and he just laughed. He said he was almost done here anyway, and he'd move on somewhere else where I wouldn't find him."

"Two *kinner*?" Petunia breathed.

"Yah. We were married for five years, and I have two little ones. Lizzie who is four, and Annie who is two."

Two little girls at home . . . and he was here in Blueberry ruining Eden's reputation!

"Come and sit down, Verna," the bishop said, and he pulled up another chair. Verna sank into it, eyeing Petunia uncomfortably.

"I wasn't sure how to tell the community about Verna, but this is as good a way as any. Verna was Ike's rightful wife. And Verna knows about Eden."

Petunia heaved a relieved sigh. "I'm glad I'm not the one to break that news to you. But Eden, the girl he was leading on, is my best friend. She's being charged for his murder."

"Then she should be punished for what she did," Verna said. "I had every reason to hate Ike, but I didn't do anything like that! She should pay." After a moment, she added, "Maybe she found out about us."

"She didn't do it," Petunia said firmly.

"Are you so sure?" Verna asked. "You say that no one knew about me. What if Ike told her? What if, after all his promises—and Ike was very good at making promises, but terrible at keeping them—what if he told her about me?"

"Not Eden!"

Verna just shook her head. "Someone did it, and I know for sure and certain it wasn't me."

No good was going to come from arguing with Ike's widow about Eden.

"How did you ever get involved with Ike?" Petunia asked instead. "Weren't there any signs of his bad character?"

"Oh, there were plenty," Verna replied. "Everyone I knew told to me to stay away from him. He drank, he smoked, he swore, he gambled . . . but there was something about a bad boy who needed me that tugged at my heart." Tears rose in Verna's eyes then. "He's easy to love."

"How did you convince your family to accept him?" Petunia asked.

"I didn't. We went into town and got married by a judge. It was legal and binding. And I was already four months pregnant."

"Oh . . . ," Petunia breathed. This was sounding awfully familiar, except Ike wouldn't run off to an Englisher court to marry Eden. He couldn't—he was already married! And this was the very solution she was thinking would work for Benjie and Priscilla . . . "It's a solution. I understand why you would do that. I do."

"It was the worst mistake of my life," Verna said. "And I don't just mean marrying Ike. I mean going against my friends and family and my Amish community and getting married the Englisher way. Marriage isn't only about two people. It's about the community that supports them, too. I didn't get any support doing it the wrong way. No one was happy for me. No one was joyfully congratulating me. It wasn't the right way to get married. Marriage is important enough to take the time and do things properly."

Not the advice that Petunia was wanting to give to Benji and Priscilla . . . but she still thought it might be good for them. When a generational argument got in the way of love, should the young people be driven apart? It was hardly fair!

"Well said," Bishop Felty said seriously.

"So no one supported you, even given time?" Petunia asked. "Even after a year or two?"

"No, not really. My family was furious with me for marrying him. They thought I'd made the biggest mistake of my life, and they wouldn't let him under their roofs. He had disrespected them and me, they said. If I wanted to see my family, I had to go see them with the *kinner* but without him. He hated that. He said he was my husband and they should get used to it. But they couldn't."

"And that's why he left Shipshewana?" Petunia asked.

"No." Verna shook her head. "He left because he's a lazy coward who doesn't want to step up and be the kind of man who can support a family. He wanted to keep drinking and gambling, and sweet-talking girls. My family might not have liked him, but if he had an ounce of character, he would have proven them wrong. No, Ike left me and our daughters because he wanted to. Plain and simple. Ike always does whatever he wants."

"He did, you mean . . . ," the bishop said softly.

"Yah." Verna sucked in a shaky breath. "He did. He's dead now. That's still a shock every time I realize it. I've spent five years deeply regretting my choices, and here I am, free of him at long last."

Right now, Verna looked like the woman with the most to win by Ike's death. Her marriage to him had ruined her entire existence, and having him dead meant that Verna could start her life again as a young widow. She could find a better man and remarry, if she dared.

"Will you miss him at all?" Petunia asked.

Verna dropped her gaze. "I loved him. If I could have made him into a better man, I would have. If a woman's love could have been enough to redeem him, he'd be at home with us, his feet up and me cooking for him with love in my heart." Her chin trembled. "But a woman isn't enough."

So Verna did love him. And not only was she the one with the most to gain by his death, but she was also a woman with enough emotional turmoil that a violent strike was more believable.

Maybe Verna was their killer!

Petunia felt a pang of guilt at her own hopefulness there. Here she was hoping that this young mother with two little girls was a murderer!

"Where are your daughters?" Petunia asked.

"At home with my mother."

Petunia nodded. "Is your family expecting you to bring Ike home?"

"I was hoping to," Verna said. "I couldn't go on alone—not if I could bring my husband home to provide for us. But now . . ."

But now, while she didn't have a husband to provide, she also didn't have any less than she had before. He hadn't done anything for her the last year, at least. And his death was an even better result for her because she could find a new husband. Petunia looked over at the bishop, but he was looking down at his hands, refusing to betray any of his own personal feelings.

"What will you do now?" Petunia asked.

"Go home," Verna said. "I miss my girls desperately, and there's nothing to keep me here."

Petunia nodded. "Understandable." But then something occurred to her. "But you might not want to leave right away. There is a murder investigation going on, and the detective will want to speak with you, I'm sure. We've been looking for you."

Verna turned away, her jaw tensed. For a moment she was silent, and she twisted her handkerchief in her white knuckled grip.

"The Englishers don't understand us," she said.

"This one will," Petunia replied. "I'm helping him."

"And how do we know *you* didn't kill Ike?" Verna demanded, turning on Petunia with fire in her eyes. "How do we know you aren't leading that detective by the nose?"

Petunia blinked at her, then looked at the bishop again.

"Verna," the bishop said quietly. "This is not the way. If you leave without speaking to him, he'll only wonder why. You should talk to him. Tell him who you are, why you were here, and why you're going home."

Verna looked up at Bishop Felty, and for a long moment, it was like they were having a silent disagreement, the bishop meeting her gaze with calm strength, and her eyes snapping with irritation. Then Verna deflated.

"Fine. You're probably right. I just want to get home to my girls. That's all."

"It's your choice, Verna," he said.

"I know. I'll stay."

Petunia breathed a sigh of relief.

"This will be sorted out soon, I'm sure of it," she said. And Asher would need to speak to Verna to make that happen.

* * *

Petunia left the bishop's office, leaving Felty and Verna alone inside. Her stocking feet were silent against the hardwood floor. The muddy water from the dog had all been mopped up. She turned back and looked toward the office. The door was shut again, and she could see a shadow in the crack of light under the door, and she could just hear the low murmur of the bishop's reassuring voice, but couldn't make out his words.

Petunia headed toward the kitchen, and she could hear some water running in the bathroom upstairs. It looked like the dog was getting the last of his bath. As Petunia entered the large, bright kitchen, she spotted Lovina at the kitchen sink, washing her hands. The older woman looked up with a smile.

"That dog is very naughty," Lovina said. "He's never done that before. The last time we bathed him, he was sweet as pie. This time he ran for the hills."

"So he's not always that naughty," Petunia replied.

"Even dogs have their bad days."

"True . . ."

How far did a bad day go, though? Was a murder in the same category—something out of character, never to be repeated? Lovina dried her hands and reached for a bowl, placing it on the counter in front of her.

"I noticed you talked to my brother," Lovina said. "Is everything okay?"

Her words seemed a little more pointed than her body language. Lovina took three eggs out of an egg basket on the far side of the counter and cracked them into the bowl. Her movements were slow, relaxed, and the majority of her focus seemed to be mostly on the eggs that she started to whisk with a pleasant shushing sound of metal against the glass bowl.

"Yah, everything is fine . . . well, as close to fine as any of us can be with a murder in our community," Petunia replied. And then something occurred to her—how much did Lovina know about Verna Smoker? "Lovina, did you know about a rumor that Ike left Shipshewana because he got a woman pregnant?"

Lovina's whisking stopped, and she looked up, her blue gaze sharp. "Really?"

"Yah, people are saying that he got a woman pregnant, you know, before marriage, and didn't want to marry her, so he ran away." It was a bit of an enlargement on the original story, but Petunia wanted to hear what Lovina would say.

"That's something . . . Wow." Lovina shook her head, and got a bottle of vanilla. She cocked her head to one side as she dribbled a little into the bowl, then screwed the lid back on. "But I suppose it might explain things."

"Explain what?" Petunia asked.

"Well . . . maybe Ike didn't want to get married, and that's why he was stringing poor Eden along. Some aversion to marriage."

The whisking started again. That was very close to an outright lie, and Petunia watched Lovina's face for some sign of discomfort or evasion, but she found none.

"Lovina, I met Verna in the bishop's office," Petunia said.

"Oh." Lovina stopped mixing and reached for baking powder. She measured with a teaspoon. "So you know."

"You were going to let me share an obviously untrue rumor with you, you were going to agree with it, encourage it, and send me away?" Petunia burst out.

Lovina's cheeks did redden then, and she looked up from her cooking. "I'm sorry, Petunia."

"You were willing to *lie* to me!" Petunia said. That was a shock. Lovina was known to be many things, but her truthfulness had never been questioned.

"I wasn't—" Lovina sighed, gave the bowl one quick whisk, then put it down and circled around the counter. "Petunia, I am part of the bishop's household. I oftentimes know far more than I should, just because I see something, or overhear it, or Felty and Rosie are discussing something . . . I can't talk openly about the things I learn here. I just can't!"

"That is understandable," Petunia said. "But gossiping with me, and letting me believe it was true—"

Petunia was investigating a murder. There could be far-reaching consequences, like sending her off on a fool's errand, and letting a killer go free. But she couldn't say that, could she?

"What I said was mostly true," Lovina said. "He did leave a woman with his children. The part you didn't say you knew was that he was married. And since you obviously know that now, yes, Verna is his wife. And he has *kinner* in Shipshewana that he should have been at home supporting."

"How well do you know Verna?" Petunia asked, lowering her voice.

"Not too well," Lovina replied. "We only just met her a week ago when she arrived. But she's a decent woman, and . . . and I find I honestly like her."

"So you didn't know Ike was married before that?" Petunia asked.

"No, of course not!"

"How did Verna know where to come?" Petunia asked.

"She came to the bishop to discuss her run-off husband," Lovina said. "All she had to do was ask where the bishop lived and someone pointed her in the right direction. As for coming to Blueberry, someone told her that he was here. People have friends from all over. Word gets out. Someone he knew recognized Ike from Shipshewana, I imagine."

"Of course." That made sense, she had to admit. Petunia lowered her voice to a whisper. "Lovina, do you think Verna might have killed him?"

Lovina sighed softly. "I can't say."

"Because you know too much, or because you don't know?" Petunia pressed.

"Petunia, please don't put me in this position!" Lovina pleaded. "Everyone likes me much better if they think I know very little. They hate to think I know things and I just won't say. So I've let people think that I'm not very bright. It smooths paths. But with you, I see I'll have to just be honest, and you'll have to understand my position."

"Yah, I do understand," Petunia said.

They were both silent for a moment, and Lovina circled back around to the counter again and reached for a bottle of milk. That would be from their own dairy—possibly even fresh from the morning. She measured two cups with a teacup into the bowl, and the whisking started again.

Petunia had to admit that she had learned something new about Lovina today. She knew far more about the people in this community than she let on. Lovina could keep a secret. Like it had been locked in a vault.

"Maybe I can ask your advice about something, then," Petunia said. "You might be a better person to discuss it with than the bishop."

"Of course," Lovina said. She pulled down another bowl, added a yellow lump of butter and a generous pour of white sugar. Then she started to blend them together with a fork. Her movements were smooth and precise—more than her measuring seemed to be.

"And you can keep this private, I presume?" Petunia pressed.

"Of course, Petunia. I have a lot of practice doing exactly that."

"Well, I'm sewing the dresses for an upcoming wedding," Petunia said. "And I recently found out that the wedding might be called off because of an inheritance kerfuffle."

"I know who you're talking about."

"Oh, that makes it easier," Petunia said with a sigh. "Then I can tell you that Priscilla had no idea anything had changed as of last night. She was excited about her wedding. She was telling me what a wonderful man Benji is. And when I saw him just outside, Benji said he was off to tell her the bad news that they can't get married, and . . . I just feel terrible! I know they love each other. Priscilla is such a happy bride-to-be. I don't know what to do!"

"Sometimes you can't do anything," Lovina replied, looking up.

"But don't you think that they *should* get married, even if the uncle cuts him from his will?" Petunia asked. "Shouldn't love matter more?"

Lovina turned back to blending butter and sugar. "Life would be very difficult for them with their extended families fighting each other. And love might matter more at the start of things, but I've watched couples marry, have babies, raise those babies, and then see those *kinner* grow up and move into their own homes. And as the years go by, and different seasons of life pass, extended family begins to matter a whole lot more. Without it? I don't know . . ."

"The family can get used to the idea," Petunia said. "They'd have their own seasons of life to pass, too."

"Bitterness can get entrenched."

"People can grow!"

"You disagree with me."

"I do," Petunia said fervently.

"You're young, Petunia."

That was the criticism she got most often. She was too young to know what older people knew through life experience. But youth didn't equal stupidity, either.

"Maybe I am, but I believe in love, too!" Petunia said. "What is the use of people getting married if they didn't love each other enough to wade through the hardest times together? Verna and Ike were been married too. There is no magic in the vows."

"You are passionately devoted to your friends' happiness," Lovina said, pouring the butter and sugar into the bowl. "And that is a wonderful thing. But I fear that this time you are wrong. You need to let them sort out their own business. If things go sour it can't be because you meddled."

"They might sort themselves right out of a marriage," Petunia sighed.

"They might."

"I hate that."

"Me too." Lovina retired the whisk and picked up a wooden spoon. "But for some, it's better to end it than to get married to the wrong person."

"I don't think they're wrong for each other."

"You might not have thought that Ike and Verna were, either, had you been in the same position with them . . ." She gave Petunia a sympathetic look. "Petunia, as you know, I'm the community Old Maid. I've seen a lot. I learned a long time ago that sometimes the most useful thing you can do is to let people sort themselves out. And just . . . be supportive while they do that. Everyone needs a kind person who cares."

"You're probably right," Petunia said, and she looked out the kitchen window to where Trudy stamped in the snow, waiting. "I'd better get going. I have to meet up with Detective Nate."

Lovina made a face. "Is that a good idea, spending so much time with that Englisher cop?"

"We have to find the killer!"

"But he's an Englisher."

"He's an Englisher with *guidance*," Petunia replied.

Lovina gaze turned knife sharp. "Don't trust him, Petunia. You don't know what he'll do to our community. You don't know!"

She slammed the spoon down onto the countertop with a bang, and Petunia jumped. Lovina stood, her hand flat against the counter, her flashing gaze meeting Petunia's. That was a rather strong reaction to an Englisher in their midst . . .

Then Lovina swallowed, lowered her eyes to the mixing bowl again, and pressed her lips together.

"I'm sorry," Lovina said, lowering her voice to just above a whisper. "But I saw that detective of yours, and I saw the way he looks at you, too. He's attracted to you. That is not your fault, but you should be cautious all the same. I know this one is hard to avoid, but you don't need to accept it so cheerfully, either."

"I'm not happy about any of this!" Petunia replied. "I just want to see Eden released."

"Just . . . be careful."

"I always am," Petunia said.

Lovina turned back to her mixing and Petunia moved toward the hall that led to the sitting room and the front door where her boots waited for her. She suddenly wanted to be out of there as quickly as she politely could be.

Did Lovina know more than she let on? It could be safely assumed she always did. But was Lovina trying to protect someone from a murder charge? Maybe she'd grown closer to Verna than she'd admitted.

"I'll see you later, Lovina," Petunia called over her shoulder, hoping to make things feel more like normal again. That had been a strange reaction from Lovina . . .

Petunia went to the front door where her boots waited, and stepped back into them, pulling her coat close around her. Her mind was spinning as she pulled the door shut behind her and headed around the house to where her buggy waited. They had found the mystery woman who had slapped Ike . . . could Verna be the killer?

But Verna would hardly admit to being at the ice house if she'd killed him, would she? There would be some sort of instinct to hide as much as possible, but Verna had opened up about her marriage, her children, and about her anger toward her husband.

Did guilty people do that?

Petunia wasn't sure, but something felt off. Maybe Asher would know more about how these things worked.

"You have a good day, Petunia," Lovina called from the side door. She sounded completely normal again, like any other day. Her hand, covered in flour, fluttered in the air in a goodbye.

"You too!" Petunia sounded cheerier than she felt. She pushed her hand into her coat pocket and felt the edges of the photo still tucked away.

Her stomach sank. The picture was still in her pocket! She hadn't meant to keep it, it had just happened . . . Had she just stolen a picture from the bishop's desk? This was not going to be easy to explain.

But there was no going back to return it now. It would have to wait for another day.

Chapter Nine

Later that morning, Petunia stood in the small stable, shoveling soiled hay into a wheelbarrow. She'd called Asher from their local phone booth, and she'd left a message for him saying that she had more information for him. That was all she could do, and since her father was out with the tour group, and the stable hadn't been cleaned out yet that morning because of a malfunctioning wind-up alarm clock, Petunia set to work mucking out the stalls.

The horses were outside munching a fresh feeder of silage, and Petunia worked in relative silence, listening to the sound of crows arguing with each other from a tree and the scrape of her shovel against the cement floor.

Her mind was spinning with her new information, and she could only pray that everything could be sorted out in time for Eden to come home to her family. That was the worst part—poor Eden sitting alone in that cell. It wasn't right! And given much longer, they might send her farther away to a real prison. That thought sent chills down Petunia's spine.

Eden had always been a little naïve. She fell in love with Ike because he was sweet to her, and she didn't seem to care how he behaved to anyone else. She thought Ike had potential to be better, if she just loved him well enough. A man's worth couldn't be weighed by how he treated one person, though. It was the bigger picture that mattered. A man could be a patient teacher in the fields and go home and be a tyrant to his family. He could be generous with other farmers and cruel to his own animals. One recipient of his best behavior didn't make a good man.

Petunia filled the barrow, then wheeled it out into the cold winter air and to the manure pile. The sun shone bright and sparkled off the snow that capped the fence posts. She heard the rumble of a car engine before she saw Asher's police cruiser come down the drive. She waited until he parked. His window slowly opened.

"Care to go for a drive?" Asher called. "You said you have an update for me."

"I can't. I have to finish the stable," she replied. "Care to muck out a stall?"

Petunia was joking about getting him to shovel out a stall, but her humor seemed to be lost on Asher because he looked undecided for a moment, then sighed. "All right." He closed his window, turned off the car, and hopped out. "So how are you doing?"

"I'm fine." She nodded toward the open stable door, and then picked up the handles of the wheelbarrow again. "I won't actually make you muck out a stall and get your work clothes dirty. That was a joke."

Asher shot her a wry smile.

"I feel like it's the gentlemanly thing to do to help you," he said, stepping through some muddy snow to get to where she stood. He looked tough, even in those dress pants and the shiny, low winter boots. There was something almost feral about Asher.

"You're no gentleman," she said with a laugh.

"Says who?"

"You're a cop," she clarified. "It's a whole different category."

Maybe that was what set him apart and made him different. He was too observant, too conniving. Part of the job, no doubt.

"Again, says who?"

Petunia eyed Asher for a moment, wondering if he was joking now. He stood there with his hands in the pockets of his black coat, his legs akimbo, and his expression curious, but not offended.

"Says me," she said, and she shot him a grin to show no ill will. "Come on, then. I have to update you and I might as well do it while I'm working."

Petunia led the way inside and Asher followed her into the stable. She pulled the door shut after them to keep the cold air out. The air was musty inside, but when she opened a fresh bale of hay with the pop of twine and it sprung open, the fresh scent of golden hay followed.

Petunia forked hay into the first stall, left the pitchfork in the first stall, and then grabbed the shovel for the second stall.

"I can do that," Asher said.

Let him get dirty if he really wanted to. She relinquished the shovel and let him shovel out the next stall while she leaned against the rail and watched him work.

"What's the update?" he asked her.

"I went to see the bishop today," Petunia said. "And he's got a visitor there—a woman from another community who has admitted to slapping Ike across the face."

"What?" He stopped short and looked over at her surprise.

"That's not the best part," Petunia said. "Her name is Verna Smoker, and she's Ike's legal wife."

Asher blew out a breath. "I knew teaming up with you was a good idea . . . She just . . . walked in and announced this?"

"No, I was asking questions, and then she walked in," Petunia said. "Regardless, she told me all about herself. She's from Shipshewana and she and Ike had two little girls together. He couldn't marry Eden because he was already married, Asher!"

"It does seem that way . . ."

"You don't believe it?" she asked. "The bishop was right there, and he confirmed it all."

"That is very helpful, but I'd like to talk to her myself," he replied.

"Yah, I thought so," Petunia replied. "That's why I told her she shouldn't leave for home like she wanted to."

"Good. That was the right thing to do."

Her mind went back to that photograph she'd accidentally taken.

"I also did something not so good," Petunia admitted.

"What did you do?" he asked.

"I stole something off the bishop's desk," she said with a wince. "I didn't mean to. There was a big kerfuffle with a dog, and I was waiting in the bishop's office—no, no, I shouldn't compound lies. I was snooping in his office while he was outside the house chasing after his wet dog. And when I was holding a picture, he came back in, and I just . . . I slipped it into my pocket."

"A picture . . ."

"A photograph."

"Does your community allow them? I know different communities have different requirements."

"No, ours doesn't allow them. And the bishop has come down hard on a family that sent their *kinner* to Blueberry Elementary and ordered school pictures. So the fact that he had a photo on his desk is . . . unsettling."

"Can I see it?" he asked.

"It's inside," she said. "It's of Ike."

He let out a low whistle. "The plot thickens."

"It would seem so," she agreed. "And on the back of the photo it said something about Ike coming, and that the bishop should be ready."

"So Bishop Felty was warned that Ike was on his way," Asher summed up.

"He was."

"How is he connected to Ike? A relative?"

"He gave us all the impression that Ike was a complete stranger!" she replied. "And there are no Smokers in the Schlabach family that I know of."

Asher started shoveling again, and his boot slipped in something wet. He made a face and looked down at his boot.

"You ready to let me muck out this stall?" she asked, holding out her hand. "I'm wearing the right boots for it."

He passed over the shovel mutely, and she continued the work. There wasn't much left to do, and then she forked hay onto the bare floor and picked up the handles of the wheelbarrow.

"Here's what I'm wondering," Asher said, holding the door open for her to pass through. "The bishop knew Ike was coming. Ike was not a good man according to Amish standards."

"He was good according to yours?" Petunia asked, passing him and going out into the fresh, chill air. She wheeled the barrow to the manure pile and dumped it.

"Not according to mine, either," he said. "Anyway, the point is, from what I can tell, the bishop could have done a lot more than what he was doing to corral Ike Smoker. But he wasn't doing much. And he knew he was coming . . . Who gave him the heads up?"

"I don't know."

Asher scuffed his boot in the snow, cleaning it off.

"There's a boot brush," she said, nodding toward the side of the stable. A boot brush shaped like a hedgehog with a cast iron body stood next to the door, partially submerged in snow.

"Thanks." He moved over to the boot brush and began to work at the boot. "There's something there, obviously. There's a connection between them."

"Or between him and whoever warned him," she replied.

"Huh. Good point. I wish we knew who it was."

"All the same, I need to return that picture. I don't want to get a reputation around here of having sticky fingers."

Asher laughed, and came back over to where she stood. "Grab the picture for me. I want to see it."

Petunia did as he asked. She'd hidden it in a drawer in the kitchen—that seemed like the safest place to hide it where her father wouldn't go rooting through. She retrieved it and brought it to the door where Asher stood, just inside, where it was warm.

"Shut the door," she said, not even thinking before she gave the order, and to her relief, Asher complied without seeming to have a problem with her forthrightness.

He took a look at the photo and exhaled a slow breath. "I see why he was popular with the ladies."

"Yah. That picture shows a rather . . . attractive side to him."

She'd seen much less attractive behavior from him, but based on physical appearance alone, Ike had been a strikingly handsome man.

Asher flipped the photo and looked on the back. "I can't understand what's written. This must be in Pennsylvania Dutch?"

"Yah, it's our language," she said. "It says, '*This is Ike. He'll be coming your way. You owe me.*'"

"You owe me . . . ," he murmured. "But the picture introduces Ike, so the bishop didn't know him, or wouldn't have known him without a picture. Presumably, they'd talked about him before. Maybe he's someone your bishop was supposed to help."

"That would be a reasonable explanation," she replied.

Asher looked up at her sharply. "But?"

"But nothing. I don't know. I suppose we have to ask him, but I hate admitting I took it!"

"We can go back, I'll distract him, and you put it back," he replied. "I'll question him about Ike, and I'll see what I can get out of him. If we need to, you can rediscover the picture and point it out to me."

"We could do that?" she asked.

"Sure. Why not?"

"Thank you!" It would certainly solve that problem, although the sheer sneakiness of the plan left her feeling a little guilty. "I do have one other worry."

"What's that?"

"Someone needs to tell Eden that Ike was married," she said.

Someone needed to break poor Eden's heart all over again. She loved the man, she'd lost him, and now she'd lose him in a different way—her blind good opinion of him would be shattered.

"We'll sort that out, but she might have known all about it," Asher said. "I did some digging, and our Ike Smoker had a criminal record too."

"What?" Petunia looked up, but she shouldn't be so surprised, she realized. It matched his character.

"Yep. Petty theft, assault, shoplifting . . . small time stuff."

"A criminal record." Petunia shook her head. "There's no way Eden knew about that, either."

"Oh, she knew about the criminal record," he replied. "I asked her about it. She was in no way surprised. She said he'd told her all about it, but he'd turned a new leaf, so to speak."

"She knew?" Petunia felt the breath seep out of her.

"Yes. She knew."

"And she continued on with him, knowing what kind of man he was?" That was said more to herself than to him, because Eden had never been the kind of woman who'd hand herself body and heart over to a man with a proven inclination toward crime! She'd talked about marrying a pious farmer for years, and the cagey ice man was departure enough.

"Well . . . she thought those were mistakes in his past," Asher said. "She thought he was reformed, she said. But yes, she knew all about his criminal record."

And Eden hadn't told her. Petunia had told Eden everything—her hopes for the future, her unrequited crush on Obadiah Schlabach, her frustration with never being a good enough woman for someone to choose her . . . She'd bared her soul to Eden, and Eden had held this back?

"Petunia?"

She looked up, startled out of her thoughts. "Yah?"

"Are you okay?" Asher asked.

"I'm just surprised she never told me," Petunia replied. "There seems to be a lot she didn't tell me . . . Like that she's pregnant." She sighed. "All the same, someone has to tell her that Ike was married. Unless she knew that too. I'm starting to feel like I didn't know my best friend very well at all."

He nodded slowly. "Then why we don't we swing by the precinct and you can have a word with her."

"You don't mind?"

"If she didn't know Ike was married, it might shake loose that loyalty of hers and she'll tell us more about him. I have a feeling she won't believe me. But she'll believe you."

Yes, Eden would believe Petunia.

"Then let's go see her," Petunia said, and she felt a well of uncertain, frustrated feelings rising up inside of her. How much had Eden been hiding? Maybe Eden wasn't quite the confused innocent that Petunia had believed her to be.

Even if it was after his death, Eden was going to face the truth about Ike Smoker. Dead or alive, that man had been a cad, and Petunia wanted to see her friend admit it.

* * *

There was a change in Eden since Petunia had seen her last. Gone were the tears and the helplessness. Now, Eden sat with her back straight and her expression resigned.

"How are you doing?" Petunia asked.

"Fine, considering," Eden replied. "I talked to a lawyer, and it doesn't look good for me."

"Why not?" Petunia asked.

"I've been formally charged with murder. All signs point to me, and they want to transfer me to a real prison."

"We aren't done looking through all the suspects yet!" Petunia replied.

Eden picked up a saltine cracker and nibbled on it dismally. "I don't know what to say."

"Well, we're still looking for who did this, and I'm not resting until we find them . . ." She watched her friend take another small bite of cracker. She looked pale. "Is your stomach upset?"

"It's the stress," Eden replied.

Another outright lie. It would be morning sickness. But Petunia was amazed at how easily Eden had fibbed. Much like Lovina, who'd lied just as easily earlier. Was Petunia the only one who still squirmed when she told an untruth?

"Asher told me about Ike's criminal history," Petunia said.

Eden's gaze flickered over to her. "Did he?"

"Eden, why wouldn't you tell me that?" Petunia asked. "How many times did we sit talking, pouring our hearts out, and you never once breathed a word about it! It must have been upsetting for you."

"Ike's mistakes were in the past," Eden said. "And you didn't like Ike. I knew you wouldn't understand."

"A mistake is a little lie, or skipping a day of work," Petunia said. "Theft and assault—those are more than little mistakes. That's a pattern of behavior that could be very dangerous."

Eden just cast her a tired look. Yah, that was why she hadn't said anything.

"I'm not trying to argue with you," Petunia said.

"Then stop talking about Ike like you knew him," Eden said frankly. "*I* knew him. And his mistakes—yes, I'm calling them mistakes—were in the past. He was changing his life. He was determined to be a better man. We say we believe in forgiveness, but that's more than simply letting go of the anger when someone wrongs us. That means letting people's mistakes go and not holding it against a man. *Letting* him be better! We have to let people grow and improve. If we keep holding everything against them, they have no chance to be any better, do they? And then all we have is one mistake per person, and everyone gets locked down and identified by their worst sin. Well, no one is that simple! Everyone is more complicated, and everyone deserves another chance to be better. But Ike won't get that now, will he?"

Eden's chin trembled.

"No, he won't," Petunia said quietly. "And you're right—no one can change if we keep holding them back in their worst behavior. I fully agree. But sometimes people are lying to you, Eden. Sometimes people haven't changed."

"Even after his death, you won't give me this?" Eden asked, then shook her head bitterly.

"Eden, he was married," Petunia said.

Eden stilled, and it was as if she'd suddenly turned to stone. There was no movement. No expression . . .

"Did you hear me? He was married to another woman."

"What makes you say that?" Eden asked, turning toward her.

"I met her today. Her names is Verna Smoker. Did he mention her at all?"

"No . . . ," Eden whispered. "Never. I think she's lying."

"The bishop confirmed it all. It's true. She went to see him at the ice house," Petunia went on. "She slapped him when he said he was moving on with you, and she couldn't stop him."

"Surely you mean they were engaged, or . . ." Eden's breath sped up.

"No, married. She said they went into town and got married after a short time of dating. Everyone was against it, but Verna was determined. They had two little girls together, and then he left her and came to Blueberry."

"Married?"

"Yah. With *kinner*."

"Then he *couldn't* have married me," Eden said, her voice shaking. "He said we'd get married somehow, even if we moved to another community together. I was positive he'd marry me now that—" Eden stopped there and pressed her lips together.

"Now that you're pregnant?" Petunia asked softly.

Eden looked over with tears in her eyes. "How did you know?"

"I pieced it together," Petunia said. "It doesn't matter."

"Yes, I'm having Ike's baby . . ." She swallowed. "And now that he's dead, there's no way for us to make it right and get married. But even if he'd lived, we couldn't have! He was already married! I would have been . . . a single mother . . ." The realization was only now registering on Eden's face. "How is this even possible?"

"How far along is the pregnancy?" Petunia asked.

"A doctor came a couple of days ago," Eden said. "They say I'm about eight weeks. So it's new. And . . . my stomach is heaving." She took another nibble of the cracker. "Apparently, that's a good sign."

"Is that what you wanted me to tell your mother you were sorry about?" Petunia asked.

Eden nodded. "Yah."

"Did Ike know?" Petunia asked.

"That's what I was going to tell him when I went to the ice house," she whispered. "I wanted him to run off with me and get married, and save me the embarrassment . . . I don't know what I'll do, Petunia. I really don't."

"First things first," she replied. "We have to find out who killed Ike and get you released. Then we can worry about other things."

Eden was silent for a moment. "How long was Ike married for?"

"Well, his daughters are now four years old and two years old," Petunia said. "So . . . five years? Give or take?"

Eden pressed her lips together and she slowly shook her head.

"You really didn't know this, did you?" Petunia said.

"Of course I didn't know!" Eden said. "And now I have to apologize to this other woman for . . . for . . ."

"*You* don't need to apologize for anything!" Petunia retorted. "Ike lied to both of you. He was the one who led you along. You wouldn't have had anything to do with him if you'd known he was married."

"How could he do this?" Eden asked, shaking her head.

"I don't know," Petunia replied. "But maybe now you can see that he wasn't the man you thought he was."

"Maybe you're right . . ." Eden rubbed her hands over her face. "Although I don't know what good that does me now!"

"I know you were keeping his secrets," Petunia said quietly. "But you can't do that anymore. He lied to you, and to Verna. Was there anyone else he mentioned who might have wanted to hurt him?"

"He didn't tell me those things," Petunia said. "He said he was a man and he'd sort it out. He didn't want me to worry about anything. He said he'd take care of it all."

"But you knew he was in trouble?" Petunia pressed.

"He owed people money," Eden said, "I knew that. And he had some people who just didn't like him. In Shipshewana, there were plenty of people who were still angry about his . . . crimes."

"What about people here?" Petunia asked.

Eden shook her head slowly. "Wait—one thing Ike always said when I worried about him paying back his debts was that someone here owed him a good deal of money."

"That's what he said? Exactly?"

"I don't remember exactly, but he said that someone in Blueberry owed him big time, and when he'd got the money from that person, paying back everyone else would be easy."

Petunia frowned. Who would owe Ike money? He seemed to be borrowing money all over the community, not the other way around.

"When he came to Blueberry, did he arrive with money that he loaned to someone?" Petunia asked.

"I don't know."

"Did he know anyone here?" Petunia pressed. "Did he seem like someone was familiar to him? Someone he'd known before?"

"Not that I could tell," Eden replied. "But I wasn't with him all the time."

"True . . . ," Petunia sighed. "Eden, I'm going to be honest with you. This looks bad. Really bad. They could argue that you knew about his wife, and in a rage you killed him. So if there is anything else you know that could help us—anything at all!—you need to tell me now. Or tell Asher, if you don't want to tell me. Because otherwise, it could look like you were hiding things to protect yourself."

"I'm not hiding things!" Eden said. "I've told you everything. I didn't know about his wife and *kinner*. I promise you that. And I don't know who owed him money, or who he owed money to! I don't know those things. I thought all of his bad behavior was in the past and he was trying to mend his ways."

"Okay," Petunia said. "I guess we just need to sleuth out who owed Ike money. That might be a motive to kill him—trying to avoid paying him back."

"It might be," Eden agreed.

Petunia looked at her friend's sad eyes, and suddenly she felt a wave of sympathy. She'd been duped by a handsome man who'd promised things he could never give her.

"What did your *mamm* want you to do?" Petunia asked. "She knew about the pregnancy."

"Yah, she knew. I told her first. She wanted me to wait. She said we could figure it out together . . . somehow, and not include Ike." Eden's eyes misted. "I said some harsh things to my mother then. But she was right, wasn't she? You were all right."

Petunia reached out and squeezed her friend's hand. There was nothing to say. Eden had trusted the wrong man, and even if she'd managed to tell him about the baby, Ike wouldn't have been able to marry her anyway.

Legally speaking, Ike's loyalties were all to Verna.

Chapter Ten

"I wonder who owed Ike money?" Petunia asked on the drive back to the acreage.

"He could have been lying about that, too," Asher replied.

"I suppose so," she agreed. "But here's the thing. I didn't like Ike. I hated the way he was treating my friend. But he did have some goodness in him, too. I'd seen his face when Eden's brother said something cutting to him, and Ike looked genuinely hurt. He covered it quickly, but there was a heart in there . . ."

"No one is fully evil," Asher agreed. "But liars lie. That's something I learned along the way. When you push a liar into an uncomfortable position, he'll lie to get out of it before he even thinks. Does it make him a monster? No, but it does make him a liar."

"But not everything a liar says is a lie, either," she countered.

"So you think there's someone in Blueberry who owed him a large sum of money?" Asher asked.

"Maybe. I think it's possible," she replied thoughtfully. "The bishop knew that Ike was coming. So Ike coming out here wasn't random. Maybe Ike knew someone out here and he thought making a fresh start in Blueberry would be easier than anywhere else . . . someone who will be trying very hard to keep their head down right now."

Someone who might have killed him!

"Hm." Asher looked over at her and gave her an approving smile. "I like how you think, Petunia."

"Thank you . . . ," she murmured, but her mind was already spinning ahead to the people in her community. Who could possibly have owed Ike money?

When the cruiser pulled into the drive, Petunia saw a buggy in front of the house next to her father's tour wagon. They had a guest, apparently.

"Thank you for taking me to see Eden," Petunia said.

"No problem," Asher replied. "I'm going to be nosing around into Ike's finances and getting a copy of his marriage certificate—that sort of thing. I'll get that done as fast as I can today, and hopefully tomorrow afternoon we can go talk to Verna. I need to go there prepared. All we have right now is her word that they were married."

"You think that might not be true?" Petunia whipped around. "The bishop did confirm it."

Asher shrugged. "As a detective, it's my job to verify it."

"Wait . . . so you weren't sure, but you let me tell Eden that he was married," she said.

"Would she have told you that someone owed Ike money otherwise?" he asked. "If she didn't tell everything she knew, we'd be no further ahead. Your friend could be seeing some serious jail time if she's convicted."

"You let me tell her because you weren't certain. You can't lie to her, so you let me take that risk," she said, the realization dawning on her. "You used me, Asher!"

"I—" Some color touched his cheeks. "You were certain. The bishop's word was enough for you. I just allowed you to tell her what you were certain of. And it did help her to open up about the rest of what she knew."

"Asher, she's pregnant," Petunia said. Anything could have happened to Eden with a big shock.

"And I'd much rather she have her baby as a free woman," he replied. "That's the honest truth."

And yet Petunia had trusted that Asher was telling her everything, when he wasn't. A whole lot like Eden keeping her own secrets, too. Maybe she was naïve to expect the full and honest truth from people in her life, but she did.

"I feel like you used me for your own ends there, Asher," Petunia said, pushing the door open and letting in a rush of cold winter air. "And I don't like being used."

"Petunia—" Asher leaned over to see her face as she stepped out of the car.

"I've said my piece!" she said. "I don't like that. You could have told me what you were doing."

"If I had, you wouldn't have pulled it off," he called after her.

"I don't care. You used me, and I don't appreciate that. Anything could have happened, upsetting Eden like that. If you want my honesty and cooperation, I don't think it's too much to expect the same in return. That's all I've got to say on the matter."

Petunia slammed the door shut and marched toward the house. She was tempted to, but she didn't look back. If Asher wanted her help, then he'd better return the respect and honesty that she gave to him.

As she went inside, she saw Priscilla sitting at the kitchen table, sniffling into a handkerchief. Elias looked up with an expression of pure relief when he saw her.

"You're home!" Elias said, a little too loudly. "Petunia is back. You can tell her all about it. I'm sure she can help."

"What happened?" Petunia asked, pulling off her coat and hanging it on a hook and stepping out of her boots, her own frustrations with Asher forgotten. Although she had an inkling of what had happened with Priscilla.

"Benji came by my place yesterday, and he . . . he . . ." Priscilla gulped back her tears.

"What did he say?" Petunia asked, slipping into the seat opposite her friend.

"He said he can't marry me." Tears leaked down her cheeks. "Just like that."

"Did he give a reason?"

"Yah. He said his uncle hates my father, and that if we get married, he won't let him inherit the carpentry shop that he's been working at all these years. And Benji says if our families don't support us, he can't go through with it."

Elias slipped out of the room, and Petunia listened to the creak of the stairs as he mounted them. Her *daet* didn't want to be in the middle of emotional drama. And while Petunia would rather tell her *daet* about her frustration with Asher, Priscilla needed her support right now.

"Tell him the carpentry shop doesn't matter," Petunia said.

"The problem is . . ." Priscilla's cheeks colored.

"It matters to you?" Petunia looked at the young woman in surprise.

"It not about me, it's about my own family," she said. "Our farm is small, and the west field is just about useless. It floods every year. Last spring, the house flooded, and we moved into the trailer . . . One thing after another! So my *daet* can't cut up the land, and my older brother is going to get that. But that leaves the rest of us . . . and as you know, there are seven of us. My *daet* is most concerned about Levi. He was going to work with Benji, and Benji said he'd make him a partner in the business. Levi's really good with his hands, you see."

So there were more than Priscilla's hopes at stake here . . . an entire family was hoping for some stability through her marriage.

"So this marriage would be more than yours," Petunia said. "Your *daet* needs your marriage to provide for some of your siblings too."

"For Levi, at least," she said. "After Levi there are three more girls, so they can get married and be cared for that way . . ."

Petunia nodded. "What did your *daet* say?"

"Nothing coherent. He's furious with Benjie's uncle Noah. Something happened a long time ago, and they can't stand each other!"

"Do you know what happened?" Petunia asked.

Priscilla just shook her head. "I have no idea. No one talks about it openly."

"But your *daet* was willing to let you marry into the family," Petunia said.

"He said we have to forgive," Priscilla said. "He said that Benjie was a good man, and he wouldn't interfere in my happiness. But then Noah started up, and my *daet* got offended, and it's all a huge—" She waved her hands in the air in demonstration. "Petunia, what do I do? It isn't fair that my marriage is supposed to fix everyone else's problems. What about me? What about who I love?"

Petunia sighed. "I don't know . . ."

How to fix problems in generations back? How was Priscilla supposed to convince her own family that they'd have to find another solution for Levi?

"How does Benjie feel?" Petunia asked softly.

"He cried." Tears welled in Priscilla's eyes and her voice trembled. "He sat down at my table, and he cried into his arms. He said he loves me, but he can't ask me to go against my family, and he can't take on a whole family feud. He begged me to forgive him."

"Oh, Priscilla . . ." It was worse than Petunia feared. They were both deeply in love, and there would be no walking away from this, getting over it in a reasonable amount of time.

"What if we just . . . ran off and got married?" Priscilla asked helplessly. "What if we went into town and got married the Englisher way, at a courthouse?"

"A little while ago, I would have suggested it myself," Petunia said. "But I've recently met someone who did just that, and everything went very, very wrong. Priscilla, if you get married without your families present, they'll always remember it. And marriage is about more than just the two of you."

"So I'm supposed to just let him go?" Priscilla asked, shaking her head.

"I didn't say that. All I'm saying is, when life begins to get rolling, you'll be grateful for a supportive mother-in-law and for your family embracing Benji and making him feel welcome. Because life can get stressful, and you'll both need family support."

"I don't want another man," Priscilla said. "This was what I was afraid of—something happening to ruin my chance at true happiness."

"Don't give up yet," Petunia said. "It's not over yet. This is just . . . a bump. A considerable one, yah, but still, just a bump. Okay?"

"I don't know how I'll convince my family, let alone his," Priscilla said weakly. "Last year I overheard my *daet* talk about a loan he took with a man he didn't know. But he was from another Amish community. The problem was, the interest rate was very high—and that's not the Amish way. But my *daet* was desperate. We'd lost another crop. And over the last year, *Daet* has been trying to find a way to pay him back, but with that interest rate, and another year of that west field flooding, then the house . . ." Priscilla shrugged. "We're in trouble, Petunia. My *daet* has been losing weight and staying up late. My *mamm* has been begging him to stop worrying, to put it in Gott's hands, but he says that's easier said than done when he's put our family into this position. All conversations that were supposed to be private, of course."

"Of course," Petunia murmured, but her pulse had sped up. Priscilla's father owed a man from another community a great deal of money . . .

"Please don't say anything to anyone," Priscilla said. "I'm upset, and I'm talking more than I should."

"He borrowed money from a man from another community?" Petunia confirmed, trying to keep her voice low and even, but not sure she managed it.

"Yah."

"Which community?"

"I don't remember."

"Could it be Shipshewana?" Petunia asked.

"Maybe. I'd have to ask my *daet*, and he'd be upset I even knew about it. I don't dare say anything. All I know is that the man who loaned it to him can't have a conscience, charging an interest rate like that."

"An unscrupulous man charging high rates to desperate people . . . ," she murmured.

"That isn't the point, though," Priscilla insisted. "All I'm trying to say is that money is very tight right now, and my family can't pitch in to help Benjie and me start out. They can't help Benjie start a business, or anything!"

"I know," Petunia said gently. "And I'm not married, or likely to get married, so I don't have any wonderful advice for you except this: I've seen people get married who didn't love each other nearly enough. I've recently met someone who married a man who simply didn't love her. He said he did. He married her, even. But he didn't love her. And that isn't your problem. You and Benjie adore each other. No man cries at your kitchen table for lack of love. That's all I know. There has to be a way through this, Priscilla, if you're patient and can wait a little bit."

"I don't see how," Priscilla said. "But it isn't like I want another man. I might as well wait. You think I have hope?"

"You have something better than hope," Petunia said firmly. "You have Benjie's heart."

When Priscilla left, Elias came back down the staircase again, and he looked at Petunia cautiously. "All fixed?"

Petunia shook her head. "I don't think so, but it's not something that I can do anything about. Benjie and Priscilla have to figure it out. They'll either tackle it together and find a way to get their families' support for a wedding, or . . . they won't."

Elias nodded soberly.

"But I did learn something very interesting," Petunia said.

"What's that?" her father asked.

"Priscilla's father, Elijah Kempf, borrowed a large amount of money from an Amish man from another community," she said.

"Yah, I know about that," her father replied.

"What? What do you know about it?"

"Just that—he borrowed the money and it saved the farm."

"Was it from a business or a loan agency?" Petunia asked.

"No, from another Amish man. He preferred to keep the matter private. But I know the interest rate was immoral. Elijah was very upset about it. He's been asking for prayer for months, for Gott to show him how to repay the loan. I've even given him a little money here and there to help them through."

So it was confirmed.

"Someone owed Ike a great deal of money, too," Petunia said. "And Eden said he was certain all his problems would be solved when that person paid him back."

Elias's eyebrows rose. "Oh. That's a big coincidence."

"Do you know of anyone else who borrowed money from someone out of town?" she asked.

Her father was silent for a moment, chewing the side of his cheek, then he shook his head.

"No, I don't. He's the only one I'm aware of. But Elijah Kempf is a good man. He's a little tightly wound, but he loves his family and he works hard."

"But the stress might have gotten to him," Petunia said. "I don't want to incriminate anyone, *Daet*, but it's only right that the person who killed Ike pay for the crime. Not an innocent woman."

"I agree with that," her father said.

Petunia thought for a moment. She didn't want to raise an alarm where there wasn't a need, especially with Englisher police. But if they didn't find the killer, Eden was going to pay for this. She'd been formally charged.

"It's a very big coincidence, isn't it?" Petunia said after a moment. "Almost too big of one?"

"I do hate to say it, but it's worth mentioning to your detective," Elias agreed.

"I think so too. I'm going down to the phone booth to call Asher and let him know what I found out. Then I'll start supper."

"Fair enough," her father said.

As she grabbed her coat, her father called after her, "And let the police do the police work, Petunia! They are paid for this kind of risk. You are not!"

* * *

The closest phone hut was about a mile down the road, and then south, down another gravel road a little way. In spring and summer, she'd walk diagonally across a field and cut her time in half, but in the snow, she preferred walking along the road.

The Amish of their community didn't keep phones in their homes. Some farmers had phones in their barns in case of emergency, but everyone else used a community phone hut that held a telephone and a record book for each person to write down their call. They used to have a tin can inside, too, and people would pay a dollar for each call, and the money in the can would pay the phone bill each month, but then someone started figuring out there was money in the Amish phone huts and started stealing it. So now, they all pitched in at the end of the month to pay the bill.

The walk was a pleasant one. There was no wind, so she stayed warm as she went along, her boots crunching against the snow. They lived close to town, and there were more cars and trucks passing this way because of the proximity, and she moved off the road as a pickup truck came whipping past.

Maybe, if Elijah Kempf was the one who'd killed Ike, the judge would have some pity on him, considering what that loan had done to his family. Maybe there would be some mercy. But as she thought about it, she realized that no matter who was charged and convicted for this murder, families would be affected, people would be heartbroken, and their community would never be the same.

But Ike—unlikable and as irredeemable as he seemed to be—didn't deserve to be killed like that, either. The Amish were pacifists. Petunia had been raised with stories of Anabaptists who had given their own lives to save the lives of people who hated them. And Ike didn't deserve to be murdered. Even if Petunia hadn't liked him, she'd find him justice. It was the Amish thing to do.

Petunia got to the big stop sign, then turned south, heading downhill toward the phone hut. She could see it from there—a little way off the road, with a parking area next to it. A buggy stood there, hitched up with stamping horses, so someone else was making a call. She idly wondered who it was.

Another open-top, two-seater buggy came down the road from the other direction. She shaded her eyes to make out the driver, then waved at Bonita Weir. Bonita waved back and then reined in to a stop across from Petunia. There were no other vehicles passing, so there was no rush.

"How are you doing, Petunia?" Bonita asked, leaning over to see her better.

"I'm good," Petunia said.

"Where are you off to? Making a call?"

"Yah," Petunia said.

"I've heard you're helping an Englisher detective," Bonita said.

"Well, I don't want him to misunderstand us and arrest the wrong person," Petunia said.

"I also know that you saw my husband at the station." Bonita's back stiffened. "I know it might be too much to ask, but I was hoping you might not tell anyone else about that."

Did she know about Jacob's sloppy kiss on her forehead? She hoped not!

"Of course, Bonita," Petunia said. "I would never use your family as gossip. I promise you that."

"Thank you." Bonita relaxed a little bit. "I hope that my husband and I don't look like suspects in Ike's murder. Everyone knew that I didn't like my husband's relationship with him, but my husband is a lamb. I admit it frustrates me that he won't stand up for himself more, but he is completely incapable of hurting anyone."

"If it makes you feel better, the detective said he didn't think Jacob did it," Petunia said.

"It does . . ." Bonita smiled wanly. "I couldn't have hurt him, either."

"Where were you?" Petunia asked, then tried to look more conciliatory. "I mean, so I can tell the detective and you'll be crossed off the list."

"Is there a list?" Bonita asked, her eyes wide.

"Yah," Petunia admitted.

"Well, I was at home in bed with my husband," she replied.

"It was early in the morning, around seven," Petunia said.

"Oh . . . well, then I would have been on my way to work at the hotel." Bonita's face blanched. "Alone . . . Oh dear, he's going to suspect me, isn't he?"

"It's okay," Petunia said. "No one was expecting to have to account for themselves. We're looking for the real killer, not someone to blame it on."

Bonita didn't look much comforted, though. She looked down at a watch on her wrist.

"Would you like a ride home?" Bonita asked. "I can wait. It's no trouble for me."

It was a kind offer, but there was something a little too direct in Bonita's glittering gaze. Bonita was worried about her alibi, and she actually looked like a rather good suspect to Petunia. She felt bad for her that she'd married such a weak-willed man, but Bonita had every reason to hate Ike, and no one to say where she was for the time of the murder.

"No, it's okay," Petunia said. "Thank you for the offer, but I enjoy the walk. I haven't been getting enough exercise since the snow came. You know how it is."

There was a beat of silence. "Yah, I sure do. I'd best get moving then." Bonita gave her a pointed look. "And you be careful too, Petunia. I know you're only helping, but murders are a dangerous business to poke your nose into."

"I'm doing my best," she replied more cheerily than she felt.

Petunia watched Bonita's buggy for a moment as it started off again, then continued on her path toward the phone booth. When she looked back again, she saw the buggy stopping at the big stop sign. And for some reason she couldn't quite name but had nothing to do with the cold, she shivered.

The wind started up again just as Petunia got to the telephone hut, and she looked over at the horse and buggy—it took a moment, but she recognized the horse.

"Hi, Arnie," she said, going over to pet his nose. It was Eden's horse—or her family's. The wind whipped around her. Arnie, being a quarter horse and having a thick coat, didn't seem much bothered. But for Petunia, the wind whipped around her legs, and she moved over to the side of the telephone hut for some shelter.

There was a time when Petunia would have been excited to see someone from her best friend's household, but today she felt more cautious. She couldn't tell anyone the details of the case—not much, at least. And so far, even considering Bonita, Eden still looked like the best candidate for the murder. Innocent or not.

Petunia leaned against the wall, and she could make out the voice of a woman inside. It was Susanna Beiler, Eden's mother—Petunia recognized her voice.

"Yah, she'd be arriving . . . well, as soon as we can get her there. She's only a few weeks along, and she would stay there for her whole . . . uh . . . until the delivery. There is a delay right now, though, so it might take another couple of weeks before we can send her out to you," Susannah was saying. "What kind of doctor would she be seeing while there?" A long pause. "Yah . . . yah . . . and how much would that cost?"

It sounded like Susanna was making plans for Eden to go to another community to have her baby. Of course . . . when Eden got home, she'd have to leave again and go give birth. But if they were sending her away, it would be a good year before Petunia saw her again, and the realization was a sad one.

Everything had changed already. There was no going back to what it used to be.

"We'll pay for any medical expenses privately, of course," Susanna said. "And what did you say the cost of room and board was? Hmmm. That's steep . . . but I know, I know. It costs what it costs. I don't know where we'll get the money for that, though . . . honestly."

How much did a maternity plan like this cost? And where did pregnant Amish girls go to have their babies? It must be an Amish community, considering that Susanna was speaking in Pennsylvania Dutch. It didn't matter where it was, of course, but Petunia did wonder, all the same.

"And we'd need this be as private as possible," Susanna went on. "You'd need to call her by a different name. Maybe Sarah. No one but her father or I will know where she is. No one." Another pause. "No, the father of the baby will not be part of her life. He's . . . He's gone. And when the baby is born, the child will return with her here."

A pause.

"Yah, but we'll explain it away. We'll say a family member died, and we're adopting the baby." Susanna's voice shook. "I've already given up my own soul to protect my daughter. What's one more lie? I will not force her to give up her child. I blame the father of this baby. Not her."

Susanna's voice shook, and Petunia's breath caught in her chest. She'd said that she'd already *given up her own soul* to protect Eden . . . what did that mean? What had Susanna done to keep Eden safe? She'd tried involving the bishop and elders—Petunia knew that. She'd tried talking to Eden . . . and then she'd discovered her daughter's pregnancy.

Had Susanna Beiler killed Ike?

Petunia felt like her breath was squeezed out of her lungs, and she stood there in the cold air considering the possibility. What if it was Susanna who'd gone to the ice house before her daughter arrived and confronted him. Susanna was older, with some life experience. What if she'd guessed the truth about Ike and demanded some answers. What if he laughed at her, like he had laughed at Verna, and Susanna had struck out in a maternal rage?

She could see it happening . . .

But would Susanna let her daughter go to prison for her?

Unless Susanna was planning on confessing later . . .

Petunia realized then that the conversation had stopped, and suddenly the phone hut door opened and Susanna took a startled step back.

"Hello," Petunia said, trying to sound as normal as possible.

"Hello." Susanna's face was white. "How long have you been here?"

"Oh, just a little while."

"And you . . . overheard?"

Petunia considered lying, but she had a soul of her own to think about, too.

"Yah, I did, and I'm very sorry to have overhead. But please believe me, Susanna—this isn't a surprise to me," Petunia said quickly. "I guessed as soon as I saw those prenatal vitamins and you claimed they were yours."

"Right . . ." Susanna dropped her gaze. "You would know that wasn't possible."

"Yah . . . and Eden told me recently about the pregnancy, so . . ." Petunia reached out and caught the older woman's hand. "Susanna, you're a good *mamm*! You really are. I know you love Eden more than anything."

"We warned her!" Susanna said, squeezing Petunia's hand in return. "She knew better than this. I made sure of it. I told her about the wrong kinds of men, about men who'd take what wasn't theirs before the wedding, and about waiting for a proper husband. She knew better!"

"I know," Petunia said softly.

"I hate for my own daughter to be a lesson for others," Susanna said. "But you should take a good hard look at what happened to Eden, and make sure you make better choices."

"Oh, you don't have any worry with me," Petunia said. "I don't have men thinking of me that way. I have too big of a mouth, and too many opinions, and I'm always certain I'm right. I also can hardly cook, and I'm only middling good-looking. You know as well as anyone that I'm downright unmarriageable!"

"The wrong kind of man never even considers marriage," Susanna said meaningfully. "That's not the protection you think. Besides, I've seen you going about with that Englisher detective."

"Yah, but he's Englisher," Petunia said with a short laugh.

"And yet, he's still a man, Petunia," Susanna said. "I know I'm not a shining example of a mother considering what happened to my own daughter, but you have no *mamm* of your own. So I'm going to give you some advice."

"Okay . . . ," Petunia said.

"Hearts can get entangled with the wrong man very easily. Don't let it happen with your Englisher detective. I know what I saw."

"What did you see?" Petunia asked uncertainly. "Was I acting inappropriately?"

"You? Never! You are very proper," Susanna said. "I saw the way he looked at you, dear girl. Be careful."

How had Asher looked at her, exactly? What made Susanna think that Asher was interested in her more than as a guide through the Amish culture? She'd never seen it from him, and she counted herself as a rather observant person.

Unless this was a distraction . . . Susanna was trying to get Petunia to think about other things . . .

"I'll try," Petunia said.

"I'd better get going," Susanna said. "Please keep this private. I know that goes without saying."

"Eden is my best friend," Petunia said earnestly. "I will find who killed Ike, no matter what it takes. I'll find whoever did it."

Susanna licked her lips uncomfortably, then nodded quickly. "I have to head home. Dinner won't cook itself. Goodbye, Petunia. And be careful."

That was the third person today to tell her that. Perhaps she should consider the overwhelming quantity of the same advice and be just a little more cautious.

Chapter Eleven

Petunia watched as Susanna's buggy rolled out before she shut the door to the telephone hut firmly. She picked up the phone log and looked down the list of phone numbers. At the bottom, of the list, Susanna hadn't filled out her phone call. She was hiding her tracks—something Petunia didn't blame her for, but she was surprised at how naturally this seemed to come to some people.

Petunia picked up the phone and dialed Asher's number. She knew it by heart now, and didn't really need the tattered business card that she referred to. The phone rang twice, and then Asher picked up.

"Detective Nate," he said curtly, and it occurred to her just then that he might be angry with her for the way she let loose on him when he dropped her off. She was used to saying what she thought and living with the consequences, but Asher was different. He might not just roll his eyes and write her off.

"Asher?"

"Hi, Petunia." His tone softened. "I didn't recognize the number right away. What can I do for you?"

It was such a relief to hear his quieter, gentler voice that it all came rushing out of her at once. She told him about Elijah Kempf borrowing money from someone out of town, and about how her father had confirmed it. She told him about how high that interest rate was—positive usury! She told him about Bonita's shaky alibi, and about Susanna, and what she'd said about giving up her own soul to protect her daughter.

"It just doesn't make sense that Susanna would let her daughter sit in a jail cell while pregnant!" Petunia said.

"Unless she has another plan to get away with it," Asher said.

"I don't know what it would be," she replied.

"Me neither, but I don't like to take a suspect off my list until I'm absolutely sure, so she's going to stay there."

"Understood," Petunia replied with a sigh. "What about Bonita?"

"It seems strange that she'd wait this long to kill Ike. She had plenty of reason before. If she killed him, then it wouldn't be a crime of passion. It would be premeditated revenge. Does that sound likely for her?"

Petunia sighed. "No. Bonita is a good woman who's had a tough life. But I can't see her plotting a murder. I just can't."

"It's still a possibility," he said, then was silent for a beat. "Look, Petunia, I feel badly about how we parted earlier. I don't want you to feel used, but there are some times I'll have to keep some information to myself. It's for your safety."

"I have to live in this community when you're gone," she said. "I have a life here."

"I know. I'm sorry if I didn't appreciate that deeply enough. But your safety matters more to me than any of that." There was something almost tender in his voice.

"Oh . . ." Had Susanna had a point?

"If something happened to you, I'd have to sit down with your father and explain myself, and I'd rather not do that. Your father is an intimidating guy."

Petunia smiled at his dry humor. "I know you can't tell me everything, but we have to protect Eden, too."

"And I am," he said. "I personally got her some healthy snacks, and I've assured her that we're doing everything we can to get to the bottom of things."

"Thank you," Petunia said.

"But to show you a little goodwill, I'm going to tell you what I dug up today."

"What did you find?" she asked.

"A marriage license for Ike and Verna," he replied. "So that is confirmed. They got married . . . let me see, July 27, five years ago. Verna has no criminal history, but she does have a driver's license."

"A driver's license?" Petunia said. "We don't drive!"

"She got one, all the same," he replied. "Maybe she got one when she was less firm in the faith."

"Maybe . . ." Perhaps Verna had a few more secrets of her own . . .

"So I think we have enough to go have a chat with her," he said. "And I want to do it sooner rather than later. I know you'll probably hate this, but I like to interrupt people at dinner time. It annoys them, and like you've seen, they tend to say more when annoyed. What do you say?"

"Yah, I think you have a point. You can come pick me up. And Asher?"

"Yes?"

"While we're at the Schlabach farm, I'm going to need a couple of minutes to return that photo to the bishop's study."

"Right. I'll do what I can. I'll see you in a few minutes."

* * *

Petunia had just gotten home and explained to her father that she needed to go out again when Asher's cruiser pulled into the drive.

"What am I supposed to eat this time?" he muttered irritably.

"A grilled cheese sandwich?" Petunia asked. "I also have those leftover biscuits in the bread box."

"Petunia, those biscuits are . . . uh. . . ."

"I know, I know. I used too much baking powder and you can taste it," she said. "Then we'll throw those out. There is leftover beef—that would be good. And there's cheese in the ice box, oh, and some leftover ice cream. It's the chocolate mocha flavor I made—"

"I'll figure it out," he said with a sigh, and there was a knock on the side door. "That's your detective."

"I'll make that fried chicken you like tomorrow," Petunia said. "To make up for it."

"I'd appreciate that," he replied. "But the way things are going, I should just learn to cook."

Petunia cast her father a wry smile at his dry teasing and went over to let Asher in. He waited by the door while she stepped into her boots and pulled her shawl around her shoulders. No coat this time. A shawl would make this easier. She wore a white apron, and she had her purloined photo tucked inside of it within easy reach for when she could return it.

"Hello, Elias," Asher called.

Her father grunted in response.

"He's upset I'm not here to cook," she said. "You see, I'd make a terrible wife. I can't even manage to feed my father at home."

"Elias, it's my fault," Asher said. "And I'd like to make it up to you. Do you like pizza? I'll pick one up on my way to bring Petunia home again. My way of thanking you."

Elias looked like he wasn't sure if he should continue being angry or not, then he smiled and nodded.

"I don't mind a slice or two. But I never eat past six o'clock. Petunia knows it."

It was true. Elias had his own ways, and even if he was starving, he'd wait until breakfast. He was stubborn.

"I'll bring pizza before six," Asher said. "I'm good for it."

Petunia went out the door first, and Asher followed. As she got into the warm car, she said, "That was very nice of you, Asher. My *daet* appreciates it, I know."

"It's not a problem," Asher said.

"He's serious about not eating past six. Even if he misses his supper, and it's two minutes past, he won't eat it."

"Why?" he asked.

"Just his way. He says it unsettles his stomach."

"Well, we'll have to make sure we're on time then. I want your . . . *daet* . . . to know I'm a good guy. That he can trust me with you."

She smiled at his use of the Pennsylvania Dutch word. "You'll feed him better than I do. He might just adopt you."

Asher chuckled. "No time to waste, then. Let's go interrupt someone's dinner."

It didn't take long to drive to the Schlabach farm. There was more traffic since it was "rush hour" and Englishers and Amish alike were heading home for dinner after work. As soon as they turned into the drive, Petunia spotted a hired van in front of the farmhouse, and she squinted, leaning forward.

"Hm. I wonder if that's someone arriving, or running for it," Asher said dryly.

"I wonder," Petunia replied.

There were two suitcases, and an Englisher man hoisted them up into the back of the van. Asher pulled up behind the van, and the man looked over his shoulder at the police cruiser in surprise. Asher stopped the car, turned it off, and hopped out.

The bishop stood off to the side with Verna, and Rosie stood a few feet away from them with her arms crossed over her chest—from the cold, or from her mood, Petunia couldn't make out. But the bishop's wife was staring at the van with a stony look on her face and her coat undone to reveal a gray work apron underneath. Her teenage daughter Hadassah stood a couple of feet behind her mother, her eyes wide and worried.

"Good evening," Asher said, and he turned his attention immediately to the Englisher driver, flashing a badge. "Where are you off to today?"

"I'm a hired service," the man said. "I'm just picking up a customer."

Petunia shut her door behind her, and glanced over at Bishop Felty and Verna. She walked over.

"You said you'd stay," Petunia said, her voice low.

"For how long?" Verna demanded. "I have *kinner* at home! I'm not sitting around in Blueberry for weeks while some Englisher cop noses around. I have a family."

"Yah, yah . . . ," the bishop said, his tone soothing, but he looked distracted.

"Well, the detective is here now," Petunia said. "I'm sure you'll be happy to talk to him and get it out of the way."

"I don't have time for that," Verna replied. "The driver is here. Now. I have to go."

"But you'll have to talk to the police," Petunia said.

"I don't see why. I have nothing to do with this."

"Ike was your husband!" Petunia was losing patience. "You have something to do with the victim, at the very least!"

Verna pressed her lips together, and she looked over at the bishop questioningly.

"He's here now . . . ," Bishop Felty said with a shrug. "You can't *not* talk to him."

Was the bishop part of trying to secret Verna away before she talked with Asher? Petunia would be surprised if their bishop went against a criminal investigation, but then the bishop was responsible for souls, not justice, and from the start his reaction to this murder had sounded . . . odd. And even now, he seemed paler than usual, and thinner .... if she wasn't imagining it.

Maybe she was . . .

"Mrs. Smoker," Asher said, coming in their direction.

Verna stiffened at the title. It wasn't the Amish way to use the titles of Mr. and Mrs., but Petunia had a feeling it wasn't that.

"Can I talk with you alone, please?" Asher asked, and he looked pointedly at the bishop first, and then Petunia. She felt the silent dismissal—and the opportunity afforded.

"Of course," Bishop Felty said.

"Maybe I could use your washroom," Petunia murmured.

"Go on inside," the bishop said.

Petunia put her hand over the photo under her shawl and hurried toward the house before anyone could follow. She didn't need the washroom at all. What she needed was thirty seconds alone in the bishop's study.

She slipped past Hadassah and went in the side door, and when she got inside she found Lovina at the stove, stirring a large pot of some sort of stew that smelled wonderful.

"Oh, hello, Petunia," Lovina said. "I see you brought your detective this time."

"He needed to speak with Verna," Petunia replied.

"Ah." Lovina looked at her for a moment—her gaze thoughtful. "I know you can't help that, dear. Don't worry. We are commanded to obey the law of the land."

Petunia let out a slow breath. "Yah, we are." She glanced toward the window. "Rosie seems pleased to be rid of Verna."

"It's been hard having an extra woman in the house," Lovina said. "Even though Felty only sees her as a part of his spiritual flock, so to speak. But Rosie guards her fence."

"Understandably," Petunia said demurely.

She needed to get that picture back to the office, but the bathroom was upstairs, and the office was on the floor level. How was she going to do this with Lovina watching? But then a plan occurred to her. Why not simply play dumb?

"Well, I came in to use the washroom," Petunia said. "Excuse me, please."

And she turned on her heel and marched directly to the bishop's office. She heard Lovina's yelp from the kitchen, and Petunia ran across the room, threw the photo under an open book, and then came back to the door just as Lovina arrived.

"This is *not* the washroom!" Lovina's face was red.

"I'm sorry!" Petunia said. "I thought . . . I thought I remembered—"

"Upstairs," Lovina said. "Right above here. But upstairs."

"Right. I feel silly." Petunia's hot face was testament to how foolish she felt playing this game, but the photo was finally out of her possession, and for that she was relieved.

She hurried upstairs, found the bathroom, and locked herself inside. For a moment, she just stood there breathing. She looked at herself in the mirror and saw the red spots in her cheeks. She washed her hands, rubbed water on her face, then dried herself on a hand towel. The bathroom had one small, high window with curtains over it, and Petunia looked outside. From her vantage point, she could see the van—still blocked in by Asher's cruiser, and the bored Englisher driver playing on his phone. The bishop and his wife now stood side by side, their shoulders touching, and the black top of the bishop's felt hat was tipped toward his wife as if he was speaking with her. Verna and Asher stood a few yards off, Asher jotting notes in a little notepad.

Would Asher tell her what Verna had said? She could only hope. When her heartbeat had returned to some semblance of normal, she opened the door and stepped out into the hallway.

She heard the creak of floorboards in the room next to the bathroom, and since the door was open, she allowed herself one peek inside. Obadiah stood there—this was his bedroom, it seemed—and he was looking out his window at the very scene she'd viewed from the bathroom. His head was cocked to one side, his arms crossed over his chest.

"Obie?" she said.

He turned, and his expression was filled with such sadness that her heart skipped a beat.

"Oh . . . Petunia. Hello."

"I was just—" She pointed in the direction of the washroom. "I wonder what they're saying down there."

"Hard to tell," he said.

"Verna seems very at home here," Petunia said. "I doubt your mother feels the same way." She forced a little laugh.

"Verna will go home," Obie said. "And that will be the end of that."

"Who was Verna to you . . . really?" Petunia asked cautiously. "She doesn't seem like just some stranger passing through."

"That's because she's not," Obie said. "And my parents think they hide that fact so well, but they don't. They have no idea how much pressure it is for me to keep covering for them."

"About what?" Petunia asked. Would he answer, or clam up then and there?

"Oh, what does it matter?" Obie sighed. "We've been hiding this for so long, and I imagine the truth is coming out down there anyway with your Englisher detective."

"The truth about what?" Petunia asked.

"About us. Our family. Our history, and . . . our imperfections," he replied.

"Every family has something," she said diplomatically.

"Well, we have bigger secrets than most. Verna isn't some passing stranger. She looks like she belongs here because she does. She's family," he replied. "She's my sister-in-law."

Petunia's mind spun, trying to figure out how that worked. Obie had two other brothers, but Petunia knew who they were married to . . . "But Verna was married to Ike, Obie."

Did Obadiah not know that? Maybe not. She sifted through her mind to remember if they'd discussed Verna before. Maybe his family kept some secrets from him, too.

"I know Verna was married to Ike," Obie said flatly. "And Ike was my brother."

"Ike was . . . ," she murmured disbelievingly.

"My brother," he repeated, and Petunia's heart thudded to a stop.

"What happened? How is that possible?" she asked.

"He's my half-brother. He has a different mother. That's a story for my *daet* to tell, though."

"How long have you known?" she asked.

"Ever since Ike arrived, the secret was out. *Daet* told us then. It was very difficult around here for a while. *Mamm* didn't take it well, as you can imagine. And when Verna showed up, that was a whole new surprise. We hadn't known Ike was married until then."

"Okay . . ." Petunia tried to sort out the details in her mind. Ike was Obadiah's brother. Bishop Felty had fathered a child with another woman some twenty-five years earlier. And then that child—Ike Smoker—had come to the same community where his father lived. Who had sent that card with the picture—was that Ike's mother? Or just someone who knew the connection?

"What about—" she began, and Obie held up a hand.

"Ask my *daet*. He'd be angry if I told his story. I've said too much already."

* * *

Petunia's sensible running shoes squeaked down the stairs. In the kitchen, Lovina stood next to the window, her hands on her hips. She turned when she heard Petunia, and give her a wan smile.

"What's happening out there?" Petunia asked.

"I don't know . . . I'm just trying to get some cooking done. I'm sure when all of this settles down, everyone will be hungry. Aren't you the one who said everyone still needs to be fed?"

"It's the truth, isn't it?" Petunia said, and she cast the older woman a tired smile. "It doesn't really matter what's going on, everyone needs a solid meal."

"It'll all be okay," Lovina said. "It's dramatic now, but it'll settle down. You'll see."

"Thanks, Lovina," she said. "I appreciate that."

Maybe Petunia needed a little bit of comfort too. Lovina went back to the counter, and Petunia headed for the door.

She pulled the door shut behind her, and Bishop Felty and Rosie both looked over at her. Hadassah still stood on the step, and she looked over at Petunia with a pale face.

Not too long ago, Petunia was worried that Ike had been flirting with young Hadassah, but now she realized she'd been wrong. Ike wasn't interested in her as a girlfriend—she was his younger sister! Everything was coming together now. Obadiah didn't need to get rid of Ike to protect his sister . . . but he might have wanted his half-brother to leave the family alone. That four thousand dollars had been a loan to his brother.

Asher was still talking with Verna, but seemed to be finishing up. He said something to Verna, and she nodded, but didn't seem pleased. Then he came over to where the bishop and his wife stood.

"Could I have a quick word with you?" Petunia asked, raising her voice.

Asher changed course and came over to the step. Petunia moved away from the door, giving Hadassah a reassuring smile, but she didn't want to be overheard. She lowered her voice.

"Did you return the photo?" Asher asked softly.

"Yah, I did, but I also talked to Obadiah. He's inside."

"And?" he asked.

"It turns out that Ike was Bishop Felty's son from another woman," Petunia said. "He was Obadiah's half-brother."

"Really now?" Asher's eyebrows went up. "I didn't get that much out of Verna. Sounds like they open up more around you, as I suspected. Care to come over and talk to the bishop with me?"

Petunia's heart skipped a beat. "He's my *bishop*, Asher."

"Play dumb. You know nothing. Act shocked when I say things. They'll assume Verna told me."

"Yah?" she asked uncertainly.

"It'll work. They have big secrets and no idea who's talking."

"Okay," she agreed, and Asher gave her a reassuring smile.

"You're better at this than you think," he said. "Come on."

Petunia followed him over to where the bishop and his wife stood, their expressions grim.

"Bishop Felty," Asher said, his voice suddenly respectful and quiet. "I wanted to have Petunia here with me because she's acting as a social translator for me. She'd asked me to let her stand apart, but I really do want her here. So please, just pretend she isn't here. But she'll give me insights into things I might otherwise misunderstand. It's helpful for you, I assure you."

Bishop Felty looked over at Petunia soberly, then nodded.

"Go ahead," Felty said.

"Ike was your son, correct?" Asher pulled out his notebook, flipped back a few pages as if consulting it, then flipped forward to a new page.

While Asher was fiddling with his notebook, the blood drained from Felty's face, and Rosie put a hand out to steady him. He looked at Rosie and she gave him a faint nod. Petunia attempted to hide every emotion possible—standing there like a statue—instead of faking emotions she wasn't feeling. Because what she really felt was deeply uncomfortable.

"Yah, I must confess that he is . . . was my son." Felty pulled off his hat and rubbed a hand over his forehead. "It's a long story."

"One I'd like to hear," Asher said, looking up with a mild, innocent look on his face.

"Many years ago, a couple of years after I married my dear Rosie, I had a time of doubt," he said. "I went to Shipshewana to work, and while I was there I met a woman named Debrah Smoker. I'm not proud of it, but she and I grew close because she was questioning her faith as well. We thought we might leave the church together." He looked over at his wife apologetically. "I'm so sorry, Rosie, to make you hear this again. I know how it pains you."

"Go on." Rosie's eyes flashed fire, and she pressed her lips together. "Tell it, if you must."

"I came to my senses, and I came home and found a local job," the bishop went on. "My wife and I were blessed with our oldest daughter, and our family—as everyone knows it—started. I didn't know about Ike until a few years later when Debrah reached out to me. I sent her some money whenever I could, and she agreed not to say anything. She let people believe that the father was an Englisher. No one would look further into that sort of claim. I thought it was all behind me when Debrah sent me a letter saying Ike was coming to Blueberry. He needed a fresh start after his own run of poor choices, and how could I not try to help him? He was my son, and I owed him!"

"Of course," Asher said. "But him being here in your community threatened everything, didn't it?"

"It did," Felty replied. "It threatened everything except my own soul. Could I reach the end of my days and face Gott with a secret like that? Confession is good for the soul. I expect Blueberry will choose a new bishop—it would be the right thing to do. And we will be shamed because of me."

"And you're willing to face all of that?" Asher asked.

The bishop nodded sadly. "Yah, I am."

But Rosie's expression was less humbly penitent. She looked angry, and she wasn't hiding a bit of it. Her lips were tightly pressed together, her jaw was tensed, and her hands at her sides were balled into fists. That was rage. Not that Petunia blamed her. It wasn't her sin being exposed—it was something deeply embarrassing, though. It was something that would make the other women look at her differently if they knew. Having a husband who'd been unfaithful was shameful to the wife too.

"Was Ike blackmailing you?" Asher asked. "Making any demands in order to keep his mouth shut?"

"No, no, nothing like that," the bishop replied. "But I was helping him get established as best I could."

"Except he was behaving badly," Asher said. "He was ruining Eden's reputation, borrowing money and not repaying it, and generally being disreputable. Am I right?"

Felty and Rosie exchanged another look.

"He grew up without a father," Felty said. "All of this pain is my fault. All of it. But he grew up with a single mother and the Amish shame of that. He came to Blueberry and I wasn't publicly owning him as mine. He was . . . acting out."

"He was twenty-five!" Rosie snapped, breaking her silence for the first time. "He wasn't a little boy. He was a grown man, and he had chosen his path."

"Even grown men deserve a path to redemption," Felty said quietly. "Even grown men have pain from what they lacked growing up."

"This isn't about your *daet* beating you," Rosie said. "You never beat your own *kinner*, did you? He had a choice as well as you did."

Petunia and Asher exchanged a look.

"So . . . about Verna," Asher said, and the couple turned to face Asher again, Rosie rigid, Felty looking deflated. "How did she find you?"

"She knew who we were," Rosie said. "I didn't know about her, and Felty claims he didn't either."

"I didn't . . . ," Felty murmured.

"Anyway, she knew who we were from Ike, I assume," Rosie said, "and she arrived on our doorstep and told us she was Ike's wife. My husband was trying to get them to reconcile."

Petunia tried to hide her surprise there. But it did make sense. Ike was legally married and should go back to his wife and *kinner*.

"What about Eden?" Petunia asked.

"We had told her ever since Ike arrived that she should find a more reliable man," Rosie said. "She wouldn't listen."

"Did you tell her he was married?" Petunia pressed.

Rosie made a little face. "Give me time, and I would have. We only found out about his marriage when Verna arrived a week ago."

"He should have told her himself," Felty said.

"We now know he was married the whole time he was carrying on with her," Rosie retorted. "What makes you think he would?"

"He has a conscience," Felty replied.

"You thought too well of Ike," Rosie said. "I saw him for what he was."

"And what was that?" Asher asked.

But Rosie shut her mouth then and looked off in to the distance. She must have realized that she'd said too much.

"He was a hurting soul," Felty said, spreading his hands. "He needed guidance—much earlier, I admit. He needed a man to show him what being a real, loving, kind man was. He'd never seen that in his own home with his mother. Not up close."

"Was he angry about that?" Asher asked.

Felty shrugged. "A little."

The side door opened, and Petunia looked over to see Obadiah coming outside in his coat and boots, and he stopped next to his sister. Felty and Rosie exchanged a quick look, and Rosie pasted a smile on her face. She smoothed her hands down her coat and took a deep breath. She was putting a happy face for the benefit of her children.

"Is that all?" Felty asked. "I'm sure I've told you everything."

"For now," Asher said. "I'll be back later to get a bit more information, I'm sure." He glanced toward Obadiah. "But we can stop for now."

Felty and Rosie both sagged just a little bit, and they moved toward the side door together.

"I got a different story from Verna," Asher said, his voice low enough for Petunia only.

"What did she say?" Petunia whispered.

"Nothing about Felty Schlabach being her father-in-law," he replied with a meaningful look. "She's hiding things."

It seemed that she was, but if she didn't open up and talk, how were they supposed to get information out of her? So maybe Verna was the one who killed Ike. She'd been his wife and he was being unfaithful to her. She was angry with him, and she'd never be free of him as long as they both lived . . .

"What do you do if she's hiding things?" Petunia asked.

"I'm going to bring her into the station to question her there," Asher replied. "That can loosen lips too."

"Oh."

"I want you there too," Asher said. "We do something called good cop/bad cop. And I want you to be my good cop. I'm going to be all business and asking questions, and I want you to be reassuring. Bring her some tea. Reassure her that this will be over soon enough and she can go back to her children. That sort of thing."

"It works?"

"Rather well."

Petunia nodded. "Okay. I can do that."

All Asher was asking was that she be nice, and that came as second nature to her.

"Besides, she'll be more comfortable traveling to the station if you're in the car, too. She won't be so alone," Asher said. "I want to get to the bottom of this, but I don't want to terrify some poor Amish woman, either."

"That's very good of you, Asher," Petunia said.

Petunia looked back toward the house. The bishop, his wife, and their daughter had gone back inside, but Obadiah stood on the step still, and he was watching them pointedly.

"We're going to head out, Obie!" Petunia called to him.

Obadiah's expression changed and he waved. "Yah. Okay! See you, then."

As if they'd just come by to buy eggs or something, and he hadn't just confessed that his family was nothing like everyone believed them to be. He was acting so ordinary that it was strange.

Asher went over to talk to Verna, and she saw him gesture toward the car. Verna balked.

"It's okay," Petunia called to her in Pennsylvania Dutch. "I'm going too. Don't worry. It won't take too long."

Verna still looked wary, but when Asher opened the back door of the cruiser, she got in.

"Where are you taking her?" Obadiah called.

"Just to the station for a chat," Asher replied. "I'll bring her back myself in a few hours. Keep some supper warm for her. Nothing to worry about."

And Asher did make it all seem so safe, but what if Verna confessed to murder? She wouldn't be back for supper then, would she?

But Eden might . . .

As Petunia got into the front seat of the cruiser, she saw Obadiah watching her. His expression had turned worried, and he didn't return her wave when she waved at him once more.

Who was she fooling? This was no trip to town. This was a trip to the police station, and Petunia was hoping against all hope that Verna would confess, the killer would be someone from outside of Blueberry, and this whole misery would be over.

Chapter Twelve

The Borough of Blueberry Police Department was busy when they arrived. There were some Englisher teenagers who'd been arrested for something, and one of their mothers was standing at the front desk shouting about lawyers and letting her son go. Officer Dot, who was working the front desk, looked annoyed, but not intimidated. It seemed that she'd dealt with angry mothers in the past, and she'd deal with more of them in the future.

"He broke the law, ma'am. He was defacing public property. He'll be charged and processed in due time."

Asher nodded at Dot and ushered Petunia and Verna through.

"Remember, you're the good one," Asher murmured to Petunia. "When we get in there, insist that I get her some water."

"Okay . . ."

This was all very confusing, and very planned. There really was no such thing as a casual chat with a police officer, was there?

Asher led the way to a room with a window in the door. It had a little black sign with white lettering that read *Interview Room 1.*

"How many interview rooms are there?" Petunia asked.

"Two." He smiled faintly and then opened the door. "Have a seat, please, Verna. I wanted to get started with—"

"You really should offer her something to drink," Petunia broke in. "It's cold outside, and these dresses don't keep in the heat very well. Get her some tea."

Had she overdone it? Hopefully not. At least Asher was encouraging her to be her ordinary outspoken self—it looked less like pretending.

"Do you want one too?" Asher asked. "Since I'm fetching tea?"

"Yes, please." She shot him a grin. This was rather fun, she had to admit. Asher heaved a big sigh and headed back out of the room again.

Verna licked her lips and looked around the sparse room. There was a table, two chairs on one side, and a single chair on the other. There was a coat rack by the door, and Petunia hung her shawl up, but almost regretted it when she felt how cool the room was. Verna kept her coat on and plunged her hands into the pockets.

"Don't worry, Asher is a really nice man," Petunia said.

"You know him?" Verna asked.

"Yah. Well, I do now. I'm helping him to look into the murder. I don't want him to misunderstand our ways and accuse someone of murder who is really innocent."

"That's a relief," Verna said. "Because I didn't kill my husband."

Or so she claimed.

"That's all you have to say," Petunia said, just as the door opened again and Asher came inside with two Styrofoam cups, steaming with hot water, and tea bag labels hanging out the side. He put them on the table, followed by a handful of sugar packets and two stir sticks. *Not terribly comforting*, Petunia thought. Tea should be in a proper cup, and the sugar should be in a bowl. But it was better than nothing.

"Now," Asher said, taking a seat in a chair opposite Verna. "When I spoke with you at the Schlabach place, you omitted some important information. I want to know why."

Verna blinked. "What?"

"Did you tell me everything?" Asher asked.

"Yah."

"Are you sure?" His tone was sharp, and Verna flinched.

"You should just tell him," Petunia said softly. "If he's asking like that, he knows already . . ."

Petunia nudged the hot cup of tea into Verna's hands.

"You mean that my husband was Bishop Felty's son?" Verna asked, looking first at the tea, and then up at Asher.

Asher looked at her silently.

"Was that what you found out?" she asked.

He was silent again.

"Look, I didn't say anything because it's private. That kind of information could ruin the Schlabach family! And they have been kind to me. The bishop was trying to get Ike to reconcile with me."

"How was he doing that?" Petunia asked.

"By talking to him," Verna replied. "He was telling him about the importance of marriage, of keeping your promises, and being a good *daet* to his little girls. He was telling him that he could never marry that floozy he was fooling around with anyway."

"She isn't a floozy," Petunia said.

"She was carrying on with a married man!"

"She had no idea he was married," Petunia replied. "And she was horrified to find out about you. She's guilt-ridden." Petunia glanced quickly at Asher. "About him being married, that is."

"I've been told you think she killed Ike," Verna said, glaring at Asher. "You have her. She was standing over his body with blood on her hands—isn't that what happened? So why am I here?"

So she'd heard the details of her husband's death . . . Or she'd watched his body discovered from a distance?

"Because I'm not convinced she did it," Asher replied.

"Well, it's wasn't me!" Verna said. "I think you've got the right person in custody already. You arrested the one who was standing over his body. She was carrying on with my husband, and for whatever twisted reason she had, she killed him."

For a moment all was silent, then Petunia felt Asher's shoe nudge hers under the table.

"Did you want sugar?" Petunia asked softly.

Verna shook her head and took a sip of the hot tea.

"Just tell Asher what you know," Petunia said. "Then you can go back and have dinner with the Schlabachs. And, Asher, you should be nicer to her."

"Am I not nice?" Asher asked, raising his eyebrows.

"Not especially," Petunia said. "You catch more flies with honey than with vinegar."

Asher sighed and sat back in his seat. "Go on, Verna. Tell me what you know."

"I don't remember where I was in the story," Verna said.

"Did you have reason to think that Ike might go home with you?" Asher asked.

Verna nodded. "Bishop Felty said that Ike felt bad about leaving me with the girls, but that he was very attached to this new girl here. Felty said that Ike might need to see me face to face in order to rattle him out of his comfortable little life here. The bishop didn't want him to stay, either. He wanted him to come home with me."

"So it was the bishop's idea for you to see Ike at his workplace?" Petunia asked, and she blushed and cast Asher an apologetic look. She wasn't supposed to be questioning her, but this detail mattered. Up until now, she'd assumed she went to see Ike on her own.

"Yah, it was Felty's idea," Verna replied. "Obadiah drove me to the ice house. I'd never have found it on my own."

"Obie drove you?" Petunia said with a frown.

"Yah. He drove me down there, and I went to talk to Ike. That's when Ike laughed at me, and I got furious and I slapped him."

So Obadiah was there too. Petunia wasn't sure how, but that felt important.

"What is your feeling about Obadiah?" Asher asked.

"My feeling?" Verna asked.

"What kind of man is he?" Asher asked. "Character-wise? How did he feel about you being there? How did he feel about his brother?"

"Um . . ." Verna looked over at Petunia, looking mildly confused at the list of questions, and Petunia busied herself with adding sugar to her tea and stirring it. "I would say Obadiah is a very compassionate man. He talked with me for hours about Ike and how he'd walked out on me. He didn't blame me for Ike's bad behavior at all. He told me that some men can't appreciate a good thing when they have it."

"Did some people blame you?" Asher asked.

"Well . . . my mother suggested that if I'd been a better wife, I might have kept him at home," Verna said. "And there might be some truth to that. I let him rile me up. I let him get me angry over silly things. He was only doing it to see if he could, and I should have let those things go. But instead I'd shout at him."

"What sorts of things riled you up?" Asher asked.

"Oh . . . little things. He'd say a woman was pretty and I'd get jealous, or he'd say something like he thought pigs would go to Heaven when they died, just before butchering, and that isn't what we Amish believe. Silly things. But things that would upset me. And maybe I was too easy to upset."

"And you would get angry?" Asher asked.

"Yah."

"You would shout?"

"Sometimes."

"Did you tend to hit him?"

"No!" Verna said. "That time I slapped him was the first time, and believe me, I'm horrified with myself for it. Whatever he did, I shouldn't have let him change me into that kind of woman."

"What kind of woman?"

"A harpy."

"A woman who'd . . . kill?" Asher asked.

Verna blinked. "No!"

"You went to see him. He humiliated you. He'd married you, had children with you, then abandoned you for a younger woman. When you tried to bring him home, he humiliated you further. He laughed at you for even thinking he'd go back—in front of Obadiah no less! You were furious. So you decided to get revenge. Maybe he made plans to meet up with you and talk privately and ensuring you'd leave him alone. You returned by yourself, and this time, he turned his back on you. Went into the ice house, and you followed him. You took the ice pick, and when he laughed again—" Asher slammed his hand onto the table, and both Petunia and Verna jumped.

"No, I did not!" Verna gasped. "I did not kill him! I couldn't do that! I was angry, yes. I shouted at him, yes. I slapped him, yes. But then I went back to the bishop's house and had a good cry! That is all! Ask Obadiah!"

"That brings us back to Obadiah," Asher said, coming quickly on the end of her words. "How did he feel about his brother?"

"He hated him!" Verna burst out. "Of course he hated him! Up until Ike showed up, Obadiah was the oldest son!"

"What does that mean?" Asher asked, looking over at Petunia.

"He'd inherit the farm . . . I suppose," Petunia said.

"And not anymore?" Asher asked.

"The bishop changed his will," Verna said. "Obadiah told me about it during one of our long talks. He said that his father put Ike in the will too, so that he'd receive enough to get a good start in life."

Ike was in the will? Petunia had to bite her tongue to keep from jumping in and asking more questions.

"How much would he inherit?" Asher asked.

"I don't know," Verna said. "But it was enough to really hurt Obadiah's feelings. He's worked hard for his *daet*—at least that's what he told me. And I overheard him talking to his *mamm* about it, and she said to just give it time. She said Ike would show his true colors, and Felty would change the will."

"How did Obadiah react to that?" Asher asked.

"He agreed," Verna said. "He said he'd just wait and pray for Gott to open his *daet*'s eyes to the kind of man Ike was."

"And what kind of man was he?" Petunia asked quietly.

"A liar and a cheater," Verna said. "I'm not going to pretend I thought he was better than he was, but he was the husband I married, and for better or for worse, I had to make the best of it. I needed him to provide for *me*, not some other woman. Me!"

"I wonder how much Ike was getting in the will," Petunia said aloud, and she looked over at Asher.

"We might want to ask your bishop," Asher replied, and he held her gaze thoughtfully. Then he stood up. "Thank you for your time, Verna. We'll give you a ride home. I told them to keep a plate warm for you for dinner."

Verna looked startled, then nodded. "Oh. Yah. Well, thank you. Can I go back to Shipshewana now? I miss my girls . . ."

"Not quite yet," Asher said. "I'm sorry, but I'll do my best to hurry this investigation along. Trust me, I have no desire to drag it out."

"Oh . . ." Verna nodded, and tears misted her eyes. She took a trembling sip of tea.

"You can wait here until I drive you back," Asher said, and he angled his head toward the door, looking expectantly at Petunia. She stood up and followed him out of the room. Asher shut the door firmly behind them.

"What do you think?" he asked.

"She told us about the will," Petunia said.

"If it's true," he replied.

"You don't believe her?" Petunia asked.

He shrugged. "I'll feel better after you talk to your friend Obie."

"Okay," Petunia said. "I'll ask him about it." She looked in the direction of the holding cells and that solid door that was closed up tight. Eden was in there . . . "Since I'm here, can I talk to Eden again?"

"Sure. Why don't you tell her about the will and see what she says," he said.

"She said she told us everything," Petunia said.

"Just ask her."

And what could Petunia do?

* * *

"Ike's wife is here?" Eden whispered. "Does she know that I'm here too?"

"I'm not sure," Petunia replied.

"Does she know . . . about me?" she whispered.

"Yah, and she doesn't like it. But the security around here is very tight. She can't very well wander in here."

Eden rubbed her hands over her face. She looked tired—there were faint smudges under her eyes, and she looked paler than usual.

"Did you tell her I was sorry?" Eden asked.

"Yah, I did. Sort of. I said you had no idea about her, and that you were guilt-ridden."

"Was she angry?" Eden asked.

"Considering she thinks you killed her husband, yah," Petunia replied. "There will be hard feelings, Eden. Even after this is sorted out."

"Is it possible she killed him in anger when she found out about Ike being with me?" Eden asked.

"It's possible," Petunia replied. "I think so, at least. And she did know about you, so . . . But, Eden, I don't have much time before I'll have to leave again. We heard something . . . something we thought might be important. Did you ever hear Ike talk about a will?"

"A will? Like the legal document?"

"Yah. Did he mention that . . . anyone . . . might have included him in a will to inherit something?"

"No . . . *Is* there a will?" her friend asked.

"Yah."

"Whose?" Eden asked.

"If you don't know, let's keep it that way," Petunia said. "So never mind that. On another topic, I saw Obadiah today. What can you tell me about his relationship with Ike?"

"You know him as well as I do," Eden replied. "Oh, Petunia . . . Obie? You were in love with him for years! And now you think he'd kill someone?"

"I just have to look at all the possibilities, Eden," she said. "I don't want to believe it, but someone killed Ike, and it wasn't you. I'm remembering his feelings for you when I was pining away for him, and he was pining away for you. You'd know him better than I ever did."

Eden's face pinked. "That was a very long time ago, and it didn't matter. I was with Ike. His feelings for me had already stopped."

Or so she thought.

"But jealousy can do big things," Petunia replied. "How did he feel about Ike?"

"Obadiah is a sweet man. He's gentle. Maybe too gentle. His father won't let him take an inch off his own path. You know that! And when it came to Ike, he . . . didn't say a word. He didn't act angry. Well, maybe he disapproved. He told me a couple of times that Ike wasn't a good man."

"Eden, what was Obie like when he was with Ike? Was he angry that you were dating Ike and not him?"

"Obie wouldn't have hurt Ike!" Eden said, then she leaned forward and whispered softly. "Ike was . . ." She licked her lips and looked up at a security camera in the corner, then back at Petunia. "They were half-brothers. They were family . . ."

"Eden!" Petunia said. "You told me before you told me everything!"

"I know."

"And you didn't tell me that." Petunia looked at her friend reproachfully. "Honestly, Eden, you held a lot of secrets back. And I never did hold secrets from you!"

"It's different when you're in a relationship with a man," Eden replied. "I thought I was going to marry him. Of course I had to keep his secrets. That's how it works."

Petunia sighed. "He wasn't going to marry you."

"I know that now. But I was upset! That's a huge thing to figure out about a man you thought loved you. I forgot what I'd told you. I didn't mean to hold things back. Things have been really overwhelming."

"Okay," Petunia said. "But I really don't have much time. So you're telling me that Obie and Ike were . . . close?"

"Not exactly close, but they understood each other, I think. Obie was resentful, but Ike understood how he was feeling. Whenever Obie acted angry and said something rude, Ike always said that I should be understanding of his position—Obie had lost a good deal."

As in, a good deal of his inheritance?

"What did Obadiah lose?" Petunia asked cautiously.

"His good opinion of his own father," Eden replied. "That's . . . that's everything!"

The door opened then, and Asher poked his head in. Petunia and Eden looked over at him. His shirt was open at the neck, and his hair looked a little ruffled. He was tired, Petunia realized.

"Ready to go?" Asher asked Petunia.

She looked back at Eden.

"Go on," Eden said. "Yah, I'm lonely here, but I'll read my Bible and pray you find out who did this. Your time is better spent sleuthing than comforting me."

Petunia leaned over and gave her friend a hug. "I'm doing my best, Eden! I really am."

As Petunia looked over her friend's shoulder, she saw Verna come up behind Asher, and she slipped under his arm and into the room.

"Is that her?" Verna's voice shook, and she kept moving, out of Asher's reach and toward the cell.

Petunia let go of Eden, and they both stared wide-eyed at the approaching woman. Asher sprang into action and caught Verna's arm just before she reached the cell. Not that she could have gotten inside. Petunia and Eden were locked in together.

"It *is* you."

Eden stared, aghast.

"Eden, meet Verna Smoker," Petunia said, her pulse coming back down. Eden, however, blanched and took a step back.

"So it is—the little hussy that was trying to steal my husband!"

"She didn't know!" Petunia said.

"I didn't!" Eden echoed. "Do you really think I wanted to try and steal another woman's husband, and never have a real husband of my own? Do you think that was my goal? I had no idea!"

"All I know is that my husband came out here, and you were stepping out with him!" Verna snapped.

"He was a liar, Verna," Petunia said. "And you aren't the only one he fooled. You're both in the same situation here."

"Are we?" Verna's eyes snapped fire. "I have two little girls to raise on my own!"

"I'm so sorry," Eden said. "I know you won't hear it now, but I am! I didn't know! I would never have done that. Ever!"

Verna launched herself at the cell, and in the heartbeat it took for Petunia to freeze, Asher caught the Amish woman neatly in a pair of handcuffs and snapped them tight.

"I think we'll keep you restrained for the moment," Asher said. "Now, are we going to keep that promise about bringing you home for dinner, or are we going to put you in the cell next to her?"

Eden gasped at that, but Verna stopped struggling. She stood stock-still and gritted her teeth together.

"Is that you behaving yourself?" Asher asked.

"Yah. I won't do that again."

"Okay, then." He opened the door that led to the station and called through, "Officer Klaus, could you please take Verna Smoker to wait for me? I'm going to escort her home."

"You bet." Officer Klaus was a petite but solidly built woman who took Verna's other arm and led her out into the office.

The door shut and Asher exhaled a slow breath.

"That was dramatic," he said, and he went over to the cell with a set of keys and opened the door. Petunia came out, and he shut it again with a clang.

"Wow . . . ," Petunia breathed.

"I'm sorry about that, ladies," Asher said. "I truly am. I didn't mean to let that happen. Don't worry, Eden, I won't be putting her in a cell next to you. That will not happen, so you have no reason to worry, okay?"

Eden's lips were white, and she sat down. "Okay . . ."

"But we did learn something," Asher said, "intentionally or not. She's a violent woman. I'm willing to bet that slap at the ice house wasn't her first break with decorum, as she claims. When she gets angry, she gets physical."

"Yah, I'd agree with that," Petunia breathed.

And after seeing the rage that had bubbled out of the Amish woman, Petunia wouldn't have been shocked to learn she was the killer.

She was capable of great violence. If there hadn't been bars between them, she would have laid hands on Eden, Petunia was sure of it.

"Eden, I want you to know that you have nothing to fear here," Asher repeated. "I mean that."

"Thank you," Eden murmured.

It was good of Asher to make sure Eden felt safe. She was pregnant, and the last thing Eden needed was another shock like that one, or simply dreading what might be coming next.

"I'll visit when I can," Petunia said.

"Just find out who did it," Eden pleaded.

Petunia sighed as she followed Asher back out into the station. Verna was waiting in a chair beside Officer Klaus's desk, still cuffed, and looking significantly more humble.

"I apologize," Verna said Asher approached her. "I won't do that again. You don't need to bring me back in handcuffs."

"All right then," Asher said. "But if this happens again, I will charge and arrest you. Understood?"

"Yes."

Asher opened the cuffs, and she rubbed her wrists. Verna's gaze moved over toward the door that separated them from the cells, then she turned her back on it.

"I'm ready to leave," Verna said.

What kind of woman was Verna Smoker? A violent one when given enough reason—that was obvious. And a strong one.

She *could* have killed her husband in a fit of rage. She *could* have grabbed an ice pick and done exactly as Asher had suggested earlier in that interview room.

But Asher wasn't holding Verna for further questioning. He was taking her back to the Schlabachs where she would most assuredly disappear back to Shipshewana.

Why? That was what Petunia wanted to know. Why was he letting their best suspect walk away?

Chapter Thirteen

The drive from town back to the Schlabach residence was a quiet one. Petunia couldn't ask questions of Asher with Verna in the vehicle. When they dropped her off, Asher got out and opened the back door for Verna to get out. He politely thanked her for her time and wished her a pleasant evening. The sun was lowering in the sky, but there was still another hour or two of daylight.

The bishop came out onto the porch and waited for Verna to come inside, and then the door closed up tight behind her. No more friendly gestures. Asher stopped and did some typing into his phone, pulled out his credit card, typed that in, and then pocketed both card and phone again.

"Why did you do that?" Petunia asked.

"Do what?" Asher put the car into reverse and turned around to drive back off the property. "You mean order the pizza for your father?"

"Oh." She felt a little taken aback now. "Thank you. That really is nice. I'd forgotten."

"I hadn't."

"But what I was asking about was letting Verna go. She's obviously going to leave town the minute she's able, and then she'll be gone," Petunia said. "She's Ike's ex-wife who came to bring him home with her. She has a volatile temper, and she was obviously incredibly jealous of Ike's feelings for Eden. She had every reason, and every opportunity to kill him!"

"And we have no proof," Asher replied.

"Then we find it!" she exclaimed. Was he really giving up? Because this felt to her like letting a prime suspect go, and Eden couldn't afford for them to make mistakes.

"Way ahead of you, Pet." Asher shot her a grin. "I've got a couple of officers watching the property. If she has bloody clothes from the night of the murder, she'll want to get rid of them before she skips town. So now that we've scared her, we're going to sit back and watch to see what she does. If she's the killer, I'm willing to bet she takes the evidence with her."

"So this is part of a plan?" she asked.

"It is."

"I'm glad . . ." She smiled faintly. "Sorry to have thought you were about to blow the case."

"You thought that?" Asher shook his head. "I should be hurt. I'm better at my job than that, you know."

"How am I supposed to know that?" she retorted. "This is the first murder I've seen you try to solve. And it's my best friend's entire future on the line."

"True. Well, just take my word for it. I'm good at this. And I've got nothing else to do to distract me from finding out who killed Ike Smoker. Nothing."

"Nothing?" She frowned over at him. "No friends? No hobbies? Not even a garden or a dog, or anything?"

Asher chuckled. "I'm making myself look incredibly pathetic, but no to both garden and dog. But that's not to say I won't get a dog eventually. It's just that I work long hours."

"Hmm." Petunia looked out the window at the passing snow-crusted fields, the early evening sunlight shining in long, golden rays. "Can I ask you something?"

"Sure."

"What if you don't see Verna go dig something up?"

"Then when she leaves, we stop her van a few miles from here and check her packed bag."

"And if there's nothing there?" she prompted.

"Then, as much you'll hate this, I think she'd be innocent."

Petunia sighed. "I don't want her to be guilty, exactly. It would just be easier if it was her and not someone I knew better."

"Hey, I get it," he said, lowering his voice. "I grew up in downtown Pittsburgh, and I was posted there after I graduated police academy. It was hard arresting guys I knew from high school. It's part of the reason I left after my divorce."

"Really?"

"Yeah."

And he'd come out here to Blueberry and settled down into a life without garden, dog, family, or comforts, by the sound of it. Who took care of Asher Nate? Who made sure he got a hot meal in his belly at the end of a long shift of chasing down murderers?

"What was the rest of your reason?" she asked.

Asher looked over at her, and by his expression seemed to be weighing his options. Then he shrugged. "I needed a truly fresh start. I loved Christy. A lot. It took me a few rounds of therapy after she left me, but ultimately, I was trying to make her into someone she wasn't—someone I needed."

"She left you?" Petunia asked. That felt almost impossible. What woman would leave a man like Asher—strong, smart, and seemingly quite principled? But there was always another side of the story.

"She left me for my best friend."

Petunia let out a slow breath. "Oh, Asher . . ."

"Yeah, yeah, I know," he said. "I didn't catch them or anything, either. They came to me together, sat me down, and told me that they'd been involved for some time, that my wife was leaving me, and they were going to get married. It was very civilized and mature."

"Just like that?" Petunia said. "We don't have those things here."

"You must have some drama," he replied.

"Of course, there's been a murder. But for us, marriage isn't for as long as you feel comfortable. When you marry, it is for life—as in the rest of your life. For better or for worse. There is no leaving after you're married. If you're frustrated with your husband or wife, you fix the problem. The rest of your life is a long time to go unhappy, and people generally don't! They might ask the bishop for guidance, or a trusted older couple to help counsel them, but they find a way to feel happy together again."

"What about Ike and Verna?" he asked.

"What Ike did was scandalous and *rare*. And he couldn't ever remarry as an Amish man. Not until Verna passed away."

"And Verna couldn't truly move on until Ike died." Asher signaled a turn.

"Yah. But even so, a husband or wife ending up dead like this is rare too. Because we don't see marriage as a string of romantic gestures. We see it as a partnership. They both work hard for the family they've created. And they're grateful for each other. Maybe she's not as pretty as another woman, but she's got a hot meal on the table when he comes in hungry and tired after a day of work. She's the one sewing up the holes in his shirts and stoking up a fire to warm his feet on a winter night. And he might not tell her beautiful things to make her heart skip a beat, but with his own two hands he'll fix the roof over her head when it leaks. It's hard not to swoon a little for that."

"Practical," he said.

"Very. And it works." Petunia was quiet for a moment. "Look at the Schlabachs."

"Not exactly an example of doing it right," Asher replied. "Felty wasn't faithful to Rosie."

"No, but it is an example of forgiveness and moving on together. Rosie forgave Felty. Felty came home to Rosie and dedicated his life to the family they raised together. They'll grow old together. They'll take care of each other, too."

"True," he murmured.

She couldn't make out what he was feeling behind the word, though. His expression had closed off like granite. Did he think she was judging his situation? Because she wasn't. She knew it was different for Englishers. They didn't have a community all working in tandem to keep a couple together.

Asher stopped at the pizza place, and Petunia waited with the heat pumping comfortably onto her legs while Asher went inside. He came out with two large flat boxes. He got back into the car and passed the pizza to her. It was warm and smelled so good her stomach growled.

"Will you need my help tomorrow?" she asked.

"I don't think so," Asher replied. "I'll give you a break. I'm going to be checking the autopsy results—not that I'm expecting any surprises there. And I have to look into a few other things. I'll be in touch when I need you to tag along again."

Petunia found herself feeling just a little disappointed at that. These last few days with Asher had been fun, and she'd felt truly needed in a way that she'd never really felt before. Was it because Asher was a man who wasn't put off by her ideas and prying, needling curiosity? It might be, and she'd have to keep an eye on that. Nursing some ridiculous crush on an Englisher cop would be incredibly undignified.

When they reached Petunia's home, Asher gave her a friendly nod.

"Thank you for all you've done today," he said. "I might need to find a way to get you paid for some of your time through the precinct."

"Could you do that?" she asked. She made her own income from her sewing, but they could always use a little extra. The first thing she'd do was restock her thread and fabric.

"I might be able to. It involves some paperwork. I'd have to pass it by my boss. I'd call you a local consultant."

"A consultant . . ." She liked the sound of that.

"I'll look into it," he said. "Have a good night, Pet."

Petunia got out, and she felt a smile on her lips as she headed to the side door. A consultant . . . a *paid* consultant. It sounded so interesting. She was well on her way to being a genuine businesswoman with multiple income sources, wasn't she? Was it prideful to enjoy this so much?

As she came inside, the heat from the wood stove engulfed her in cozy warmth. She took off her shawl and boots, and carried the pizza boxes into the kitchen. Her father brightened at the sight of the pizza.

"That does smell good, Petunia," her father said. "How did everything go today?"

Elias took the boxes from her hands and carried them to the table.

"Oh, *Daet*, you wouldn't believe my day!" she said, hanging up her coat and following her father into the kitchen. They put plates on the table, and each took a hot slice of pizza.

"Before you tell me, let's say grace," Elias said.

She bowed her head, and silence descended on the kitchen—the comfortable kind that was filled with goodwill, grateful hearts, and all the beautiful things she'd grown to count on. Then her father raised his head, and they each took a bite.

Then Petunia told her father all that had happened—from Verna's attack on Eden, to the story of the Schlabach marriage and Ike's relation to the bishop. Her father listened and ate, stopping sometimes to stare at her in shock, shake his head, and take another bite.

"Do you think Verna did it?" her father asked.

"I honestly don't know!" Petunia replied. "The bishop's whole world was turned upside down when Ike came. Could he have done it?"

But even as she said it, she couldn't imagine their thoughtful bishop plunging an ice pick into his own son's chest. Impossible!

"How sad is he over Ike's passing?" her father asked.

Petunia frowned. "He's doesn't seem to be grieving now . . ." But then she remembered what Lovina had told her about her brother's reaction to the murder when they'd talked in the dry goods store. "But Lovina told me when all this began that the bishop had gone into prayer and dropped to his knees when he heard about it. I'd thought it was a strange reaction, but Ike being his son does explain those extreme emotions, doesn't it?"

"But he doesn't seem sad at the moment?" her father asked.

"He seems . . . sad, but not overcome," she replied. "And Rosie was just angry about the whole situation—and I don't blame her a bit. I think she hides a lot of emotion under her anger. It's probably holding her together."

"Hm," her father said, chewing a bite of pizza.

"You don't think Rosie did it?" she asked. "In anger over Ike coming back and maybe threatening to expose everything?"

Her father just shook his head.

"And then there's Obadiah. He's bitter, very bitter. But again—do you blame him?"

"Not really," Elias agreed.

"Oh, and I forgot to add that when we talked to Verna, she told us that the bishop had put Ike in his will."

"That would affect Obadiah's inheritance," he said. "And maybe his pride."

"It only gets more complicated, doesn't it?" Petunia said. "And we need proof, not theories! Because Eden was on the scene with blood on her hands. When I saw her today, she looked pretty shaken up. And she almost begged me to find the killer, *Daet*."

"I can only imagine," Elias said. "I saw her father today, too. Her brother Jonathan is thinking of moving to a new community, he's so upset."

"What?" she asked, dropping her crust onto her plate. "Where would he go?"

"His wife has a cousin out in Idaho, and apparently, he just wants to get away from all the ugliness."

"Before his sister is set free?" she asked.

"I don't know. Apparently, there's a job that's open now, and it's a matter of timing."

"Or is he running away?" she asked. "Maybe he killed Ike, and he doesn't want to face the consequences."

"And let his sister stay in prison?" Elias shook his head. "I don't know about that. If he killed Ike in anger over how Ike was treating Eden, then leaving her in jail doesn't seem consistent."

"Unless it was in a rage," Petunia said, "and he realized that if they find him out, he'd go to jail and his pregnant wife would be alone."

"His sister is pregnant, too," Elias countered.

"True . . ." But Jonathan leaving town wouldn't sit right with her, either.

There was more to this. She could feel it.

"I just can't make sense of it, *Daet*," she said. "I need to talk to Jonathan—alone. Without Asher. That way I can give Asher a full explanation of what happened."

"And if Jonathan is the killer?" her father asked with a frown.

"Like you said, he wouldn't leave his pregnant sister in prison. He just wouldn't. I don't think it's him, but I need to know why he's leaving."

"You can go tonight, but I'm coming with you," her father said. "I understand not bringing Asher along, but you are not going by yourself."

"Okay, *Daet*," she agreed. "*Danke.*"

Just then she heard a buggy turn into the drive, and she looked out the window in the lowering light. It was Priscilla with the reins in her hands. She was sitting up straight, her shoulders back and her chin high. Something had changed since Petunia last saw her . . .

"We go after you've spoken to your friend," her father said.

She nodded. Yah, she had a good *daet* who wasn't going to let her go running into danger on her own. She felt safer already.

* * *

"Would you like some pizza?" Elias asked Priscilla as she came into the house.

Priscilla wore a black woolen shawl wrapped around her, and thick stockings under her dress. Her cheeks were pink from the cold, and she pulled off her mittens, revealing cold reddened fingers. But her eyes sparkled.

"No thank you, Elias," Priscilla replied, and then she turned to Petunia and lowered her voice. "I don't think I could eat if I tried!"

This was either good news or bad, but by the brightness in her friend's eyes, Petunia thought she knew.

"What happened?" Petunia asked. "Something has changed . . . How is Benjie?"

"Good." Priscilla looked politely over at Elias. This was not a conversation to be had in front of Petunia's father, who was pulling a new slice of pizza out of the box, and over to his plate.

Petunia nodded toward the sitting room.

"Let's go talk," she said.

Petunia led her friend into the sitting room, leaving Elias at the table. Petunia lit a kerosene lamp on the table with a match—the light was low enough inside now that they needed it. Then she sat down on the couch and Petunia patted the seat next to her.

Priscilla sank into it.

"So what's going on?" Petunia asked. "You look like you're about to burst!"

"I had to tell you about it," Priscilla said. "You're the only one who will really understand."

"So . . . everything is okay now?" Petunia guessed.

"Well," Priscilla said, "we don't have the blessing of Benjie's uncle Noah for us to get married."

"Oh, dear . . . Did Benjie ask you to run away with him?"

"No, no," Priscilla said, "but we have decided to have a yearlong engagement."

"*Another* year?"

"I know! I hate it." Priscilla smoothed her hands over her knees. "I don't want to wait another year, but it's either wait and marry the man I love, or lose him completely."

"Oh, Priscilla . . ."

"Maybe we'll change his uncle's mind," Priscilla said. "I'll do my best. I intend to bring him some of my baking once every few weeks, and whatever he says to me, I'm going to forgive. But he'll see that I'm a good person, and that I love his nephew, and that I won't retaliate. He'll *have* to see it."

"You still don't know what happened to cause such bad blood between your families?" Petunia asked.

"I've learned a little bit. Apparently, Benjie's uncle Noah had wanted to marry my aunt, and my father advised her against it."

"Oh!"

"And she married my uncle, and they went on to have ten *kinner*. So there is no going back on that, is there?" Priscilla sighed.

"But Noah married Marie," Petunia said. Marie had since passed away, and they'd never had children, which was why Benjie had been set to inherit.

"Yah, he did," Priscilla agreed. "That was just the beginning of a back and forth. My *daet* was trying to get a loan from the bank, and Noah told the bank manager a lie about my *daet*'s credit. Then my *daet* told the bishop, and Noah denied doing it. Then Noah did something else, and it went on for about ten years. Back and forth. My *daet* eventually stopped it and tried to make peace, but Noah couldn't forgive him."

"I didn't know they had such history!" Petunia said.

"I knew a little bit, but I didn't think Noah would hold that kind of grudge against my *daet*, considering my *daet* didn't hold any ill will against Noah anymore."

"Do you think you can smooth him over?" Petunia asked.

"I'm going to try. It's high time this ended. Why keep fighting? I'm not Noah's enemy, and neither is my father."

Long-held grudges could be hard to uproot.

"I hope it works, but what if he doesn't give Benjie the land?" Petunia asked.

"Benjie and I have a plan for that," Priscilla said. "And it's actually thanks to you."

"Thanks to me?"

"Yah. I've been watching you run your own sewing business for a few years now, and I've always admired your ability to take care of things so professionally. And I thought, why can't I do what Petunia does?"

Petunia's stomach gave a flip. "You're going to be my competition?"

"No!" Priscilla laughed. "I'm not going to be a seamstress. I'm not as good as you are with a needle, and you know it. I want to take a bookkeeping course. It takes nine months to complete, and then I'll be able to open my own bookkeeping business. I can work from home, and I can make some money too. I know as the wife I'm supposed to just stay home and keep the house and let my husband deal with the money, but . . ."

"But you intend to make the money your business too," Petunia concluded.

"Yah, I do. If my husband can't inherit that land, I intend to make enough money on the side that we can save up a down payment for another plot. That's my plan."

"And your brother?" Petunia asked.

"I'll hire him. I'll teach him! Maybe he can take the course too, and we can work together. You never know! But there are worse things in the world than starting from scratch and working your way up. You've proven to me that you can take the situation you're dealt and make the most of it. You don't try to change yourself—you just step on up and keep moving. I want to be strong like you, Petunia."

"Oh, that is very sweet . . ." Petunia reached out and took her friend's hand. "But you realize I'm no man's wife."

Priscilla squeezed her hand. "Give it time. You're far too smart, and far too good with a needle to be left on the shelf."

Petunia sincerely doubted this, but she didn't want to ruin a beautiful moment by pointing it out. She was more concerned with the timing of the wedding right now, because that would affect the timing of Petunia getting paid.

"I'm glad you've got a solution," Petunia said. "I'm almost done with your dresses, though. What do you want me to do with them?"

Would Priscilla be able to pay for them? That would be a hit to Petunia's bottom line if she didn't get paid for a very big order like this one. Even if Priscilla put off paying for another year. Not only was there the time involved in making all the dresses, but the fabric cost, too. Six *newehocker* dresses as well as Priscilla's blue wedding dress added up to a lot of fabric.

"Could you bring them to me when you're done?" Priscilla asked. "I'm going to put them aside and pay you. Don't worry about that. Because those dresses are for my wedding, and unless Benjie backs out on me, I'm getting married next year. I'm working toward it."

That was a relief . . . for her own financial situation. But she cared more about making sure her friend's wedding went forward.

"You don't think Benjie would back out, do you?" Petunia asked.

A smile lit up Priscilla's face. "We talked last night, and he was so happy I'd help him work for our future that he almost took me to the bishop and married me then and there! But no, I don't think he's going anywhere. We've finally got a solution. You were right. Waiting and finding a way forward was the right thing to do."

And here was hoping that Petunia's advice would work for finding Ike's killer, too. Patience and being stubbornly optimistic had helped Petunia a great deal in the past, but wise advice was often easier to give than to take. May it help her now.

Chapter Fourteen

When Priscilla left, Elias put the plates into the sink and Petunia put the last of the pizza into the ice box. She had to admit, with the sun setting, she did feel better knowing that she'd be out in a proper buggy with her father. The last thing she wanted was another frightening night like when she went to the ice house . . .

Jonathan had been there that night too. And she'd never told anyone that part. But now Jonathan was thinking of leaving town and going to another state, and she had to wonder how that was connected.

And what about poor Eden?

She'd find out what she could, and then she'd fill in Asher.

"Are you ready to go?" Elias asked. "We don't want to be out too late."

"Yah, I'm ready."

Elias hitched up the buggy, and Petunia waited until he hopped up next to her and flicked the reins. She put a thick quilt over her lap, and her father did the same. It was a cold night, and even with the enclosed buggy, there was no windshield to stop frigid air from blowing in from the square opening in front.

The night was bright and the sky clear, with a half moon hanging in the sky among a wash of stars. This far from town, there was no light pollution to ruin the view, and Petunia settled back as her *daet* drove them in the direction of the rented house on another family's land where Jonathan and Beth Beiler lived. She couldn't see much in the enclosed buggy, and she looked over at her father's reassuring profile. He was a tall, lean man with a gray-streaked beard that touched his chest. She wondered if he'd ever remarry. It had been ten years since Petunia's *mamm* had passed away, and there had been plenty of single women who'd been interested in Elias.

Was Petunia the one holding him back, she wondered? If she was provided for, would her *daet* decide to remarry? He deserved some comfort and happiness too . . . except Petunia had inherited her unique personality from him. Elias did things the way he did them, and he refused to alter his ways for anything short of a visit from the elders.

Like when he cooked the same meal for three months, every single day in a row because he liked it. *I like pork chops* was the only explanation he ever gave. Petunia learned how to cook from her aunts, and her father would still request the same meal—pork chops. And he wouldn't eat a minute past six. He claimed it upset his stomach, and even if guests came by and brought a freshly baked pie, not a morsel would pass his lips until morning. Petunia didn't even think it upset his stomach anymore. He was mostly just stubborn. That was just Elias being Elias.

Or there was the time their dog had puppies, and instead of selling them, they ended up with eight puppies taking over the property. That had been when Petunia was small and her *mamm* was still alive, but she could still remember her mother throwing up her hands when the puppies dug up her garden, because Elias refused to be reasoned with.

That was just the way he was.

Ironically, Elias had decided that Petunia should be allowed to pursue her own ways, and now it was the entire community throwing up their hands with him, because Petunia was a problem to be fixed. But Elias would be Elias.

So while Petunia doubted she'd find her perfect marital match, she did hope her father would. She wasn't sure what kind of woman would be able to handle him after her *mamm*, but she prayed that this mystery woman would come along anyway.

None of the homes in the district were very far from each other. That was how Amish districts were separated—geographically. The point was to keep a community close together, physically and in their loyalty. If you needed help, your neighbors wouldn't be traveling far to lend a hand. And if someone's barn burned down, you wouldn't have far to go to help them rebuild it. Proximity mattered even more than natural affinity for a person. You might be lifelong good friends with someone from another district, but you'd be attending church and pitching in with those who lived closest to you. Period.

They turned into the drive that led to Jonathan's little house. They had to pass the main Kauffman farm, from whom the Beilers rented. Leroy Kauffman was walking back toward the house from the barn, and he waved at them. Elias reined in and talked to him through the window for a couple of minutes—it was only polite—and they covered the topics of the weather, the cold, and, of course, the murder.

Then they carried on past to the little house located down a road that curved away from the barn, and sat nestled in a copse of spruce trees.

Elias parked the buggy under the shelter and threw some blankets over the horses' backs. It was too cold not to protect the animals. Jonathan poked his head out of the little house, warm light glowing behind him, and he already had his coat on. He helped them give the horses some hay to munch on before they all went inside together.

"I'm sorry to come by so late," Elias said. "But my daughter wanted to see you and your wife, and I didn't want her to come alone. Not with . . . the murder."

"I don't blame you," Jonathan said. "Of course. But Beth has gone to bed early tonight. She was really tired out this evening."

"That's okay," Petunia said. "It's understandable. Really, I wanted to talk to you."

She gave Jonathan a meaningful look, and Jonathan looked over at Elias uncertainly. He was probably wondering how much she'd told her father.

"I could just warm up by the stove," Elias said, and sidled off toward the kitchen. It was a small house—one story, and one bedroom. So there wasn't far to go, but Jonathan led the way into the sitting room.

"What can I do for you?" Jonathan asked.

"Well . . ." She hadn't rehearsed this before arriving. "Jonathan, I heard you're moving."

"It's not for sure," Jonathan said. "It's just a possibility."

"A strong one?" she asked.

"What is it to you, Petunia?" he asked bluntly. "My wife's family lives out there. We're expecting our first baby. She'd like be closer to her own mother and sisters. Is that so strange?"

The timing was a little strange, but it didn't seem helpful to point that out just then.

"Have you talked to Eden recently?" Petunia asked.

"No." Jonathan dropped his gaze. "Look, I wanted to keep this private, but all of this murder drama has been incredibly hard on my wife. She's done her best to stand by our family and be brave, but she just wants to go home. And I don't blame her."

"It is rather ugly," Petunia murmured.

So Beth wanted to hightail it out of Blueberry? She hadn't considered her as a suspect yet.

"Did she know Ike?" Petunia asked.

"Not especially."

Or not that she told her husband about . . . If Beth had a reason to hate Ike enough to kill him, she might also be willing to leave

Eden in prison and run away. She couldn't believe she hadn't thought of it before . . . but what reason would Beth have to hate him? That would have to go on the back burner for now.

"How is my sister doing?" Jonathan asked. "Is she holding up okay?"

"You should go visit her!" Petunia said, but Jonathan didn't answer. So she continued, "She's all right. A little rattled, of course, but she's begging me to get to the bottom of this."

"Do you think you will?" Jonathan asked.

"Yah, I do."

He nodded slowly, but didn't look comforted.

"I did learn something I thought you might like to know," Petunia said.

"What's that?"

"Ike was married."

"To my sister?!" Rage flashed in his eyes.

"No! To a woman named Verna. She's been in town for a little while."

"What?" Jonathan looked stunned.

Petunia nodded. "She's been staying with the bishop's family. The bishop was trying to reunite Ike and Verna."

Jonathan thought for a moment, then sighed. "Come to think of it, I shouldn't be surprised that Ike would have a secret wife, I suppose. It matches his character."

Petunia was forced to nod in agreement.

"But this woman—Verna, you say? Did she want Ike back?"

"Yah. She wanted her husband to come home."

"Did she know about Eden?" He narrowed his gaze then, scrutinizing Petunia as if she might try to hide something.

"Yah," Petunia replied. "She did know about Eden. And she wasn't pleased about Ike stepping out on her. But it wasn't fair. Eden had no clue he was married! You know Eden better than I do, and she's got moral fiber. In fact, when I told her about Ike's wife, she was incredibly upset."

"Did she see Verna?" he pressed.

"Yah . . . sort of." There was that big scene when Verna shouted and threatened.

"Did my sister recognize her?"

Petunia frowned and tried to remember. It had been a tumultuous meeting.

"Um . . . I don't know if Eden recognized her, but come to think of it, Verna asked if this was where they were keeping her husband's girlfriend, and when she saw Eden, she said something like, 'It is you.' I think Verna recognize *her*."

"Because before Ike died, Eden told me that a strange Amish woman she'd never met walked up to her in the drug store and said that she had a gift of knowing when a woman was pregnant, and she 'knew' that Eden was."

Petunia blinked. "How awful!"

"Very. Eden was upset. I think that might have been Verna. How many strangers do we have around here? Not many. And Verna would have reason to try to upset my sister if she saw her as her competition."

"That's a good point," Petunia said. "Plus, Verna has a terrible temper. I'd normally ask who would do that kind of thing, but honestly, I think Verna would. We just have to ask Eden about it."

"I wonder how long she was lurking around," Jonathan said. "Watching, and plotting, and wishing ill on my sister . . ."

"She went to go talk to Ike, too, and they had a confrontation," Petunia added. "She slapped him. Mary Hilty saw it."

"That doesn't mean it was the first time she visited Ike, though, does it?" Jonathan asked.

"Or the last," Petunia added.

"Was he in contact with his wife all this time?" Jonathan asked. "He could have been playing both his wife and Eden."

"I don't think so. Verna said he just disappeared."

Petunia was silent for a moment. The more she talked with Jonathan, the more likely it seemed that Verna was the killer. Besides, Jonathan had been a friend for most of her life. She'd been best friends with his sister, and even attended his wedding. She was at his grandparents' funerals, too. They were connected, and maybe it was time to start seeing the people she could trust. Jonathan was a good man. He had information she needed, why not just ask him?

"Jonathan, can I ask you something?" Petunia asked.

"Sure." He stuck his thumbs into his suspenders.

"What did you find in the ice house that night when I saw you there?"

"What are you talking about?" he asked.

Was he going to pretend that hadn't happened?

"You had something in your hand," she said. "Come on, Jonathan, I saw it. When I asked about it, you put it into your pocket. You found something out there, and considering the lack of evidence in this case, besides blood on Eden's hands, we need everything we can find."

Jonathan met her gaze for a moment, then shook his head. "I didn't find anything."

He was lying. She knew it in her bones. He had found something, and he wasn't going to tell her.

"Please, Jonathan. You know I want to prove Eden innocent! We're on the same side here."

He shook his head. "I didn't find anything."

So he wasn't going to tell her, and what could she do about that? Not very much. But he was also eager to move away from Blueberry . . .

Was he trying to avoid justice . . . or was he protecting someone else? Like his wife, pregnant with his first child?

Petunia saw the bedroom door open a crack and then shut again. They'd probably woke Beth up, but if she'd gone to bed early, she wouldn't be dressed for guests. It was time to leave.

"I'm sorry for staying so long," Petunia said. "*Daet*, I think we should head home, don't you?"

"Yah, yah. Sounds good," he said. "It was nice to see you, Jonathan. Give our best to your wife, please."

"Yah. Good night." Jonathan's voice was strained, and Petunia noticed the bedroom door open an inch again.

They put on their boots again, bundled up into their coats, and headed out into the night. After tossing the horse blankets into the back, they were on their way, the horses trotting with their knees high.

"What did you learn?" her father asked once the turned onto the main road.

"First of all, we think Verna had been harassing Eden before Eden knew who she was," Petunia said, and she told the story. Her father stayed silent. "I also learned that Beth is eager to get away from here. That's why Jonathan is considering moving."

"I guess I don't blame her," Elias replied.

"I also learned that Jonathan lies to me very easily," she added.

Her father gave her a surprised look. "Those are strong words, Pet."

"Murder is a strong thing, too, *Daet*. He found something at the crime scene. I saw him find it. He put it in his pocket. But when I asked about it, he said he hadn't found anything. I asked him about it again tonight. He still said he hadn't found anything."

"Maybe he's telling the truth?" Elias asked.

"Nope." Petunia sighed. "It was a bold-faced lie."

* * *

That evening, Petunia sat up late doing the last of her sewing for Priscilla. She finished the hemming, and checked every dress for stray threads. She'd take everything to Priscilla in the morning along with a bill.

There was a tap on her workroom door, and Petunia looked up in surprise to see her father standing there.

"Hi, *Daet*," she said. "I thought you were in bed by now."

"It's hard to unwind when you're wondering which one of your neighbors murdered Ike Smoker," he replied.

"Isn't that the truth," she replied. "On the plus side, I finished the dresses for Priscilla."

"Is that wedding going forward?" he asked.

"Yes, just with a longer engagement."

He swirled his finger through a bowl of little odds and ends. There were hooks to fasten the backs of dresses in there, and a couple of thimbles. There was loose change, some sewing machine needles, a small bar of sewing soap to mark fabric with, a spool of thread, the color of which she liked but was poor quality . . . Just a dish of odds and ends, and whenever her father came into her sewing room, he would pick through that dish before he came to his point.

"Is something bothering you, *Daet*?" she asked.

"Just one thing," he said. "I talked to Eden's father yesterday. I was offering him my condolences about how hard things were right now. We've been friends for years, as you know. We've always been open with each other. Anyway, he told me that he thought we'd both done wrong by our daughters. Obviously, he saw Eden being attracted to Ike as his own personal failing, but he also seemed to think I'd done wrong by you."

"You haven't done wrong by me," she said.

"Well, he said that maybe both our girls would find good Amish husbands if we fathers did better," Elias said.

"*Daet*, there are worse things than being single," Petunia said earnestly. "I've seen it! I could be a married woman abandoned by my husband. I could be in a marriage where I had an awful lot to forgive. I could be trying so very hard to be someone else in order to please a man, and grinding my own spirit into the dust . . ." Petunia shrugged. "I could run off and go English, or I could take up gambling and impoverish you completely." She shot her father a grin. "I could be so much worse, *Daet*. Being single is not the worst thing to befall a woman. I'm happy."

"Are you?" Elias met her gaze earnestly. "Are you really happy?"

"Mostly," she said. "Less so thinking my friend might go to prison . . . but overall, yah. I'm happy."

"If I start . . . I don't know . . . getting in the way of you settling down with some nice Amish man, let me know, okay?" he said.

"I will do that, *Daet*."

Her father picked up something from the dish on her shelf and turned it over in his fingers.

"What's that?" she asked.

"One of those little cows that Obadiah carves." He held it up. It was a miniature cow, about an inch long. He'd been whittling it during a youth group event a few years ago, and she'd asked for it. He'd given it to her.

That was back when Petunia had a little crush on Obadiah. That was the same summer she'd learned that Obadiah had feelings for Eden. She felt a wave of melancholy. Back then, Obadiah had filled all of her thoughts, and every youth group event, every bonfire, every hymn sing, every volleyball game, she'd hoped and prayed that Obadiah would suddenly realize he was in love with her.

Silly. He'd been crazy about Eden, not her. It was after she nursed that heartbreak that she decided to be honest with herself. It was less painful.

"Can I see that?" Petunia took the small cow from her father's fingers and looked at it.

"Well, Pet, I'm going to bed," Elias said. "Don't stay up too late."

"I won't. Good night."

Her father closed her workroom door behind him and she looked down at the carved cow, and then she dropped it back into the dish.

A lot had changed over the years, including Petunia's willingness to pine after a man. She wasn't going to do that anymore. Her time was far too valuable to waste on unrequited feelings.

* * *

The next morning, the temperature had risen to a comfortable twenty-six degrees, and Petunia carried the finished dresses, wrapped in plastic to protect them, out to her little courting buggy.

It felt good to get outside in this warmer weather, and the sun shone cheerily, filtering through the bare branches of the trees. Trudy was in fine spirits too, and when Petunia hitched her up, she stamped her big hooves in anticipation.

Petunia's melancholy from the night before had evaporated with her dreams, and she made a clucking sound with her mouth to get Trudy moving.

The Kempfs lived on a single acre that was chopped off the side of a crop field. In the summers, corn grew high and green right next to the fence, but this time of year, the snow was broken by the stumps of corn stalks that would be tilled under in the spring getting ready to plant again. But the cornfield didn't belong to the Kempfs. Priscilla's father, Elijah, worked at the canning factory, as did her eighteen-year-old brother, Levi. But the canning factory wasn't very steady work. When the employees weren't striking, there were lay-offs, and the company seemed to be struggling to keep itself afloat. Hence, Elijah's insistence that Levi find something else as quickly as he could. But reliable employment that paid a living wage while only requiring an eighth grade education—which was what the Amish got—was hard to come by.

The Kempfs owned their single acre and the double-wide trailer that they lived in. A welcoming tendril of smoke rose up from the chimney, and behind the trailer came the sound of chopping wood. *Thwack. Thwack. Thwack.*

The front door opened—there was no side door—and Priscilla waved from the doorway. Behind her, the home was bright, and Petunia knew from experience that it would be neat as a pin, too. Priscilla's mother, Lily, made the most of everything in the home, from every last item that came from their garden, to the scraps she bought to make quilts for sale at the farmers market. She once made such a lovely quilt out of old dish towels that everyone was astonished.

And Petunia was coming to be paid . . . She felt a pang of guilt. She knew the family struggled, and they'd been saving for Priscilla's wedding for a year and a half now, which was why they could afford to get Petunia's help with the sewing. Priscilla would have a proper wedding. Petunia would struggle, too, without the full pay for this job, but she had a father to provide for her.

Petunia reined in Trudy, and then reached quickly into the bag of dresses and pulled out her bill. She crumpled it and dropped it into the bottom of her buggy. Then she picked up the dresses and carefully crawled down from her little buggy into the wet snow.

"I can't wait to see them!" Priscilla called as Petunia made her way up the path that had been shoveled out before she arrived. One of Priscilla's little sisters stood leaning on a snow shovel, so Petunia could guess who she had to thank for a clear path, and she smiled at the girl.

"Come in, come in!" Lily said, looking over her daughter's shoulder. "We are so excited to see the dresses!"

No mention that with an extra year now, Lily could have sewn them herself.

Petunia pulled the plastic off the hangers and held up the first dress—the blue wedding dress. Amish women wore a blue dress on their wedding day, and that dress would be worn every Sunday after when she attended church. When it started to get worn, she'd put that dress away and keep it very carefully, because one day when she died, she'd be buried in that very dress she was wearing when she got married, and when she worshipped. This blue dress would begin a heartful of memories for Priscilla.

"Oh . . ." Tears shone in Lily's eyes. "It's perfect . . ."

"I understand that you could have sewn these yourself—" Petunia began.

"But I didn't," Lily replied. "And we're grateful for your hard work. Let me get my checkbook."

"Do you have the bill?" Priscilla asked.

"I—" Petunia licked her lips. "I lost it."

"What?" Priscilla shook her head. "I'm sure you remember what we owe you. It's—" Priscilla quoted an amount very close to the one Petunia had calculated.

"It was less, actually," Petunia said.

The front door opened and the little girl who'd been shoveling came inside and slammed the door behind her.

"This fell out of your buggy, Petunia," she said, holding up the wadded-up bill.

Priscilla scooped it up before Petunia could take it, and she looked down at the wrinkled page. "Yah, that's what I thought. I was close." She gave Petunia a knowing look. "Thank you for your generosity, Petunia, but you are running a business too, and you're worth every penny. You hear me? Soon enough I'll have a business of my own as well, and I'll need to be paid, won't I?"

Petunia felt her face heat.

"Yah, you will."

"And perhaps by that point, you'll need a bookkeeper. You never know! But you won't get there without charging people what you're worth."

Priscilla went over to where her mother stood by a window, and for a moment they focused on writing the check. Then they returned and Lily handed it over with a smile.

"We owe you more than that," Lily said. "Thank you for being a good friend to Priscilla. Because of you, she and Benjie sorted things out, and we're all so happy they did."

Petunia accepted the check with a smile of thanks, and she tucked it into her coat. She was glad she was able to give Priscilla some advice that had helped her to resolve things with Benji, but right now she felt like she was failing as Eden's friend. Eden's entire future was in the balance.

"I heard you are looking into the murder," Lily said.

"Yah," Petunia replied. "I have to find some way to prove Eden didn't kill Ike Smoker."

"It's very sad that Ike died," Lily said.

"You might be the only one besides Eden who's said that," Petunia admitted. Well, besides Eden and Hadassah.

"I know of his faults," Lily said, "and if it was my daughter he'd charmed to her detriment, I might feel differently. But I'm old enough to be his mother, and he was kind to me."

"Kind how?" Petunia asked.

"My buggy got stuck in a pothole, and he stopped and helped get me out. It took him a full hour, and he was covered in mud, but he did it. And when I thanked him, he said something like, even a rebel has a good day now and then." Lily shook her head. "He reminded me of my own son. He was getting in trouble at school a lot, and when the teacher thought he was a bad boy, it was very hard for him to fix his ways. Children—and grown men, I dare say—are self-fulfilling prophecies. And I might be the only one who thinks so, but I think Ike wanted to be a better man than he was. I think that in his own way, he was trying to be."

"Do you really think so?" Petunia asked.

"I really do," Lily replied. "Over the years I have learned that everyone has more than one side to them. Everyone."

Cheating on his wife, running away from responsibility . . . it didn't seem like Ike had succeeded too well in becoming a better man, but everyone had to turn around somewhere. Maybe Lily was right, and given a little more time he might have come clean with Eden, broken her heart, and gone home to Verna and the girls.

It was certainly something to think about as Petunia drove her buggy on the back roads toward home again. Ike had been easy to dislike, but even in marriage, the Amish said that life was long and solutions could be found. What about in the life of a rebel Amish man who needed to get back onto the right path? Would Ike have gotten there? Would Verna have had a chance to get over her hurt and anger, and start over with a better version of the man who left her? Would her girls have finally had their *daet* at home again?

The day was bright, and as she passed farms and acreages, the Amish *kinner* were outside throwing snowballs while they were supposed to be doing chores. That soft snow, so close to melting, was perfect for a good snowball, and she smiled as she saw some little girls rolling big balls to make into snowmen. Their mittens were covered in clinging, wet snow, and their laughter filtered over to Petunia.

Petunia reined in at an intersection and waited while a stream of cars whipped past. Trudy stamped in the soft snow, moving them backward a few inches, and when the traffic had passed, Petunia flicked the reins again and they turned onto the road. The bishop's house was this way, and Petunia idly wondered if Asher's prediction would come true and she'd head back home with the evidence of the murder in her bags.

The next section of road was a quiet one. There were no *kinner* outside playing, but Petunia did see an old Amish woman refilling her bird feeders in the trees, a swarm of sparrows fluttering around her as she worked to give them more food.

Everyone had more than one side to them. Wasn't that what Lily had said? And that was the problem. Because someone they didn't expect was a murderer.

As she got closer to the Schlabach property, she could see some of the hired workers carrying hay out into a field, horses plodding through the sloppy snow. The cattle were perking up at the sight of the incoming food.

The Schlabachs had a greenhouse and two large chicken coops. Petunia could see Rosie coming out of one of the coops, a basket at her side. All was quiet. Petunia raised her hand to wave, but Rosie didn't see her, and she dropped her hand again.

Would she ever be welcome at the Schlabach home again?

Trudy balked, and Petunia jerked to the side as the horse took a sudden step into the road. A car was coming toward them, and Petunia hurriedly reined in her horse. She should have been paying better attention!

"Trudy!" she said. "That's how people get into accidents, you know!"

The horse couldn't understand her, of course, but delivering a lecture helped to settle her own racing heart.

Trudy danced to the side a few more steps, and the small buggy slid along with her on the slippery road. Petunia leaned forward to see what was spooking the horse, and that racing heart skipped a beat and then thundered in her ears.

Lying in the snow, face down, was a figure. At first Petunia couldn't make out anything about the figure except for some long brown hair lying out across the snow. Her first irrational thought was that the woman hadn't tied up her bun very well. And where was her *kapp*? She spotted it a foot away, muddied and tattered.

Petunia jumped out of the buggy and hurried around to Trudy's head to calm her. But Trudy seemed to sense death, or perhaps she smelled blood, because even with Petunia holding her bridle, Trudy shivered, her coat trembling.

Petunia let go of Trudy's bridle and crept closer until she could see the face. The eyes were shut, and the face looked strangely peaceful, albeit too pale.

"Oh, dear . . ." Petunia breathed.

It was Verna. She was dressed in a coat and boots, and in the tangle of bare bushes beside her Petunia spotted a small, worn leather suitcase. She'd been making a run for it, but she hadn't gotten far.

Verna Smoker was dead.

Chapter Fifteen

The phone hut was half a mile down the road, and without thinking about actual speed, she left Trudy and the buggy behind and headed in that direction on foot. Halfway there, she realized that it would have been much faster to take the buggy. It no longer mattered as it would take just as long to go back as to keep going, and by the time she got to the phone hut, she was out of breath and her legs felt like rubber.

The phone hut—a small, white building with a single window for light—was unoccupied, and she pushed inside and picked up the phone with trembling hands. It took her a moment to remember Asher's number, and then she punched it in and waited breathlessly for him to pick up.

"Detective Nate," he intoned.

"Asher?"

"Petunia, is that you? Every time you call me it's a different number."

"I know. It's a phone hut," she said. "Asher, I'm near the Schlabachs' farm, and I found a body."

"A body?"

"Yah. A body. Verna Smoker's body, to be precise."

"Are you sure she's dead?"

"Positive." Petunia shivered at the memory. "But you'd better come quick. I'm on my own here!"

She heard the sound of a siren through the phone. "On my way," he said. "I'm five minutes out, and I'm radioing in for support. I'll be there soon, okay?"

He sounded so confident, so sure of the process, that she felt better already, and she hung up the phone and headed back the direction she'd come. Soon she could hear the far-off wail of a siren, and then another added to the chorus. She knew they were coming for Verna's body, but somehow it felt like they were coming to her defense, too.

Petunia stood by Trudy's head and felt the reassuring warmth of the horse's breath against her hands as she waited. She didn't want to look at Verna directly, but she wasn't quite willing to turn her back on her, either. So she stood there with Trudy, looking straight ahead until Asher's cruiser crunched to a stop next to her buggy.

"Are you okay, Petunia?" he asked as he got out.

"Better now," she admitted. "This is the second body I've stumbled across in the last week. It's starting to get to me."

Asher squatted down next to Verna. He was silent for a moment, then stood back up and walked over to where the suitcase lay. He cocked his head to one side as he looked at it.

"I'm curious to go through her traveling bag," he said. "But we'll have to take pictures of the scene first and gather all the evidence. Then I can get my hands on that suitcase."

"You said that she would run away, and she did," Petunia said.

"Well, I was banking on her being the killer," he replied. "But if she's dead, we're looking for someone else."

"Doesn't that mean that Eden is innocent?" Petunia asked.

"In my mind, yes," he replied. "But I can't just let her go yet. Any good lawyer would argue that just because she couldn't have killed Verna doesn't mean she didn't kill Ike. It's a big tangle of technicalities. We still need to figure out who did this to save her from going through a murder trial. The fact that we have her in custody means she couldn't have killed Verna, though."

"If she'd been at home, she could be blamed for this murder too." Petunia thought for a moment, then sighed. "I hate that you're right."

Asher shot her a rueful smile. "But I am."

She shook her head, refusing to give him more satisfaction than that.

"So what do you think happened?" Petunia asked.

"She was hit over the head with something," he replied. "We'll look around and find it. I'm guessing a piece of wood. It's probably in the ditch." He walked over to the ditch and scanned for a moment, then looked back at her. "But as to who did it, and why they targeted Verna, I don't know. Do you have any ideas?"

Petunia shook her head. "Who knew who she was? I think that's the question. If she was just a visiting Amish woman, who'd have a problem with her? It had to be someone who knew she was Ike's wife and why she was here."

"Or she saw something." Asher walked back over to where Petunia stood. "Did she mention seeing anything, or knowing anything we didn't?"

Petunia shook her head. "Not to me."

"Hm."

"We could ask the Schlabachs if she did," she suggested.

"Yep, that's an option. We'll have to ask them when they saw her last and all that . . ." He looked thoughtful. "But why Ike and Verna Smoker? That's the question, isn't it?"

An ambulance arrived next, the siren turned off, but the lights flashing, and two more police cruisers weren't far behind.

Then it was a bustle of activity. A big, black body bag came out, and a stretcher. Some officers were putting down little numbered tags and taking pictures.

Bishop Felty came out of his house, and he and Rosie walked up the drive together toward them.

"Bishop!" Asher called.

Felty picked up his pace and when he reached them, out of breath and red-faced, he looked around in confusion.

"What's happening, Detective?" he asked.

"When did you last see Verna?" Asher asked, angling the bishop so he couldn't see the body.

"Verna?" Felty shook his head. "She didn't come down for breakfast, and we thought we'd let her rest. Her husband is dead, and while she was very angry with him, she's also grieving his loss. Let the poor woman sleep."

"Did you hear anything last night?" Asher asked.

Felty shook his head, then paused. "Wait . . . I heard someone up—getting water or something. I heard the dogs next door start to bark."

"What time was that?" Asher asked.

"I don't know. It was dark."

"Right. No electronic clocks."

"No, not for us."

Rosie moved away from them, and Petunia saw the expression on her face the second she saw the body. Rosie froze, and then a look flickered across her face that surprised Petunia. Just for a moment, Rosie looked relieved. Then sadness took over, then horror, then sadness again . . . But Petunia had seen that relief.

Was Rosie glad to be rid of Verna? Had Verna been promising to continue being a difficulty in Rosie's life, even with Ike dead?

"Felty?" Rosie said. "Felty!"

The bishop pulled away from Asher and looked toward his wife. Then he spotted the body, and his eyes widened.

"Oh no . . ."

The bishop looked immediately saddened. His face fell and he seemed to deflate.

"Rosie, could I have a word with you?" Asher asked, and Felty led his wife back, away from Verna. Rosie stood there, stoic and resolute.

"When did you last see Verna?"

"When she went to bed last night."

"And you didn't think to look into her room this morning?"

"I didn't dare . . ."

"Why?"

"We argued last night," she said, her voice shaking. "She was furious, and I said some harsh things. I didn't think she'd want to see me."

"What were you arguing about?" Asher asked.

"Telling the community who Ike was to my husband," she said. "Verna thought he deserved to be owned after death, even if we never publicly acknowledged him in life."

"And you were against that."

"Of course I was! What was there to be gained by humiliating us further?"

"And what did you think?" Asher asked, turning to Felty.

"I was on my wife's side," he replied quietly.

Petunia saw Obadiah coming in their direction from the barn. He stepped high through the wet snow, coming across the yard toward them.

"What did Obie think?" Petunia asked.

Felty and Rosie exchanged a look. "He was on our side, of course. He didn't want to have our family humiliated any more than we did."

"So all three of you were strongly opposed to this idea, and Verna was threatening to tell?" Asher concluded.

"Threatening is a strong word," Felty replied. "She was suggesting it. That was all."

"And that was enough to cause an argument with you?" Asher asked, turning to Rosie. "You strike me as a woman with more self-control than that."

"It has been a long week," Rosie said. "This has been a lot for me to handle. I fear I spoke more harshly than I should have."

Obadiah arrived at the fence then, pushed down the barbed wire, and stepped over, having to stop and unhook himself where his coat caught. But then he spotted Verna. He looked down, then looked back at the body again.

He didn't look at Verna again, and he joined his parents.

"Is that . . . ," he started.

"Yah," his father replied.

"She wasn't sleeping in after all," Rosie said.

"She was leaving with a suitcase," Petunia said helpfully. "Do you know who might have been picking her up?"

"The person who killed her, I'm guessing," Felty said. "You should talk to that Englisher driver!"

"We will," Asher replied. "We've got his information, and we'll dig around to see if he's connected to Verna or Ike."

"Where is Aunt Lovina?" Obadiah asked.

They all turned and spotted the older woman standing on the step, her thick shawl wrapped around her. She started toward them, and Rosie sighed. "Go tell Lovina to stay back. She doesn't need the shock. And keep your sister inside too."

For a few more minutes Asher asked additional questions. He questioned Lovina while she stood in the drive, and she hadn't heard or seen anything. She was saddened to hear that Verna was dead and seemed to be much concerned about informing her family about what happened, and what would become of her two daughters. There was some crying, and then Lovina begged Rosie to send for the girls, but Felty pointed out that Verna had plenty of family in Shipshewana, and it wouldn't be right to take them from their maternal grandparents. Then Lovina cried some more. Hadassah didn't say anything. She just stood there, looking shaken.

The body was taken away, and the officers took the last of their photos. The Schlabachs went back to their house, and Asher draped a blanket around Petunia's shoulders, over top of her coat.

"I'm okay," Petunia said.

"This is all rather shocking," he said. "It's good to stay warm."

Asher looked out over the field toward the Schlabachs' home thoughtfully.

"Oh, Asher . . ." Petunia winced. "I forgot to tell you that I went to see Jonathan yesterday."

"Jonathan . . . Beiler?" he asked. "This is Eden's brother?"

"Yah, that's right," she said. "And . . . I hate to say this, but we were talking about Verna. He said that a strange Amish woman had told his sister that she knew that was pregnant. She said she was gifted that way, or something. He thought it was Verna. And maybe she was just trying to upset Eden. But Jonathan was asking me how long Verna had been in town. It was very important to him. He thought she'd been harassing his sister."

"And today, Verna turns up dead," Asher concluded.

"Yah."

"Hm."

"I was going there to talk to him because my *daet* heard that he was planning on taking a job in another community—just leaving while his sister is in jail! I didn't believe it. I wanted to see why."

"And what reason did he give?"

"His wife, Beth, is pregnant, and she just can't handle any more stress," Petunia said. "She wanted to go back to where her mother and sisters were, and Jonathan understood."

"So . . . Beth wanted to leave?" Asher asked.

"Both of them wanted to leave," Petunia said. "But I hardly think a pregnant woman would have gone out on foot or even in a buggy to the Schlabach home in order to kill another woman."

"You'd be surprised," Asher murmured.

"Really?"

He shrugged. "Really. But I agree that you talking to Jonathan about Verna the day before she turns up dead is a thread to pull on. Care to come with me?"

"Yah, sure," she replied.

"Good. Because we're getting closer. It's a tragedy that Verna was killed, but it also means that the murderer is getting uncomfortable. And we have to catch them before they kill again. "

Who would be the next person to drive a desperate person into a corner, asking too many questions, and demanding answers? She knew what her father feared.

"Hopefully not me," Petunia said and shivered. "But you're right—we need to hurry this up, don't we?"

* * *

Petunia drove her buggy back home, and Asher's cruiser crept along slowly behind her. She was glad that Asher wasn't leaving her on her own at a time like this. Her mind was still on her visit with Jonathan and their discussion of Verna. And now Verna was dead . . . Would Jonathan really have killed Ike, and then been willing to leave his sister to pay for it? Or was it more complicated than that? Was Asher right that a pregnancy didn't necessarily need to hold a woman back if she had reason enough to want to kill a man? And would Jonathan really have lashed out at Verna if she was leaving town?

Why strike out at her at all? Unless there was far more to the story than she was aware of. She was beginning to get used to finding that she knew far less than she thought about other people's lives.

Maybe Jonathan was protecting his wife. How well did they really know Beth? She was nice enough to chat with, and she was cordial at social events, but did any of them really *know* her? Maybe she hid another side that the rest of them hadn't seen. Lily Kempf had pointed out that every person had more than one side. And someone in this community had a side to them that killed. There was no getting away from it.

Petunia arrived home, and she unhitched the buggy, moving quickly.

"Do you need a hand?" Asher asked.

"No, it's easier to do it myself," she replied.

"Well, I think we need to go talk to Jonathan together, now, while everything is still fresh. Are you okay with coming along?"

"Yah, we can do that," she replied.

"Are you sure? I can do it alone. Your presence would be helpful, but if you're feeling too shaken about finding Verna, I can drop you off at a friend's home, or a family member's . . ."

"Asher, I'm fine," she said. "Tea and a piece of pie isn't going to calm my nerves, but finding the killer sure will. Let me just get Trudy into the stable, then we can go."

Asher stood back, but he didn't seem to like just standing there, so he paced back and forth until she was done. Then he ushered her back to his vehicle that he'd left running. Petunia got into the passenger side and heaved a sigh.

"Kind of shocking, huh?" he asked, and he put the car into reverse to turn around. The tire crunched over the gravel drive.

"Definitely," Petunia replied. "If Verna had just let Ike go and had lived her life in Shipshewana, she'd still be alive."

"Is that what you would have done?" he asked. "Just let your husband go off with someone else and stay home and accept it?"

Petunia considered for a moment. "That's not a fair question."

"Because you're the youngest old maid in all of Blueberry," he concluded.

"Exactly."

"Well, let's say you did marry some fellow, and he knew exactly what you were about, and he signed on for it. Then he ran off on you. Would you have just demurely let him go?"

Petunia tried to imagine what she would do, and she had to admit, she'd look an awful lot like Verna in that situation.

"I'd go after him," she admitted. "And I'd have some choice words."

"A slap might be in order?" he asked.

"Now, Asher, that is not nice to say. I'm not a violent woman, and I wouldn't go launching myself at the woman he'd taken up with, either."

"So there are limits," he said.

"There are certainly limits. But I do sympathize with poor Verna's situation. And maybe it's easier said than done to just stay home and endure the insult, especially when you know where to find him."

"Did he have any other romantic entanglements here in Blueberry?" Asher asked.

"Um . . . for a while he was flirting with Beth Beiler. Jonathan put a stop to it, though. Apparently, Ike didn't know she was married."

"And she didn't tell him?"

"She didn't know how to handle it," Petunia replied.

"Hm."

"You're thinking *Beth* might have killed them both?" Petunia asked.

"Maybe there was more to it than just flirtation. Maybe they'd started something."

"Asher, do I need to explain Amish marriage to you again?" she asked, exasperated.

"Petunia, some things aren't Amish or English. They're just sordid."

She couldn't help but chuckle at that. "All the same, we don't treat marriage like a temporary thing. It isn't for as long as it feels good, or for as long as your spouse still makes your heart flutter. It's for *life*."

"Then if it isn't Beth—and I do agree that a pregnant woman violently killing two people is a stretch—then maybe it was her husband."

"Is this what you do, Asher?" she asked. "Put yourself into people's shoes and wonder what you'd do?"

"Pretty much," he replied. "You put enough pressure on anyone, and they're capable of snapping."

"So what do you think would drive Jonathan to murder both of them?" Petunia asked.

"A whole lot of rage when that Amish promise for marriage doesn't pan out," he said.

"Did you feel that angry?" she asked. "With your wife, I mean?"

"Anger covers pain," he said quietly. "It's the brain's way of protecting itself. Anger isn't so hard to endure, so the brain kicks into anger instead of letting you feel the emotional pain right away. Murder tends to be about three things: love, money, and jealousy. And then once in a very long while you just get a sociopath who feels nothing and doesn't fall into any category. But for the most part, when normal people are driven to great extremes, it's for love, money, or jealousy."

It sounded so ordinary . . . so terrifyingly ordinary. People were pushed to the limit on a semi-regular basis.

"But you didn't kill anyone," Petunia said.

"No, of course not," he replied.

"So what's the difference between someone like you who didn't resort to violence, and someone who . . . snaps?" she asked.

"If we knew that, we'd be able to stop it before it happened," he replied.

They arrived at the Kauffman farm, and turned into the drive that led around to the Beilers' little house. There was no one to stop and chat with that day, and when they parked in front of the house, the front door opened. Beth was in an apron, and she looked tired. She ran a hand over her belly and gave them a wan smile.

"Hello, Petunia," she said, and her gaze flickered toward Asher.

"I'm Detective Nate, if you remember me," Asher said.

"Yah, of course. Hello."

"We were just hoping to talk with your husband," Asher said. "Is he home?"

"He's working," Beth said, shaking her head. "He's out in the barn, though. I know that. He was just home for a quick bite to eat, and he was headed there straight."

"I heard that you're moving," Petunia said.

Beth blanched. "That's not supposed to be public information. Who did you hear from?"

"It doesn't really matter," Petunia said. "I'm sorry. You know how things get out . . . We'll be sorry to lose you. That's all I wanted to say."

"Oh." Beth's cheeks colored and she looked down. "Thank you."

"You miss your family?" Petunia asked.

"So much!" Beth sighed. "Jonathan's family is wonderful, but a mother-in-law will never be like your own *mamm*, will she?"

"I suppose not." But Petunia's *mamm* had passed away, so she couldn't be sure. "Has it been difficult here?"

"Well, everyone has known Jonathan since he was tiny, and I'm the new one in the community. Everyone has been very nice, but it's not the same."

"I suppose Jonathan would get to experience that if you leave," Petunia said.

Beth sighed. "I don't want him to be lonely like I am. It's just that I'm having the baby, and everything feels so much bigger, and more emotional, and more impossible. I need my *mamm*. That's what it comes down to."

Asher cleared his throat, and Petunia nodded. "I guess we'd better go find Jonathan. But if you do decide to stay in Blueberry, maybe you and I will get to be better friends."

"Yah, that would be nice," Beth said, and her smile looked more natural then.

Petunia led the way toward the barn, and since the ground was getting muddy, she stuck to the snowy patches.

"Maybe she's just lonely," Petunia said.

"Maybe," Asher said, but he sounded noncommittal.

"Do you trust anyone at all to be a good person, Asher?"

"Sure. I trust my mother." He shot her a grin. "And you're proving yourself to be quite principled, too."

"I'll take that as a compliment," she said.

"As it was intended." But he looked like he was joking.

The barn was at the top of a hill, and when they opened the door, the smell of cattle and hay met them. Petunia had to let her eyes adjust after the bright outdoor sunlight, and when they did, she spotted Jonathan across the barn, his back to them. He was wearing his shirtsleeves and suspenders, and his hat was pushed back on his head. He seemed to be looking at something.

"Hello!" Asher called.

Jonathan startled and pushed a wad of cloth into a corner. He stepped away from it and came toward them.

"Hi," Jonathan said. "Can I help you?"

Jonathan looked at Petunia curiously, then back at Asher.

"We were hoping to ask you a few questions," Asher said.

"Sure."

"Where you were last night between the hours of"—he consulted his cell phone—"the preliminary investigation is suggesting between the hours of midnight and four AM this morning?"

"In bed with my wife," he replied.

"What time do you get up for work?" Asher asked.

"Four thirty."

"And you were sleeping in the same bed?"

"There's only one bed in our little house," Jonathan said with a chuckle. "Why do you ask?"

"Because Verna Smoker is dead," Asher replied.

Jonathan blinked. "What?"

"It's true," Petunia said. "She was murdered. I found her this morning on the road."

"Dead?" Jonathan sighed. "Wow. My wife is going to be so upset . . ."

"Did she know Verna?" Asher asked.

"No, it's another murder!"

"Are *you* upset?" Asher asked.

"Me? Sure. Of course. It's upsetting and horrible. I don't know what you want me to say."

The men were going back and forth, and Petunia slipped past Jonathan while he defended his outrage at a murder in their community, and she headed toward the corner where Jonathan had been standing. She was just reaching for the wadded-up shirt when Jonathan called out, "Petunia! Leave that!"

"Why?" she shot back, and grabbed the shirt. It fell open and something tiny fell out onto the cement floor. It bounced away, and she bent down to pick it up. It was a tiny wooden carving—a little Amish couple standing side by side, the woman's dress melting into the man's pants. It was detailed, perfect, and familiar. Her heart pounded in her ears.

"Oh, that . . ." Jonathan laughed uncomfortably. "I guess I lost it."

"You were hiding it," she countered.

"No, I was just . . ." Jonathan's face colored, and he licked his lips.

"This is what you found at the ice house, isn't it?" she demanded. "I knew you found something, and you said you hadn't. But you did. It was *this*."

Jonathan was silent.

"At the ice house, when exactly?" Asher cut in.

"The day after the murder, I went back," Petunia said. "And Jonathan was there. He'd used his sister's key for the ice house to get inside, and we both had a look around."

"You never told me that," Asher said.

No, she hadn't. She'd kept her own counsel on that one. She shot Asher an apologetic look. "Jonathan didn't kill Ike."

"What makes you so sure?" Asher asked. "Friendship?"

"Partly," she replied. "But I recognize this—the style of it, at least. It's a carving made by Obadiah Schlabach. Isn't it, Jonathan?"

Jonathan sighed. "He gave one like it to my sister years ago. I don't know what she ever did with it, but it wasn't a prized possession. But if they found this, I was afraid they'd assume it was hers, and they'd have more evidence against her."

"With Verna dead, I'm more inclined to think your sister is innocent than ever before," Asher said. "She couldn't have killed them both, and I'm pretty sure we're looking for one person for both murders. So if it didn't get into the ice house with your sister, how did it get there?"

"Obadiah . . . ," Petunia breathed.

"Let's walk through it," Asher said. "Why would he want to kill Ike?"

"For the same reason our whole family hated him," Jonathan said. "He was taking advantage of Eden. Obadiah was in love with her."

"In love?" Asher's eyebrows went up.

"I knew he had a crush—" Petunia started.

"In love!" Jonathan said firmly. "He asked me a few times to help Eden see that Ike was a bad seed, but she just wouldn't open her eyes to it. Obadiah was more than infatuated. He would have taken Eden even after all she'd done to embarrass herself with Ike Smoker. He loved her."

Petunia handed the small carving over to Asher, and he turned it over in his hands.

"It's newly carved," he said.

"Yah. That's what I thought," Jonathan said. "But it wasn't my sister's. I know that. If anyone brought that into the ice house, it was Obadiah Schlabach. As much as I hate to say it, because I really wanted to see my sister with Obie. I thought he was a good guy."

"It seems that he's got a violent side to him," Asher said thoughtfully.

"But why would he kill Verna?" Jonathan asked.

Petunia knew why. Because Verna was planning on telling everyone exactly who Ike was. And Obadiah had a lot to lose from it. His family's reputation would be ruined, and Verna would keep taking and taking from the Schlabachs, taking advantage of their guilt and feelings of responsibility. And Obadiah was sick of it.

Or maybe it was about the will . . . Ike was in it. Was Verna too? Or with Ike's death, would his part of the will revert to his wife? That would all depend on the will's wording, but Obadiah might have had some very real fears.

"Maybe this murder was about money," Petunia said, meeting Asher's gaze.

Asher nodded thoughtfully. "Maybe so," he agreed. "Maybe so." Then he turned to Jonathan. "Thank you for your time. Would you be willing to testify that you found this carving in the ice house that night?"

"If it clears my sister."

"Good," Asher replied.

But Petunia noticed that Asher didn't give any reassurances.

Chapter Sixteen

Once back in the car, Asher put the vehicle into gear and drove faster out of the property than he'd driven in. He paused at the road, then turned onto the asphalt with a spin of gravel. Petunia felt a surge of sadness. Obadiah had been a friend over the years. She'd dreamed of more than friendship with him once upon a time, too. She'd respected his family, and looked up to his parents. The sight of the Schlabachs arriving for service Sunday had always made her feel secure and happy. They were a pillar around here.

And now, a lot of that would change. The bishop had a secret son. The bishop's wife had secret pain. And everyone had been hiding the truth for a very long time, including Obadiah.

"I grew up with Obadiah," Petunia said softly. A lump stuck in her throat.

Asher's gaze flickered toward her. "I'm sorry about that."

"I knew when we found the killer it was going to sting," she said.

But with Obadiah, it more than stung. It cut.

"I knew it would be hard," Asher said. "If you hadn't helped me, though, we might never have figured it out. I needed you to get into people's homes and get them to talk. I needed your insights. Honestly, if you hadn't helped me, I think Eden would be going away for a very long time."

"I know—" She cleared her throat. "I should be focused on getting Eden out, not on how sad it makes me to find out who actually did it."

"Does it make sense to you?" Asher asked. "Knowing him, and all the facts we've uncovered, does it ring true for you?"

Petunia thought for a moment. Obadiah had lost a lot . . . and even the brother he'd gained was an embarrassment. What could the men have had in common besides some DNA? Maybe their taste in women, because they'd both been drawn to Eden. But Eden had fallen for the wrong brother—injury added to insult. And then to lose part of his inheritance, and to have Ike's volatile wife threatening to uncover all of their embarrassment for everyone to see . . .

"It all adds up, except for our proof," Petunia said. "That little carving doesn't actually prove anything. I might know who made it, but you can't prove that Obie was the one who dropped it. He's made all sorts of those little carvings. One year, he even sold them at the farmers market. Is that enough to outshine a woman with the victim's blood on her hands? This convinces *us*, not the whole court system!"

"True," Asher said, but his eyes were flinty and he kept them on the road. He slowed for a buggy, eased past, and then stepped on the gas again.

"So how do we prove it?" she asked.

"Well, first of all, I got a chance to go through Verna's bag, and there was nothing in there to incriminate her. Everything was folded, and by all appearances, she was heading home. Now, I can't prove it yet, but I think someone in the Schlabach home told her that a van was coming for her—then hit her on the head while she waited."

"You think Obie lured her out there . . ."

"It's the only explanation that matches the evidence," he said.

"Unless she called for the van herself from the phone hut," Petunia said.

"I'll check the outgoing calls from that number," he replied. "In fact—"

He picked up his phone, hit a button, and stuck it onto a magnetic holder on the dash. It rang on speaker, and an officer picked up.

"Hi, it's Asher. We need to look into some phone records for an Amish phone hut about half a mile from the site of the murder . . ."

There was a short discussion about getting a court order to allow it, and then Asher hung up.

"Will that prove anything?" she asked.

"It'll help build a picture," he replied. "But if we're going to prove beyond a reasonable doubt that Obadiah murdered both Ike and Verna, then I think we're going to need a confession."

As if that was easy to come by! If confession was as good for the soul as everyone said, Obie should have broken down and confessed it all by now. Mind, his father had kept the secret of his son's existence for quite some time, too. The Amish believed in being accountable to each other, but the Schlabachs hadn't lived up to that yet.

"And you think Obie will just come out with it?" Petunia asked. "If he killed two people and has kept his mouth shut this long—"

"He won't confess for you or me," Asher replied. "Obviously, I won't scare him enough because I have no proof, and he knows it. If he was willing to let us know about his relationship to Ike, then he's smarter than I gave him credit for."

"Smart how?" she asked.

"If he'd kept his secret and we found out about it, he'd look guilty," Asher replied. "But he told you about it first. That makes him look like just some innocent guy who's tired of the drama."

It was smart . . . and looking out that window, he'd known that the truth was bound to come out. He was just revealing it first.

"So you think he's been one step ahead of us?" she asked.

"I think he's been trying to be, and you started closing in. He's going to be feeling pretty desperate right now. There are two dead bodies, the woman he's loved for years is sitting in prison to pay for it, and we're coming closer . . . We'll have to be careful. Desperate men who've murdered twice don't tend to stop from killing again."

"So how do we get a confession?" she asked.

"Someone he trusts needs to talk to him and get him to open up," he said.

"Me?" Petunia asked.

"No, he knows you're helping me. It has to be someone he thinks will help him stay out of our way . . . ," he replied thoughtfully.

"Maybe his father," she suggested. "He might be able to convince him that confessing is what he needs to do on a spiritual level."

"The good bishop will never help us," Asher replied. "He was willing to let Ike run amok for two years and hadn't disciplined him like he would any other man behaving the way Ike did, all because he was his son. There is no way he'd throw Obadiah under the buggy, so to speak, just to help us find justice. He'll be loyal to his son."

"Then who?" she asked. "Because Rosie and Lovina will be loyal to him too! And I don't think poor Hadassah can handle any more. She's quite young."

"I'm thinking that if Jonathan is right about Obadiah's feelings for Eden, he just might fess up for her."

"You think?" She ran the idea over in her mind. Obadiah had had feelings for Eden for a long time. Had the guilt of leaving her in jail been eating away at him? "Yah, he might . . . In fact, Eden might be the only one who could."

"But I'll need you to help me convince Eden to cooperate with this," he said. "She's an honest woman, and I know that being deceitful—even for a good reason—is going to be tough for her. But we've got to get at the truth somehow."

He was right. It would be tough, but the next twenty years of Eden's life, and that of her unborn child, was on the line. Eden deserved to raise her baby. Her baby deserved to have a mother.

"I'll do my best," Petunia said.

When they got back to the Borough of Blueberry Police Department, Petunia was still thinking over her argument to convince Eden to help them, and she wasn't paying attention to their surroundings. Asher parked the car, then slammed his hands into the steering wheel.

"Seriously?" he muttered, and opened the door and got out.

Petunia sat there for a moment in surprise, then pushed her door open. What had just happened? She'd never seen Asher give in to frustration before.

"Come on! Hurry up!" Asher called. "You see that van?"

There was a green Pennsylvania Correctional Institution van parked in front of the station.

"What's happening?" Petunia asked breathlessly.

"They're transporting Eden to the prison until the trial," he said. "And we need one last interview with her before she goes."

To prison . . . Petunia's heart thudded to a stop in her chest. They were transporting poor Eden to some vile place where angry, violent criminals were kept. Petunia scurried to catch up with Asher, and strode into the station behind him.

"I need twenty minutes with Eden Beiler," Asher announced as he swept inside. "Then you can take her."

"We're on a schedule here," a uniformed man said. He looked down at a digital watch on his wrist.

"Then get your boss on the phone. I'm not releasing her just yet. Soon, I promise, but I need to speak with her once more before you transport."

There was muttering and heaved sighs, but the man dialed on his cell phone and turned away from them.

"Good," Asher said. "I don't know how much time I bought us, but we're going to make the most of it. Let's go."

Asher unlocked the door to the cell room, and he led the way inside. Eden's cell was bare now—no more quilts, no more books—and she sat on the edge of the bed looking pale.

"Petunia!" she jumped to her feet. "They're taking me to somewhere far away. I don't know where!"

Petunia had a good idea, but she didn't want to be the one to tell her. She reached through the bars to hold Eden's cold hands.

"Eden, we think we know who did it," Petunia said.

"You know? Who?"

"Obadiah Schlabach."

"Obie?" Eden frowned. "I don't get it. Why on earth would Obie do that?"

"I think that the details of why should remain private for now," Asher cut in. "The less you know right now, the better. Besides, we don't have much time. They're here to transport you out, and if we're going to prove anything, we need your help."

"Mine?" Eden asked. "What can I do?"

"Unfortunately, we're going to need you to lie . . ." Petunia winced.

"No. I won't do it." Eden shook her head.

"It's a misleading statement meant to draw the real killer out into the open," Asher said. "And if Obadiah is innocent, he won't take the bait. You'll be helping yourself, and possibly helping him if he hasn't done anything."

"What am I supposed to say?" Eden asked hesitantly.

"I want you to write Obadiah a letter," Asher said, handing her a pad of paper and a pen. "I want you to tell him that we've discovered that you're innocent, and you're going home. And then you need to tell him that you know who killed Ike. You saw it happen. And you need to talk to him alone."

"That *is* a big lie . . ."

"Would you rather have your baby in prison?" Petunia asked. "Would you rather have Ike's killer walking around free? What about justice?"

"I hate what this will make me," Eden said. "I'm not a liar."

"You aren't a killer, either!"

It took Eden a moment, but finally she nodded. "Okay . . ."

Eden wrote the note quickly, and toward the end of it she asked, "Where should I say we need to meet?"

"At the ice house," Asher said. "Tonight at eleven."

"Okay . . ." Eden added the line, then signed her name. "There." She handed it through the bars just as the door opened and the uniformed man came inside.

"Sorry, my boss says we move now," he said.

Asher nodded. "Okay, go ahead."

Asher opened the door, and snapped some handcuffs on Eden's slim wrists. He tightened them and gave her a sad smile.

"Good luck out there, Eden," Asher said. "We'll do the best we can here."

"Where am I going?" Eden asked, panic in her voice.

"You're going to the penitentiary," the man said. "Easy now. No funny business."

As if Eden would suddenly try to fight a man with a gun. Petunia blinked back tears as Eden was led out of her cell. Eden looked back over her shoulder, her eyes wide and her chin trembling.

"We're going to get him!" Petunia called after her. "I promise!"

Because if they didn't, Petunia was not going to be able to live with this memory of watching Eden led to prison. She'd see the right person behind bars!

"Do you think it will work, Asher?" Petunia asked quietly.

Asher looked down at the letter, then he folded it and slipped it into an envelope and handed it to Petunia.

"I sure hope so," he said. "Now, you need to take that to Obadiah, and I'm going to hold off on telling Eden's family about her transfer just yet. In my original plan, I wanted Eden to wear a wire and get Obadiah's confession."

Petunia's stomach dropped. "But she can't . . ."

"I know," he said. "Here's hoping that in the dark, at the place of the first murder, you'll be able to get him to confess."

So now it all hung on Petunia? She stared at Asher in horror.

"You can do it," he said. "You'll wear the wire, and I'll be concealed and watching everything. You'll be safe, I promise you that."

"I'm less worried about my own safety," she said. "I'm more concerned about getting the truth out of Obadiah!"

"It's all we've got," Asher said. "Here's hoping it's enough."

* * *

Petunia knew where to find Obadiah on a winter afternoon. The farmers market was slow. A few older couples strolled among the vendors. Petunia knew the Amish families there. There were even a few from the next district over—one that sold scarves, shawls, and mittens made from hand-spun alpaca yarn, and another that sold specialty cheeses. But other than those, the Amish families were ones she worshipped with every other Sunday when they met for service on various local farms.

Outside, snow spun down in lazy pirouettes. She'd come in her buggy—they couldn't take any chances on someone seeing her with Asher just after delivering that letter. It would look too suspicious. It was a perfect winter day, without a breath of wind. While Petunia would ordinarily enjoy such a peaceful day, her heart was far from peaceful.

She'd watched that prison van with the metal mesh over the window driving away, and she's sent up an earnest prayer that they'd get Eden back quickly. Even one night spent in that jail was one night too many.

But there would be at least one night. And Eden would have to simply wait, and hope and pray that Asher and Petunia pulled this off.

Petunia wound her way past the other vendors, heading toward the Schlabach Farm stall, and she found Obadiah sitting behind the cash register. Behind him was a freezer filled with frozen meat, and a fridge that held eggs and dairy products. He held an open book in his hands, but he wasn't reading it. Instead, he was looking off into the distance, his brow furrowed.

"Hi, Obie," Petunia said. Did that sound natural? She wasn't even sure anymore. Obadiah saw her then, and he put the book down. It was about animal husbandry—he was building up his knowledge base for running the farm, it would seem. Very responsible of him.

Was he more confident now that he wouldn't be sharing that inheritance after all?

"Hi, Petunia." He gave her a faint smile. "How are things?"

She nodded. "Good." Then she forced a smile. She had a role to play, after all. "Really good."

"Yah?" He looked at her expectantly. "What's going on?"

"Eden's being let out of jail," Petunia said, the necessary lie curdling her stomach just a little. "We got enough evidence to free her. She obviously didn't kill Ike. There was no way she could have, and the police now agree."

"Just like that?" Obadiah asked, squinting at her.

"Well . . . yah." She wasn't really prepared with a detailed story of how this occurred, and all she could do was hope he didn't ask for more information about it.

"I'm . . . I'm relieved!" Obadiah said. "How is she?"

"Shaken. Scared. Relieved. Kind of a wreck—" Petunia was just making it up as she went now. It was surprisingly easy once she got started. "She's just glad she'll be back in her own bed tonight."

"I can only imagine. I'd been praying for this!"

He might want to curb his mention of Gott. That was not only offensive to someone who knew what he'd been up to, but it was dangerous to boot. Petunia knew better than to play with the Almighty.

"Eden asked me to give you this." Petunia pulled out the sealed envelope and handed it over.

"Eden did?" Obadiah grabbed he envelope. "What did she say?"

"She said, could you give this to Obie?"

"Oh." He nodded and smiled sheepishly. "I thought—" He cleared his throat and looked down at the paper in his hand. "Do you mind if I read it now?"

"By all means."

Petunia watched as he tore open the envelope and pulled out the sheet. He turned away slightly as he read it, and she saw the color in his cheeks deepen. This letter was making him feel something, that was for sure.

"Hello, Petunia."

Petunia startled and looked over to see Rosie standing at her side. She had walked up quietly enough that Petunia hadn't heard her. She was wearing a thick woolen sweater over her gray cape dress, and her face looked tired and more lined than usual. A graying tendril of hair had slipped out of her *kapp*, and hung unnoticed behind one ear. Rosie gave Petunia a tight smile. It looked like all was not forgiven yet.

"Hello, Rosie," Petunia said quietly. She'd pushed into the Schlabachs' lives, and she now knew more than anyone wanted her to. All of that family shame, all of Rosie's embarrassment, all of Felty's regrets. She knew the worst, and she'd never be able to look at them the same way again, but that wasn't because she judged them. She was amazed at how much they'd gone through, how much they were currently enduring, and how close Felty and Rosie remained, even while working through tough issues. Not every season of marriage was an easy one, but Petunia could tell that they'd get through these hardships. But it wouldn't get any easier if the police arrested Obie for the murders.

"What are you doing here?" Rosie asked curtly. Obviously, Petunia wasn't wanted, and at any other time, she would have taken her leave. But she wanted to see Obadiah's reaction to that letter. His reaction mattered.

"She brought me this—" Obadiah said. "Eden's being released."

"What?" Rosie's eyes widened. "Released? What is that letter?"

"It's private," Obadiah said, folding it. He met his mother's gaze, and his face colored. "It's from Eden. She's just saying she's coming home. That's all."

"I thought they needed to find the killer before that happened," Rosie said. "Isn't that what you said? Did they find who did it?"

It was what Petunia had said. And that had been the truth . . .

"They found enough evidence that she didn't kill Ike," Petunia said evasively. "And she certainly couldn't have killed Verna, since she was locked up at the time. That's an airtight alibi."

"Is that what she said in the letter?" Rosie turned to her son again.

It would seem that Petunia's word was not to be trusted anymore.

Obadiah's expression turned to annoyance. "*Mamm*, the letter is private. She says she's coming home, and—"

Rosie held the hand out. "Give it to me."

Obadiah met his mother's gaze, and for a beat they stared at each other in silence. Rosie beckoned with her hand, hurrying him up to hand the letter over.

"*Mamm*, I'm grown. You can't do that."

"Obadiah." That was an order.

"No." But there was sadness in Obadiah's eyes as he said it. Was this the first time he'd openly defied his mother? It might be. "*Mamm,* it's private, okay?"

He was trying to soften the blow, but he wasn't handing the letter over. Rosie's eyes misted and she dropped her hand. "We'll discuss this with your father."

"I'm just glad she's getting out of that awful place," Obadiah said.

"Well, I'm worried," his mother replied. "We're talking about accusations of murder right now. When is she coming back?"

Rosie could sense something wrong here, and Petunia desperately hoped Obadiah's mother wouldn't see through the ruse.

"She's coming back today," Petunia said. "This evening."

What was happening to her that lying had become so easy? Petunia needed to get out of here, get away from the necessity to keep spouting untruths.

"You are not to visit her just yet, son," Rosie said. "I know you were probably considering it already. Your *daet* and I will go welcome her back, after she's had time with her family."

Obadiah didn't say anything, but Petunia recognized that defiant set to his lips. Petunia's work here was done. He'd go to the meeting place at the right time. He wouldn't give up a chance to see Eden.

If he were a more dutiful son and listened to his mother, he might get away with two murders. But he wouldn't listen. He'd go. And here was hoping that when he got there, he was talkative!

* * *

Petunia was glad to get back outside and into her little open-top buggy. The snow fell onto her coat and settled onto her bonnet. It was wet, thick snow, and she'd be drenched by the time she got home, but she was glad to be away from the questions and the tension.

When this was over, would anyone see *her* the same way again? Very likely not. Some boundaries, once crossed, could never be mended. But what choice was there? Petunia was already the youngest old maid in all of Blueberry. This was just making it all the more inescapable.

The drive home was quiet—the kind of quiet where noise of any kind got absorbed by the falling snow, and even the clop of Trudy's hooves sounded like it was muffled by pillows in the distance.

When Petunia got home, she saw that her father's wagon was there, and Petunia saw a selection of small wooden bird houses, and her father looked up as he took some cash from an older man.

"Where did you get those?" Petunia asked.

"From Benjie Stutzman," he replied. "He's earning some money for his wedding next year."

"And you'll sell some of them in the tour office?" she asked.

"If you don't mind sharing a shelf with Benjie," he replied. "Your dresses have been selling so well, I thought I'd let Benjie use some space, too."

"I don't mind at all," she replied.

Let someone get a sweet, innocent, happy life. And if anyone in Blueberry deserved it, it was Priscilla and Benjie.

"That's nice that Benjie is finding a way to make extra money," Petunia said, heading to the stove to start dinner.

"Priscilla is working on some crochet projects for me to sell, too," Elias said. "Between the two of them, they'll do this."

"Yah . . ." Petunia was happy for them, but her heart was too burdened down with other worries to be able to really feel it.

"I found out what caused the rift between those two families," her father said.

"I know—Benjie's uncle Noah wanted to marry Elijah's sister, and Elijah advised her against it."

"There's a little more to it," Elias replied. "That was the major drama that everyone knew about, but did you know that Noah's father left his family when he was young and went English?"

"What?" Petunia blinked.

"Yah, he left. It was terrible for Noah, and he became the man of his family when he was all of twelve. Anyway, when Elijah advised his sister not to marry Noah, that was the reason he gave. He basically said that Noah was too risky, that he might end up like his *daet*."

"Ouch . . . So that's why Noah was so deeply hurt . . ."

"Yah. He always felt that stain on his family. It's strange how far people will go to defend their family honor, even when it doesn't make sense to anyone else. He made himself look less reliable and honest by that feud he had with Elijah, but he figured he was defending his honor. Pride goeth before a fall . . ."

Indeed it did. Obadiah had some family honor at stake too.

"*Daet*," she said, pulling down a pot to start some potatoes. "I have to tell you where we're at with the investigation."

He wasn't going to like this one bit.

"What's happening?" Elias asked.

"Well, there's an upside to this, and a downside. The upside is that we're pretty sure we know who killed Ike and Verna. The downside is that I'm going to be the bait to catch him."

"You!?"

"Me, but with Asher in the wings to make sure I don't get hurt."

"And how can he guarantee that?" Elias demanded.

"I'll be wearing a wire, and a bulletproof vest," Petunia said. "So everything said will be recorded, and nothing will get through that vest."

Elias frowned. "Explain this to me. Every detail."

So Petunia did—why they were so certain of Obadiah, exactly how the plan would work, and how they hoped that Obadiah would be emotional enough to admit what he'd done. There was a very high likelihood that he'd threaten to kill her, but they'd be surrounded by cops, and at any sign of real danger they would all come running in with their guns drawn. She'd be really very safe. She was sure of it. She wasn't afraid at all.

At the end of it, Elias sighed.

"I will allow this on one condition," he said.

Allow it? There was no other choice! If she backed out now, Eden would end up in prison until she was middle-aged and her child was grown!

"What's that?" she asked warily.

"That I wait in the wings with your Englisher detective. He might think he's fast, but I can well assure you that a father is faster still. You can catch Obadiah Schlabach, but if he so much as raises a hand to you, I'm dealing with him myself!"

Petunia gave her father a teary smile. "Oh, *Daet* . . ."

He really was the best father in all of Amish Pennsylvania.

Chapter Seventeen

That night, Petunia and Asher arrived at the ice house an hour early. They crept through the underbrush to make sure Obadiah hadn't done the same, and Asher set up his position where he'd be able to watch everything that happened. Three more officers were positioned at other locations surrounding the ice house. If Obadiah ran, he wasn't getting far. And Elias sat next to Asher, as Petunia had promised he could.

Asher didn't like that setup. He thought that Elias might make some noise, or hold him back, but Elias had more hunting experience than Asher gave him credit for. If he could stalk a buck for hours and not make a sound, he could do this.

Petunia had a wire taped to her chest. It felt funny—a little bit itchy. And the bulletproof vest was heavy and inflexible. Luckily, her coat covered the bulk of it, and she'd looked ordinary enough when she'd seen herself in the mirror in the women's bathroom at the police station.

Petunia sat on an upturned piece of firewood next to the locked ice house. Moonlight filtered through the bare trees. The earlier snow had stopped, and the night was crisp and clear. Looking around, she appeared utterly alone, but she knew she wasn't.

"Petunia, how are you doing?" Asher's voice came softly into her earbud.

"I'm okay," she whispered.

"It's five minutes to eleven," Asher said. "So he'll be arriving soon . . . Just breathe. Everything will be fine. And even if he doesn't cooperate, we're getting you out safely, okay?"

Except Petunia wasn't willing to leave her post until she knew her friend would be free. Asher was misunderstanding her request that her father be present. She wasn't scared of Obadiah. She just loved her *daet* too much to let him worry at home.

A brisk wind wound its way through the trees, and Petunia shivered. At the top of the drive she saw the bobbing headlamps of a buggy. The lights turned off but the clop of hooves and crunch of buggy wheels surfed the night breeze. This was it . . . he'd come, just as they knew he would. She sucked in a breath and willed her heartbeat to slow down.

"Just stay calm . . ." Asher's voice was a low whisper in her ear. "You've got this . . ."

The buggy came to a stop next to hers, and she noticed that it blocked her off from any kind of exit. Was Obadiah trying to intimidate her?

But then the door opened, she saw the flash of pink, and a pair of broad hips descended from the buggy. This wasn't Obadiah at all, but a woman! Petunia couldn't make out who it was in the darkness, but then a lantern came on, the woman turned, and Petunia looked in shock at Lovina Schlabach.

Lovina frowned, looked around.

"What are you doing out here at night?" Lovina asked.

"I could ask you the same thing," Petunia said.

"I'm looking for someone."

"Eden?" Petunia asked.

"Ah." Lovina smiled faintly and shook her head. "It was you, wasn't it? You wrote the letter. It wasn't Eden at all."

"No, Eden wrote it," Petunia replied. "But she's not here."

"I take it you're the one who saw Ike die?" Lovina asked.

What was happening here? Was Lovina here to defend her nephew?

"How did you see the letter?" Petunia asked.

"I just took it," Lovina said. "Rosie is silly. She asked him for it. You don't ask with children."

"Obadiah's not a child anymore," Petunia said.

Lovina eyed Petunia, but she looked different than she normally did. Gone was the gentle smile and the deferential ways. She walked purposefully toward Petunia, and it was then that Petunia spotted the piece of rusty pipe in her gloved hand.

"Did you see the murder?" Lovina asked.

So that Lovina could get rid of her too?

"Why did you do it?" Petunia asked, stepping back. "Why kill Ike? Verna would have gotten him home sooner or later. He didn't need to die. He would have gone away."

"Oh, naïve Petunia," Lovina said, slowly shaking her head. "He wasn't going away. When a lazy, angry man finds a way to pump someone for money, you can be sure he'll come back again and again."

"And Verna?" she asked.

"She was planning on continuing the extortion. I couldn't let my family suffer like that. They were too good to do what needed doing."

"Too good to kill?" Petunia asked.

"A family runs well because of more than just a *mamm* and a *daet* and a house full of *kinner*. A family also needs maiden aunts and resourceful uncles . . . It needs people willing to do what's necessary for the good of the family, and Ike was ruining everything for his father."

"Ike couldn't help being born."

"But he could help coming to Blueberry and demanding his share of the inheritance!" Lovina shot back. "And when Verna heard about it, she thought she deserved a piece of it too!"

"It's only money . . ." Petunia took another step back.

"If it were only money, they'd still be alive," Lovina barked out a laugh. "It's never only money. They wanted my brother, the bishop, to pay with more than cash, and more than the inheritance after his death. They wanted him to pay with his dignity and his reputation, and I could not allow that to happen to my family!"

"So killing Ike had nothing to do with Eden?" Petunia asked.

"What do I care about Eden?" Lovina shook her head. "No, I did it for *my* flesh and blood. Ike could have ruined Eden for all I cared, as long as he went away, and I went to see him that night to tell him so. I told him he should run off with her and marry her where no one knew who they were. He said he wanted the money more than he wanted Eden. And I couldn't let him do that. I didn't actually mean to kill him, though." The gentle look was back on her face now. "I didn't think I would. I wanted to scare him. I wanted to show him who he was dealing with, but then I—" Lovina shrugged. "I stabbed him with the closest thing at hand."

"And Verna?" Petunia asked.

"She was so stupid. All I had to do was tell her I'd ordered her a ride and paid for it myself. I said I wanted her away from my family. She was eager to go at that point, but you can't trust these women to stay away, can you? And Rosie had dealt with enough. Felty was so heavenly minded that he was no earthly good. So I told Verna to be out there at midnight for her ride, and used a piece of firewood. Easy enough. She never saw it coming."

"So it was . . . a kindness?" Petunia only wanted to keep her talking.

"It was easier than Ike. I had to look him in the face." Lovina grimaced. "I didn't like that."

"So why come see Eden?" Petunia asked.

"Well, whoever wrote that letter saw what I did. It turns out that person is you."

"If you hurt me and I can't talk, they'll blame it on Obadiah," Petunia said.

"He's at a youth group event this evening. I made sure of it. He's there with his father and several cousins. He's not going anywhere, and he'll have forty or fifty witnesses to that. This has to end. It has to stop. People have been through enough and Blueberry has got to get back to normal."

"People will want to know who killed me," Petunia took another step back and Lovina closed the distance again, testing the weight of the pipe in her hand.

"No, they won't. You've run away," Lovina said. "You told me about it before you left. You jumped the fence and went English so that you could find an Englisher man willing to marry you."

"That's a little mean," Petunia said, dodging back another step. "You're as single as I am."

"Blueberry needs only one certified old maid," Lovina said, and the pipe came whistling through the air just past Petunia's face.

"Hands up! You're surrounded!" Lights suddenly flared up all around them, and the sound of feet moving through the underbrush made Petunia almost wilt with relief. But then Lovina leaped toward her with more agility than Petunia imagined the older woman had! And then there was a blinding crack, and everything went dark.

As consciousness faded, Petunia's last emotion was annoyance.

* * *

Petunia awoke in a white room, and for a moment she wondered if she was dead and this was Heaven, because she felt very comfortable, but then she heard the chirp of a machine, and smelled the faint scent of disinfectant, and she knew otherwise.

"Petunia?"

Petunia opened her eyes to see her father sitting by her hospital bed, and he caught her hand. "My goodness, you gave us a scare." Then he turned and called, "Asher! She's awake!"

There was one window with blinds slanted open just a little, and outside it was still dark, with the glow of yellow lights coming from the parking lot.

"What time is it?" she asked.

"Almost two in the morning," Elias said, looking down at his watch.

The hospital room door opened and Asher came striding in. Petunia struggled to sit up, and discovered that her head was bandaged, and while she did have a dull headache, it wasn't too bad. She was wearing a hospital gown, and she pulled up the blanket just a little bit higher.

"She's awake?" Asher said, and when he looked at her, she thought she saw a mist of tears in his eyes.

"I'm awake," she confirmed. "What happened?"

"Lovina Schlabach cracked you over the head with an iron pipe," Asher said. "That's what happened. But she didn't reach you very well, thankfully. And we got her entire confession on tape. She's going to prison for a good long time."

"It was Lovina!" Petunia said, the memory coming flooding back. "All this time!"

"I'm sorry, Pet," Elias said. "I know she was a friend to you."

"Not as good and true of a friend as I thought, though," she replied, touching her bandage. "I feel bad for her going to prison."

"Don't," Asher replied. "She killed two people and would have killed you if we hadn't taken her down when we did. And she shows no remorse at all."

"Really?" Petunia sighed. "And what about Eden?"

"She's coming home," Asher said. "For real this time."

"I thought it was Obie who killed Ike. I was so sure . . . ," Petunia said.

"Me too," Asher said. "Turns out, he was completely innocent. In fact, he's eager to see Eden. We accidentally let slip about her pregnancy, and he doesn't care. He says that if she'll have him, he'll marry her tomorrow."

"Wow . . . ," Petunia murmured. Even after her fall from grace, Eden had an honest and earnest proposal coming her way. Good for Eden. She deserved some happiness, and maybe she'd even let Petunia sew her wedding dress for her.

"What can I say?" Asher said with a wink. "Maybe you were right about Amish marriage being something different altogether."

Petunia smiled ruefully. "It is. And you should know that I'm almost always right, Asher." She looked around the room—a radiator under the window, a garbage can next to it, and a little bathroom opening off her room . . . that was it. It was very clean and empty. "Where are my clothes? I'd like to get home."

"You have to stay a bit longer for observation," Elias replied. "The doctor says you fared very well for getting that clunk on the head, but they want to be sure."

Petunia sighed. "Who will feed you, *Daet*?"

"I'll survive," he replied. "I've decided to learn how to cook a few meals."

"Oh, *Daet* . . . you don't have to!"

"What if I'm good at it?" he asked. "You never know. You're rather good at solving a murder case, and you didn't know that until you tried it. I'll make you a meal when you get home. We'll see how it goes."

Asher stepped forward then, and he pushed his hands into his pockets. He cleared his throat.

"Petunia, I'm really sorry that I let you get hurt," Asher said.

"I'm feeling pretty good, actually," she replied.

"All the same . . ." Asher looked uncomfortably toward Elias, then stepped a little closer. "Look, my boss says we can bring you on as a consultant. It would pay, and we'd really love your insights into local cases."

Petunia looked over at her father, and Elias shrugged. "He already told me. I don't see any way to hold you back. If you want to do it, I won't stop you."

"I think it sounds fun, myself," Petunia said with a hopeful smile. "And I'd like to contribute to Blueberry—more than just my sewing."

"You mean more to everyone than you think," Elias said. "Just being you. Believe me."

"Oh, *Daet* . . ." She cast her father a fond smile.

"All right, gentlemen, visiting hours are over," a nurse said from the doorway. "Out, out, out, and we are going to let our patient rest."

There was the scrape of a chair and the rustle of a coat as Elias put his on. Asher didn't move, though, and while Elias went toward the door, Asher bent down a little closer.

"Feel better, okay?" he said gruffly, and he caught her fingers in his. It was first time he'd touched her hand, she realized, and his grip was strong and sure. "I don't know what I'd do if anything happened to you. Next case, you aren't going anywhere without me."

"I have my own mind, Detective Nate," she said, and she was trying to joke, but she wasn't sure she managed it with Asher looking down at her with that direct stare of his.

"Let's keep you calling me Asher," he said. "I think we might count as friends now, don't we?"

His flinty gaze met hers, and her breath caught. Friends . . . Yah, they were. But this felt different, somehow—something that might lead to more if he were Amish.

Then the nurse called, "Let's go! She needs rest. Tomorrow you can come back, but my patient will get her sleep."

"I have to go," Asher said.

She wished he didn't. She wished he could sit on the chair next to her bed and banter with her for a few more minutes, and hold her hand, and talk about the case, but hospitals had rules, and the nurse was looking pointedly at them from the doorway.

"Yah, she sounds like she means business," Petunia agreed.

"They have my number. I'll drive you home when they're ready to release you. And don't worry about your father. I'll order him some pizza," he said with a smile.

"*Danke*, Asher. I really appreciate that. He'll burn the house down, otherwise."

Asher chuckled. "Good night, Pet."

Petunia watched Asher leave with a lump in her throat. How ridiculous was it that the first man to truly appreciate and understand her besides her father would be an Englisher detective?

An Englisher detective she'd work with again . . .

She smiled and let her eyes drift shut. She was the youngest old maid sleuth in all of Blueberry . . . and she was happy.